2

D1440762

Published 2018

Treasured Lies

© 2018 by Kendall Talbot

ISBN: 9781072442448

This is a work of fiction. Names, characters, places, and incidents are either the product of the author's imagination or are used fictitiously, and any resemblance to actual persons, living or dead, business establishments, events, or locales is entirely coincidental.

❀ Created with Vellum

About the Author

Kendall Talbot is a thrill seeker, hopeless romantic, virtual killer, and award-winning author of stories that'll have your heart thumping from the action-packed suspense in exotic locations and the swoon-worthy romance.

Kendall has sought thrills in all 46 countries she's visited. She's abseiled down freezing waterfalls, catapulted out of a white-water raft, jumped off a mountain with a man who spoke little English, and got way too close to a sixteen-foot shark. When she isn't writing heart-thumping suspense in exotic locations, she's enjoying wine and cheese with her crazy friends, and planning her next thrilling international escape.

She lives in Brisbane, Australia with her very own hero and a fluffy little dog who specializes in hijacking her writing time. Meanwhile, Kendall's two sons are off making their own adventures – look out world.

Kendall's book, *Lost in Kakadu* won the acclaimed title of Romantic Book of the Year 2014, and her books have also been finalists for Best Romantic Suspense, Best Crime Novel, Best Continuing Series, and Best New Author.

I love to hear from my readers!

Find my books and chat with me via any of the contacts below:

- www.kendalltalbot.com
- Email: kendall@universe.com.au

Or you can follow me on any of the following channels:

- Amazon
- Bookbub
- Goodreads

Books by Kendall Talbot

Maximum Exposure Series

(These books are stand-alone and can be read in any order):

Extreme Limit

Deadly Twist

Zero Escape

Other Stand-Alone books:

Jagged Edge

Lost in Kakadu

Double Take

Waves of Fate Series

First Fate

Feral Fate

Final Fate

Treasure Hunter Series:

Treasured Secrets

Treasured Lies

Treasured Dreams

If you sign up to my newsletter you can help with fun things like naming characters and giving characters quirky traits and interesting jobs. You'll also get my book, Breathless Encounters which is exclusive to my newsletter followers only, for free.

Here's my newsletter signup link if you're interested:

http://www.kendalltalbot.com.au/newsletter.html

TREASURED LIES

Book two in the Treasure Hunter Series

KENDALL TALBOT

Chapter One

Nox's eyes stung. No, that was an understatement. It was more like glass shards were shredding his eyes to pieces. He wanted to open them. Had to open them to see where he was. But the agony made it impossible. He went to reach up, to rub his eyes, but his arm didn't move.

Nox clawed at his memory, trawling for details of what had happened. Images, like a faulty 8mm film, flicked across his mind. It was a crazy mix of blood and water, lots of water, oceans even. Then there were stars, clouds and the sun, so hot and intense it burned him until he shriveled up like a dying toad. The other memory. . . the one that shot acid to his stomach, was the pain. Brutal, excruciating pain that ran in relentless rivers down his legs.

Strangely, there was nothing now. He couldn't feel anything. Not his arms, his legs, his feet. The acid in his stomach shot to his throat and Nox fought the urge to throw up. He gasped for air, forcing back the bitter bile. His tongue was a solid, useless lump and Nox rolled it around his mouth, trying to create some moisture.

A tear rolled out of his right eye and over his nose. It was only then that he realized he was on his side. Again, he tried to move, literally centering all his focus on his arms, but it was like a great concrete blanket was pinning him down. He couldn't stand it anymore. He forced his eyes open and blinked. But there was nothing but blackness.

Blink. Blink.

Tears pooled in his eyes as horrid thoughts petrified him.

What if they aren't tears?

What if it's blood?

What if I'm blind?

Nox forged the agony and blinked some more, desperate to achieve clarity. And then he saw it, a faint glow, low down in the distance.

Blink. Blink.

He trained his eyes on it and gradually the glow became a solid horizontal line.

The gap beneath a door.

Other objects emerged from the blackness. A chair. A table. Not a normal table though. This one was rough, with jagged edges and mismatched wood. Driftwood maybe, and the way it looked, it must have been put together by a couple of kids. He saw the ladder next and traced its line upwards to a landing, or a loft of some sort.

Am I in a barn?

At the top rung of the ladder hung a lamp. It was old. Ancient even. One of those types that required fuel and a flame. The smell registered somewhere back in his brain. Kerosene. But that wasn't all he could smell. He also smelt rotting fish, or was it death?

Or is it my own foul body odor?

Having lived with Trimethylaminuria all his life, it was rare for him to detect the pungent stench that poured from his skin in times of stress or excitement. What he was smelling now, though, was nothing like his Fish Odor Syndrome.

No. This was worse. Beyond worse.

The putrid stench flooded his nostrils and Nox heaved. Pain rippled through his body. He bucked at the agony. A scream burst from his throat but it was nothing but a strangled croak.

Nox heaved again.

He gasped. His world spun.

And when a creature scampered across the floor before him, Nox slipped into blackness.

Chapter Two

Rosalina tugged her hair into a ponytail, curled it over her shoulder and then braced for the weight of her scuba tank. It didn't matter how many times she'd done this, it always amazed her how heavy a tank of air could be.

"Ready?" Archer lifted the tank and her buoyancy vest to his knee with such ease that for a fleeting second, she wondered if it were empty. But it wouldn't be, Archer was meticulous in his pre-dive safety checks.

She fed her arms through the vest and braced for the weight. "Ready."

Archer lowered the tank and she leaned forward to avoid toppling backwards. He quickly came to her front and helped her click the buckles into place.

"Here we go, baby." Archer cupped her cheeks and kissed her, just a very brief kiss. His eyes twinkled with both the brilliant sun reflecting off the ocean and the excitement of what they were about to do. When he stepped back, Rosalina popped her regulator in her mouth and breathed in to ensure her air was flowing. Satisfied, she dropped the regulator to her side, and careful not to trip over her fins, she shuffled forward to the edge of the dive deck.

She glanced up at the three people watching her from the saloon deck of *Evangeline*. Jimmy was leaning on his hairy muscular arms, but that was about as far as his relaxed state went. His bloodshot eyes confirmed he was still in pain. If he wasn't, he'd be right there with Rosalina and Archer, helping them with the scuba gear. Rosalina was honored to be at Archer's side on this dive, because if Jimmy wasn't riddled with stitches and recovering from a serious bullet wound, she'd have to fight him for the coveted place.

Alessandro stood beside Jimmy. He too was recovering from injuries, but he didn't mask his hurt as well as Jimmy tried to. Alessandro had always been more of an indoors man. As a professor of ancient history and architecture, he spent his life in museums and lecture halls. Him being here, in the middle of the ocean, surrounded by the Greek Islands, was probably never on his life's agenda. What they were about to do put him so far out of his usual daily life, it was a wonder he could think straight.

Maybe Ginger, who was hanging off his arm, was feeding some bravado into Alessandro's veins. There was a naïve excitement about her that reminded Rosalina of her twenty-year-old self, and it was hard not to like her bubbly, though sometimes ditsy, personality.

The only other person onboard *Evangeline* was Archer's mother, Helen. But Helen rarely ventured from her bedroom. She barely did anything, for that matter; she was a tormented soul, trapped in a horrific past that now consumed her present.

Ever since she'd found that gold plate, the first solid proof of the location of the Calimala treasure, Jimmy had barely spoken of anything else. Now though, he looked about as uncomfortable as a bear in shackles. Rosalina dragged her gaze away, fighting a rollercoaster of both excitement and guilt over diving without him.

"Don't go messin' things around down there." Jimmy's gruff voice rained down from the upper deck.

Archer stood at her side, all kitted up and ready to drop into the deep blue Mediterranean Sea with her. He glanced up at Jimmy. "You know we won't, big fella." By the look on Archer's face. . . the beaming smile, twinkling eyes and wriggling eyebrows, he looked like he was high on drugs. This was his drug.

Hunting for treasure was in Archer's bones.

Today they were hoping to finish off a treasure hunt Archer's father had started nearly twenty years ago.

"Come on you two lovebirds, what're you waiting for?" Jimmy was an impatient man. She'd bet her shiny new engagement ring that he'd throw them overboard if he could. As she tugged her neoprene glove on, the brilliant diamond danced in the sun. It was a spectacular single stone in an elegant setting and she still wasn't used to wearing it. She couldn't wait to show Nonna. Her grandmother would be delighted by the classic style Archer had chosen all by himself. *Maybe I should've taken it off.* But it was too late; it would be impossible to delay the dive any more. She tugged the glove securely over her fingers; certain it was safe.

Archer saluted his old mate. "Calm down big fella, you'll pop your stitches." Jimmy huffed and Archer turned to Rosalina. "After you, madam."

Rosalina blew Jimmy a kiss, pulled her mask up to her face, pushed the regulator back into her mouth, inflated her vest, took one step forward and then, with a giant stride, she dropped into the ocean. The warm water hugged her in its welcome and seconds later she bobbed to the surface and gave the 'okay signal to Archer. He then dropped in beside her and replicated the 'okay' signal to Jimmy. Even with the regulator concealing his mouth, Archer was smiling. A halo of gold flecks danced around his coffee-colored irises.

Archer flicked his thumb downwards. It was time to descend. She let the air out of her vest and gradually lowered beneath the surface. With one hand on the anchor line, she followed Archer toward the sandy bottom. The water was a comfortable seventy-five degrees and visibility was excellent. She guessed she could see at least a hundred feet into the deep blue around her.

Right from the moment she submersed Rosalina saw the coral-covered ocean floor. A sense of contentment embraced her, taking her into a world that was as leisurely and tranquil as it was colorful. Pinks, blues and purples were bountiful and the more she descended the more prolific the colors became. Fish were in abundance too. Blue fish no bigger than a Brazil nut darted about in a large synchronized school. When one shot left, hundreds of the little fish instantly copied. Next second, they'd all dart to the right as if all their moves were choreographed. It was an amazing natural spectacle. Larger yellow fish, decorated with black spots, chased each other about the coral, darting in and out of the plant life as if playing a game of tag.

Before she reached the bottom, she spied the pair of board shorts Archer had tied to the coral the last time he was here. She remembered laughing at him as he tugged those bright shorts over his fins. That had pretty much been when the fun had ended though.

Realizing she was biting down on her mouthpiece, she tried to shove the incident from her mind. The incident. That's what they'd started to call it. What else do you call the moment you killed a man to save the people you love?

Archer caught her attention, pointed to the wafting board shorts and gave her the okay signal. Obviously, her fiancé wasn't sharing the same apprehension she was. She followed him to the marker and as she neared, she noticed the change to the sandy bottom. The last time Archer was here, he and Jimmy had dug several valuable items from the sand and the decent-sized divot they'd made was still there. She had thought the steady current would've removed any signs of their last visit. This area was obviously well protected. Hugging this close to the shore of Greek's Anafi Island sheltered this location more than she'd realized. It also explained why the precious pieces they'd already discovered were in pristine condition, even after being submerged in sea water and buried within the fine sand for nearly seven hundred years.

Rosalina followed Archer to the sandy bottom and knelt beside him. She imagined all manner of precious treasures just begging to be found amongst the grains of sand at her feet. The desire to start digging right there and then was like putting a six-tiered gateau cake, laced with cream, chocolate and liquor in front of her, giving her a fork, and then telling her not to taste it. That was her idea of torture.

But this dive was a planning one. A dive to mark out the area, dividing it into bite size pieces to ensure a systematic approach to their search. Archer was an expert at this, having done it many times over. Rosalina, though, had never laid gridlines before. Archer briefed her before the dive on the process, and all she had to do was wait for his signals and follow his lead.

Archer pushed a spike into the soft sand and with a hammer he tugged from the net bag at his hip he drove the spike deeper. Satisfied it was secure, he tied one end of white cord around the spike and, with a signal for Rosalina to follow, he pushed off and swam away from the marker.

After a distance of two yards or so he stopped and drove another spike into the ground, and then tied the cord around it too. Rosalina's job was to monitor the surroundings and make sure they stuck to their strict time limits.

A circular shadow moving slowly across the sand made her look up. Above her, cruising along in the current, was an enormous sea turtle. The largest she'd ever seen, its shell had to be at least as big as her torso. Despite its size the beautiful creature moved with the grace of an eagle, gliding its fins through the water as if it had all the time in the world. Maybe it did. A big turtle like that had obviously been doing something right.

Archer waved his hand in front of her face, dragging her attention from the turtle. He indicated he was moving onto the next point. The process was repeated over and over and fifty minutes of their dive time lapsed quickly. Rosalina caught his attention and indicated they had ten minutes left on the dive. Archer tugged his regulator from his mouth, blew her a kiss, then grabbed her hand and pulled her back to the first square they'd marked out in the grid.

He dropped to his knees at the edge of the hole he and Jimmy had made last time. They would spend the last ten minutes digging. Rosalina had been surprised he'd lasted this long. After what he'd pulled from the sand last time, it must've been killing him not to start digging the instant they revisited the spot.

He wiggled his eyebrows, grinned at her, then sunk his fingers into the soft sand and dug back a handful. Rosalina began at her own spot and pushed her gloved hands into the sand too. Just the thought of discovering a piece of treasure: gold, silver or a gem of any kind that'd been buried beneath the sand for seven centuries set her heart racing.

The large plate she'd removed last time, heavy with solid gold and etched with intricate patterns, was priceless. It was now secured within the safe on Archer's yacht. Along with the fourteen other items Jimmy and Archer had removed last time they were here.

Rosalina felt something, a thread or maybe a cord. She brushed back the sand and waved the dispersed particles away in the current.

7

The cord revealed itself quickly and the gold glimmered in the filtered sunlight like the birth of a dawn over the ocean. What she'd thought was a cord was in fact a chain. The links were significant in size, equal to her little finger or, dare she believe, even bigger? She hooked her fingers beneath the chain and teased it from the sand. Rosalina pulled and wriggled the chain with equal measure but it refused to leap from its clutches. Digging at a frantic pace, inch by inch along the chain, she found herself holding her breath. It was the jolt she needed. She inhaled a few calming breaths and took the moment to wave Archer over.

Archer launched to her side and his eyes twinkled when he saw the gold links. They worked together, she pulled on the roped gold while he brushed at the sand. Moments later a link in the chain was revealed that was different to the others. It was thicker, wider and smoother. Archer must have seen it as well because he stopped with the frantic brushing and slowed down to a more delicate touch.

The thicker link was attached to a dome, at least that's what was gradually being revealed. All of a sudden it released from the sand in a swirl of debris and Rosalina fell backwards. She grappled to get back upright, desperate to see what it was. When she looked up Archer was cupping it in his hands as if it were a sleeping kitten. What she had thought was a dome was actually the crown of a man's head on a gold bust. It was too big to be a necklace, but she couldn't work out what else it could be.

The bust filled Archer's hands and was crafted with incredible detail. The hair was symbolized with dozens of gold rosettes, curled together with detailed precision, and the beard was hundreds of tiny pearls of gold. By contrast the face was smooth gold, created with obvious expert craftsmanship and in the filtered sunlight, it came alive in Archer's hands. Rosalina frowned when Archer pointed at the horns on the statue's head. She hadn't noticed them until then. They were a strange addition to the beautiful figurine. It was most likely a statue of some kind of mythical god.

She looked at Archer and their eyes met. He oozed boyish exuberance. Twinkling eyes, wriggling eyebrows, and although she couldn't see his mouth, his dimples were a sure sign he was smiling. He tugged his regulator from his mouth and she did the same. They shared an underwater kiss, not lingering, or sensual, or erotic. But a fun kiss to celebrate their lucky find. When he pulled back, he poked his tongue at her before he put his regulator back in his mouth. She did the same and when she looked at her dive watch her heart skipped a beat. They'd exceeded their dive time limit by three minutes.

Rosalina shoved her dive watch before Archer's mask, drawing his eyes to the time. He nodded and handed her the golden statue. She grasped the figurine and threaded it and the chain into the net bag at her hip. Then she signaled 'boat' and together they pushed off the ocean floor and glided toward the surface. Fifteen feet from the fresh air, they clung to the anchor rope as they waited out their decompression for five minutes.

As she waited there, watching an abundance of fish scoot about, another giant turtle, as big as the last, cruised past. It came so close she could see it blink. It was as if the ancient creature was winking at her. Rosalina felt very welcome in the turtle's home. It always amazed her how unafraid sea creatures were in her presence. Whenever she dived, she felt a true sense of contentment and belonging.

Time was up.

Archer cupped her elbow and with a gentle kick they glided to the surface. They popped into the open air and the instant she dropped the regulator from her mouth, Archer laughed, cheered and kissed her all at once.

Chapter Three

Nox woke with a start and snapped his eyes open. Every flick of his eyelids was an excruciating gritty slice. Through blurry tears he scoured his surroundings. He was still on his side. Still trapped in a numb state of inertia. And still surrounded by blackness. The faint glow beneath the door had barely changed.

Maybe I hadn't blacked out for long.

He remembered the creature that had scampered across the floor and with his heart in his throat he searched the blackness.

He felt a presence in the room with him. Fear stung his stomach like an angry wasp as he searched for a reason behind his panic. But there was nothing. Nothing but the whistling wind that cut through the silence like an ice pick. It was the only sound he'd heard since he'd woken earlier. It was unnatural, eerie. . . spooky.

Where the hell am I?

Why am I alone?

Why aren't I in hospital?

Whoever put him here must have noticed his condition.

In the dim light, he stared at his outstretched fingers, willing them to move. Suddenly they did. With stiff jolting movements they curled and straightened as if they'd been shocked to life. Nox took a moment to let relief sink in. He concentrated on his arm next, urging it to lift. It did, and the surprising ease with which it happened had him believe he was going to be all right.

Pushing up from his side, jagged pain ripped up his back and he howled, torturing his throat with a scream. Nox fell back and clawed at the wood beneath him, begging the agony to go away. It was an eternity before it subsided and he could breathe again. It was even longer before he dared risk moving once more.

While he lay there, pinned down by fear, he begged for recall, seeking something, anything that would make sense of what was happening. What he got was a crazy concoction of events. Pain, blood, gold and water were the constant. None of it made any sense.

Clenching his jaw, he raised his arm slowly. He reached up to his face and touched his eyes. Crusty sand lined his eyelids. He brushed it away, flicking it out from his eyelashes. He turned his attention to his cheeks which, like his eyes, were covered in the fine grit. As he wiped it away, his skin began crawling with fire.

Shit! The sharp grains are salt!

Whimpering, he scrubbed his face, desperate to rid his flesh of the blazing heat.

Soon blood covered his fingers. His blood. From his face.

Nox gasped and stared wide-eyed.

He was gripped with disbelief. Horror attacked like a hunting leopard.

It was an assault to his senses. Pain was king.

Pure agony propelled him to a pain threshold he didn't know he had.

He bit down on his knuckles, forcing himself to stop rubbing his face.

His heart pounded in frantic beats. It took forever for the pain to subside.

It was an eternity before he convinced himself to resume his excruciating exploration.

With trembling fingers and a delicate touch, he felt his face, starting at his forehead, down his nose and over his cheeks. It was like examining someone else's skin.

Scabbed, peeling, swollen. None of it felt real.

His lips felt foreign too. They were puffy slabs of meat, cracked and painful. He tasted blood and with a mixture of horror and relief he sucked on the moisture, grateful for the salve to his cracked tongue.

Nox carried on the self-examination. Inch by inch he rolled his fingers over his body, assessing the source of the throbbing pain in his back.

What he discovered, set his heart to explode.

Chapter Four

Archer helped Rosalina remove her tank and buoyancy vest. He then pushed it up to the dive deck. Ginger reached for it but the young Australian struggled with the weight. For a woman in her early twenties, Ginger wasn't anywhere near as fit as Rosalina, who was seven years older than her. But as both Jimmy and Alessandro were banned from lifting anything heavy, Archer was grateful to have her around helping.

Ginger was an interesting woman, often saying ridiculous things, but then, out of the blue, she'd come up with something brilliant. He had a feeling there was a whole lot more to her than she let on.

Jimmy leaned over the railing. "Don't keep me in suspense man, how'd you go?" He wasn't a beat-around-the-bush kind of guy.

"We mapped out six squares and--"

"I know you did some digging! Did ya find anythin'?"

"Sure did. Hopefully Alex won't pass out with excitement when he sees it."

"Alex!" Jimmy said with mock hurt. "What about me? Get your ass up here so I can see it."

"Hold your horses." Archer and Rosalina shrugged out of their fins and masks and tossed them up to Ginger.

Ginger squinted against the sun. "You guys okay now? I'll go get Alex."

"We're fine," Rosalina said. "Go get him."

Ginger scurried away.

As Rosalina climbed out of the water, Archer admired her cheeky bottom. He'd never tire of that view. Rosalina wasn't all skin and bones. She embraced her curves and he loved that about her. She looked healthy, athletic and in proportion. Her height was perfect too. Perfect for her to nuzzle her face into his neck when he held her to his chest to inhale her delicate scent. Perfect also for buying her favorite maxi dresses, which he liked to do from time to time. And even better was easing her out of those flowing dresses and tossing them onto the floor.

Once they were both on the dive deck, he helped her out of her shorty wetsuit, then zipped out of his.

"Leave it here." Archer referred to the equipment Rosalina was gathering up. "Jimmy will have a coronary if we don't get up there."

"He's an impatient bugger." She chuckled.

Archer allowed Rosalina to climb the stairs up from the dive deck first. Now that she was out of her wetsuit there was even more of her body to enjoy. He didn't mind that her bikini bottoms rode between her cheeks a tad either. So damn sexy.

Jimmy was at them as soon as they reached to top step. "Let me see."

Archer placed his hand on his mate's shoulder. "Careful Jimbo, you'll pop your stitches."

"I'll pop you with somethin' if you don't hurry up."

Archer huffed out a laugh, though Jimmy probably meant it.

"*Buongiorno*. Did you find something?" Alessandro arrived at the doorway with one arm over Ginger's shoulders and the other gripping his stomach. His olive skin still looked gray even though it'd been over three weeks since his operation.

Between the two of them, Jimmy and Alessandro were sorry sights. The bullet wound Jimmy suffered had done more damage than the knife wound inflicted on Alessandro. Not that it was obvious from looking at them. Alessandro seemed to be in much more pain. But then again, although Jimmy had recently hit the fifty-year-old milestone, he was as tough as any twenty-year-old Archer had ever employed. So tough, the doctors had opted to leave the bullet in him. Archer secretly believed Jimmy was chuffed about that.

"All right you lot. *Mi scusi*, let me through." Rosalina whisked past them all, no doubt heading toward the saloon. "Give me a minute or two," she yelled over her shoulder as she strode away.

"Help me out man." Jimmy clutched Archer's wrist.

Archer hooked his shoulder up under Jimmy's arm and helped him hobble along. By the time Archer, Jimmy, Alessandro and Ginger met Rosalina in the saloon, she was waiting for them at the dining table.

Archer's eyes were drawn to her breasts and how they heaved with her breathless excitement. The dampened bikini top helped. Her glistening eyes confirmed she was itching to show them what she'd hidden beneath a white towel on the table.

"Show me!" Jimmy puffed.

Archer couldn't wait to get him seated; the brute was solid muscle.

"When you all sit, I'll show you." Rosalina said it like a teacher commanding an unruly bunch of children. Jimmy and Alessandro had to be constantly reminded of their doctor's orders to rest. The only reason they were out of hospital and on Archer's yacht in the first place was because of the assurances both Rosalina and Archer had made to the hospital staff that they'd be well looked after. A doctor flew in every second day to change their bandages, administer medications and check on their wounds. Although it was costing him a fortune, Archer would pay ten times the amount if he had to.

Jimmy would've kept a nurse on board too, if the one that turned up hadn't resembled a prison guard rather than someone he wanted to play doctors and nurses with. Not only did she look like she'd break his ball if he misbehaved, she didn't smell too crash hot either. The poor woman only put up with his schoolboy antics for a week, but Jimmy wasted no time in sweet talking Rosalina into taking over the nursing duties. Rosalina didn't mind. Looking after people was in her blood. It was one of the things Archer loved about her.

Rosalina splayed her fingers on the table and cleared her throat. "Archer and I started digging in the same spot as last time, Jimmy."

"Ah, for God's sake, will you just show us."

She smiled a cheeky smile, then gradually peeled back the towel, revealing first the chain then the golden bust.

Alessandro gasped. "*Dio mio.* It's the statue of Achelous. The patron deity of the Silver Swirling or Achelous River. . . like, ummm, what you call, River God, I understand."

"Is it gold?" Ginger's high-pitched voice hit a new level.

"Of course it's gold, honey." Jimmy played expert. "It would've wasted away to nothin' if it was anything else."

"Not exactly." Alessandro was quick to defend his new love interest. "Those nails Archer and Rosalina brought up last time are testament to that." He thrust his chin in defiance.

Alessandro had a good point. In many other locations those nails would've crumbled away to nothing in the current. Archer reached for the gold chain and glided the relatively smooth links between his fingers. This dive spot performed its own natural preservation techniques, and hopefully that meant there was a whole bounty just sitting there, waiting to be discovered.

It was a sobering thought. Just sixty or so feet below where he was standing was a hoard of items that'd been stolen from an Italian church seven hundred years ago. Hopefully they were the lucky bastards set to bring them all back to life.

Moments like these, and he'd had a couple of them in his life, made him wish his father was still alive to share the joy.

Chapter Five

Nox was being tortured. Physically and mentally. Not knowing what happened, where he was, or why he was all alone caused as much agony as his injuries.

But what drove him to delirium and nausea with equal intensity was both shocking and brutal. When he'd found the spear sticking out of his stomach, he thought he was hallucinating. Until he touched it. Barbs of pain had shot from his lower back, down his legs.

Every inch of that smooth rod, from the twenty or so inches that protruded from his stomach, to the length that stuck out his back, was very, very real.

Movement out the corner of his eye had him darting his gaze toward it.

"Hello." His voice was a jagged croak.

He couldn't move enough to turn around to see it.

"Who's there?"

The damn wind alternated between howling gusts, like forced whispers piercing the cracks in the building walls, to protracted quiet. . . like now. Sweeping silence played tricks on his mind.

He'd had endless silence before, and usually cherished being alone and devoid of any incessant noise. But as the whistling wind paused in its freakish onslaught, and he was stuck on his side and trapped all alone in this strange room, fear engulfed him. He was drowning in unanswered questions and couldn't claw his way out.

He froze at a new noise. Jerking his head backwards, agony pierced his lower back. He fought the pain, desperate to see who was there.

"What do you want?"

A sound shunted into the silence with a strange repetitive motion. It was like someone shuffling in slippers. But as suddenly as it started, it stopped.

Father Benedici had often wandered the halls of their church in his slippers. Nox lost count of the amount of times he'd had to clench his jaw to stop himself from yelling at the father to pick up his damn feet. The old fool would trudge to the restroom several times during the night. Nox should have killed him many years earlier than he did.

Clenching his teeth, he focusing solely on the shuffling. It stopped again.

"Talk to me, damn you." He slammed his fist on the wooden table and searing pain blazed down his legs. He howled at the agony.

"Help. HELP ME!" he screamed as loud as his tortured throat could suffer.

Nobody came. Tears oozed from his stinging eyes. His tears became sobbing. . . something he hadn't done since he was a child.

Why can't I recall how I got here?

Yet I can remember the last time I cried my eyes dry.

He was only ten years old at that time, locked in a cupboard, sitting on the floor with his knees tucked to his chest. It was a vivid memory. He went back there now, taking in the cold stone floor and the cramped space that seemed to nudge in that little bit more with every breath he took.

With the absolute darkness, he'd lost all sense of time. Minutes ticked by; hours dragged on. For the entire day he was imprisoned in that cupboard.

It had felt like a week.

But he'd do every second of it over again, as it turned out to be the most important lesson of his life. He'd ridden all the emotions while hugging his knees in the darkness: fear, disbelief, embarrassment, utter uselessness.

But one emotion grew like a festering wound — anger.

By the time Father Benedici found him, he was no longer a sniveling little boy. He was driven. Driven by rage like a pride of lions was driven by hunger.

His anger empowered his revenge. And when he claimed his retaliation, that little boy who locked him in the cupboard, a fellow orphan who was supposedly his friend, had been begging for his forgiveness.

He'd never forget his name, Shyain. Until the day he'd killed him, Nox repeated his name all day long. Shyain would whisper off his tongue with his first breath of the day and it would be the last word he spoke before he succumbed to sleep at night. When Nox wrapped his fingers around Shyain's scrawny neck and squeezed until his eyes bulged red, he'd repeated that name over and over like an evil chant. Once the deed was done, there was no need to utter that ridiculous name ever again.

That was the first time Nox had killed a person. And the ease with which he did it surprised him. There was no emotion, just pure analysis of the situation and outright satisfaction once it was done. Even the dilemma of getting rid of the body unfolded with ease. The hardest part had been lifting the lid off the stone crypt. He did it though. Driven. That's what he was. Even as a child he knew how to harness the power of determination.

To this day, some twenty-eight years later, no-one knew Shyain's body, though most likely nothing more than dust by now, shared an ancient crypt with Robert The Wise. It was an ironic resting place for a stupid little boy. But so be it.

The bulky ring on Nox's finger banged on the wooden table, launching him decades forward to his current hell. The precious ring contained poison. Poisonous mushroom powder to be exact. He'd made it himself. The ring was a clever design. A passing inspection would miss the little hinge that served to raise the decorated lid on a hidden compartment. The ring was at least seven hundred years old. It had been personally designed for Crisofora della Revere, a thirteenth century Italian aristocrat who apparently had as many enemies as he'd had children.

Nox wondered if just a mere taste of the powder, maybe a small spattering on the tip of his tongue, wound take the edge off his pain. All it would take was to pop the lid and dip his finger in. The magic potion may be his savior. He licked his cracked lips, weighing up the idea.

But as much as he wanted to, a niggling command in the back of his mind told him to save it. He had no idea what he was up against, and his poison could come in handy very soon. He'd been in worse situations before. Never with this much pain. But he was a survivor.

When Nox found the antique ring, it had been used to secure an ancient scroll. That scroll, and in particular what was written upon it, had been driving him for decades. And as he lay in agony and apparent neglect, he directed his focus to the scroll and finding the Calimala treasure listed in great detail upon it.

Sometimes, when a ray of light hit the ring in a certain way, the three red jewels in the lid glowed. As if they were reaching out to him; telling him to have faith. But in this dingy room the jewels were lifeless. Just like the gloom threatening to engulf his spirit.

A new noise caught his attention. A low hum, like a nesting wasp. But it wasn't a wasp, it was too consistent and gradually growing louder. It was an engine. Not as heavy as a car engine, but something smaller, like a motorcycle or scooter. He focused on the noise. *It's coming closer.*

His breath shot in and out in frantic gasps.

Relief mingled with a fresh sense of panic.

"Help." His voice was nothing more than a broken whisper. He rolled his tongue around his mouth, trying to produce moisture.

"Help me."

The noise grew louder, yet it was still some distance away. When the noise stopped his mind slammed from one unanswerable question to the next.

Fear tumbled like jagged rocks in his stomach.

A series of thumping noises replaced the engine drone. A scraping sound akin to something being dragged over rocks followed that. Footsteps crunched on what must be gravel.

His breath snagged in his throat as he stared at the light beneath the door. Dread and desperation became one in his mind.

It was a long time before two feet appeared in the gap. He could just make out their shape in the dim light. . . dirty, bare, flat and with long, disgusting toenails. The feet stayed there for a long time. Too long.

What are they doing? Why weren't they coming in?

"Help me."

The door cracked open.

Nox squinted against the glare and the figure in the doorway was nothing more than a black silhouette.

His blood drained. A prickle crawled up his neck as the person hobbled into the room with a disjointed gait. Is it a woman?

The boxy figure said otherwise. The man shuffled across the small divide; back hunched over, lopsided shoulders and long hair as bedraggled and fizzy as the matching beard.

The person stopped before him.

Nox gasped at the redness of the stranger's cheeks. Weathered, sunburned, diseased, whatever it was, the skin on his face looked painful. Nox stared wide-eyed at the hideous face. *Maybe this man has suffered the same torture as me.*

A second person lobbed into the room. Nox blinked against the glare. Either they were identical twins or he was hallucinating. "Who are you?"

"Γεια σας μπορούμε να σας βοηθήσουμε."

Whatever the man had said was impossible to decipher, not just the language, but the way he said it. It was a brittle whisper, as if talking was agony.

Fear scraped through Nox's veins.

The second man held up something. A blade glinted in the glare.

A tortured scream burst from Nox's throat.

Chapter Six

Rosalina was exhausted. Scuba diving day after day was physically draining, and her hair and skin were paying the price too. She prayed that the visiting doctor this afternoon would give Jimmy the go ahead to get back into the water. Not only to save her own sanity, but if she had to listen to him grumble one more time about not being able to dive, she'd probably throw him overboard herself. He was like a caged gorilla and his steely gaze convinced her he was trying his hardest not to rattle the bars. She couldn't wait to see him free again.

Jimmy's frustrations were justified though.

In the previous two weeks, her and Archer had coaxed thirty-eight ancient relics from their watery graves. It really was a treasure hunter's dream. And the pristine condition in which the items had been preserved was a miracle. For seven centuries they'd been exposed to the elements and yet some of the pieces, especially the smooth gold ones, looked like they'd been tossed overboard yesterday.

Alessandro, was the opposite to Jimmy. He was like a ferret on speed. He couldn't keep still, fidgeted constantly and babbled nearly nonstop. It was a world away from the Alessandro she'd known back home in Italy. Before they went on this treasure hunt, nearly all Alessandro's knowledge about history came from books.

Now he was making history.

Each item they discovered represented a puzzle. And Alessandro was a master at solving them. The ancient diary they'd stolen from the crypt in the Church of St Apostoli helped, as did the extensive research notes left behind by Archer's father.

Alessandro was applying his vast research skills to providing a detailed manifest of the haul. It was already impossible to fathom what the treasure would be worth. And there was still so much more to find.

When they were finished, they'd have an incredible showcase for a museum.

Rosalina popped her regulator in her mouth, stepped overboard into the ocean, and upon resurfacing, she gave the okay signal. Archer jumped in at her side and they descended once again to the ocean floor.

Before the dive, Archer had decided they'd exhausted their exploration of section four. It was time to move onto the fifth square they'd mapped out. Swimming along, hand in hand, they swept their metal detectors in a synchronized arc along the bottom. Dozens of small stingrays, camouflaged within the sand popped free and scooted off like Frisbee's.

The ocean floor abruptly dropped away and the change in the terrain was striking. A large collection of moss-covered boulders littered the canyon and the marine life increased dramatically. Fish of all shapes, sizes and colors added to the magnificent vista. Some darted away, some came right up close to nibble on her wetsuit. Rosalina paused along a coral wall to touch a clam. It snapped shut and she giggled. She would never get tired of seeing that.

A blue eel darted out of the coral wall. Gasping, she shoved back. Its attack was as abrupt as it was shocking. Unlike last time, she avoided the eel's razor-sharp teeth. It disappeared back into its hole as quickly as it had appeared.

As she studied its escape, something strange about a large coral fan that swayed with the current caught her attention. She pulled the plant aside and stared wide-eyed at a cave that was big enough for her to swim through. She'd seen caves in rock walls before, but none had been as big as this one looked; she couldn't even see its back wall. She unclipped her dive light from her vest and shone it into the cavernous hole.

A large crab scurried up the inside wall as her flashlight tracked its intended escape. Cobalt blue fish, with a yellow stripe that ran like a Mohawk down the length of their backbone, rubbed their bodies along the coral that lined the cave. As pieces of coral flaked off with their vigorous rubbing, a school of white fish ate in a feeding frenzy, snatching at the shrapnel that floated about as if it were their first meal of the day. Or maybe their last.

The entire cave was a beautiful kaleidoscope of color and movement against a black backdrop and she panned the light in a slow arc around it. The cave was about thirteen feet high and so deep she still couldn't see where it ended.

A section of the cave wall, devoid of any coral or plant life caught her eye.

Her breath hitched.

The cave wasn't a cave at all, it was the upturned hull of an enormous ship. An ancient wooden ship. Like the *Flying Seahorse*.

Her skin tingled with excitement. It was several breaths before she dragged her eyes away to go in search of Archer. As she eased backwards, a strange shape at the side of the entrance snagged her attention. It was a statue, standing erect as if it had been placed there intentionally. It was an ugly thing, with the head of a monkey and an oversized round belly, but the details in its decoration were extraordinary. She wanted so badly to examine it more thoroughly. But she'd wait for Archer.

Furious that he hadn't stuck to her side like a dive buddy was meant to do, she retreated from the cave and with her mind piecing together a safety lecture, she went in search of her fiancé.

But her anger melted away when she found him and saw what he was digging out from the sand. It was a cannon; black as chimney soot, smooth as molten metal, and still looking as powerful as it would have when it was first built.

Archer clutched her hand and with bulging eyes and muffled noises he pointed out aspects of the cannon. Despite the numerous golden relics they'd already salvaged, it was obvious this was his most exciting find. It must be a guy thing.

She glanced at her watch. They had twenty minutes left on the dive. She'd let him have a few more before she dragged him to her cave.

The cannon was much bigger than Archer and would weigh a ton. How they'd get it aboard *Evangeline* was a mystery to her. Knowing Archer though, he'd already have a plan.

Rosalina helped Archer scoop the sand from the barrel of the cannon for five minutes. But she couldn't wait a moment more. She dug her gloved fingers into his arm to get his attention and indicated for him to follow her. He shook his head. She tried again but his stubbornness was on overdrive.

Fighting her frustration, she removed her regulator and mouthed, 'trust me'.

He rolled his eyes, heaved a sigh with a rush of bubbles, then indicated for her to lead the way.

She swam back to the coral fan, tugged it aside and shone her flashlight into the large cave. As much as she wanted to take her time, they simply didn't have enough, so she aimed straight for the wooden slats.

Even with the regulator in his mouth she heard him say, "Holy shit."

The flashlight beam accentuated his golden-flecked eyes as he reached for her. They pushed off and glided over the cave threshold hand in hand. She tapped his arm as she played her light over the statue at the beginning of the cave. It was a bizarre sight, to see the monkey statue sitting right there. As they kicked toward it, she had to shove aside the notion that someone had actually put it there on purpose, as if guarding the treasure.

Archer fell to his knees beside the statue and a small puff of sand blossomed around his legs. His eyes widened in awe and she suddenly regretted not having her underwater camera.

Damn it! We should've taken hundreds of photographs already. Inwardly kicking herself, she made a mental note for the camera to make the next dive.

Instead, she tried to take in and memorize every aspect of this moment. Her breath was the only sound as she inhaled smooth and slow and then released a steady stream of silvery bubbles.

Archer reached out to touch the statue and it may've been the distortion in the water but he seemed to be moving slowly, as if he too felt some reservation about the statue's positioning.

Rosalina eased in for a closer look, and just like Archer she paused.

The body of the statue was decorated in Egyptian hieroglyphics. That was strange. All the Calimala treasure documented in the ancient diary was of European origin. There was no mention of anything from Egypt.

Rosalina frowned as she tried to picture how this item came to be here. Once again, the idea that someone had placed it there on purpose tumbled into her thoughts. But it was a foolish notion. If someone had found this shipwreck before them, they would've taken everything, not left gold statues behind.

The statue was at least three-foot tall and with Archer kneeling beside it, he matched it at head height. He trailed his fingers over a line below the monkey's head. With his hands on the monkey's cheeks, his knuckles bulged. He was trying to twist it.

The monkey's neck had a rim to it, as if it was actually two pieces.

Was it an urn? Did it have more treasures inside?

The monkey's head didn't shift, but the whole statue did. Archer tried to stop it but the weight must've been more than he could handle because it fell over, triggering a cloud of sand and particles. Rosalina matched Archer's efforts to fan the debris away.

When they could see again, Rosalina checked her watch. Five minutes to go. She turned her attention from the monkey statue to the rest of the cave. Her flashlight beam fell on a white object barely three feet away. She glided to it and her eyes bulged.

It took all her concentration to keep breathing.

The item was a heart shaped box in white ceramic and decorated with blue flowers. The edges were trimmed with gold. She prized its gold claw feet from the sand and was surprised at how heavy it was. The box was as big as her outstretched hand.

The clasp at the lower point of the heart shape was unlatched. She placed her light on the sand, dropped to her knees and utilizing the light beam, she pinched the decorated gold clip between her fingers and lifted. The lid resisted, but only briefly and she rolled the lid back.

A large bubble burst from her mouthpiece as she gasped.

Pearls of all shapes and sizes filled the heart shaped box. Small ones, large ones, black, white, both smooth and irregular shaped. All retained a lustrous shine. The only other two items in the box were gold clips. It was the remains of a pearl necklace. The threading had long ago disintegrated, but the pearls and gold clasps were in perfect condition.

With the lid open, she swam over to Archer who was still trying to lift the monkey statue back upright. She touched his shoulder and held forward the jewel box. He gave up his attempts on the statue and reached for it.

A frown rippled his forehead as he looked inside.

She imitated placing a necklace around her neck and Archer nodded his understanding. With his index finger he twirled the pearls around in the box and maybe it was the water distortion, but he seemed to be dismayed, rather than elated by the pearls.

When he handed it back to her, a puzzling look drilled across his eyes.

Something like this would normally result in boyish excitement.

She tucked the observation aside when he glanced at his watch. Something he didn't usually do.

Was that a deliberate distraction? She was normally the clock watcher.

He motioned boat with his hand signals.

She closed the lid, and guided the jewel box into her bag, placing it with care at the bottom of the netting. Archer reached for her hand, and when he squeezed, she searched his eyes. Even with the mask on she could tell he was distracted.

With their flashlights panning out before them, they left the cave. Once outside, sunlight filtered through the blue haze, lighting up the water like a mystical oasis. Rosalina studied the ocean floor below her as she floated upwards, but despite knowing exactly where it was, the shipwreck had once again vanished, completely concealed by coral and plants. It was nature's little disappearing act. Without their lucky find, it may have been lost forever.

Back aboard *Evangeline*, Alessandro made an enormous fuss over the jewel box. He cradled the piece in his hands like it was a newborn baby.

"Hey Jimmy, you won't believe what we found." Archer rested his palm on his mate's shoulder.

"A cannon."

Rosalina did a double take. *How did he guess that?*

"Actually, yes." Archer laughed. "But that's not the exciting bit."

Jimmy scratched his bare chest, and even from three feet away, Rosalina heard the dry rustle of his gray hairs. "Well, don't hold out on me, what'd ya find?"

"We found the *Flying Seahorse*. The whole friggin' hull. She's upside down but intact. We went in through a decent sized hole in the side. It'll be like plucking treasure from a museum display."

"Fuck me," Jimmy blurted. Normally he'd apologize after swearing like that in front of Rosalina, but the dreamy look on his face indicated he probably didn't even realize he'd said it.

"The doc had better give you the all clear today, Jimmy." Archer ran his fingers through his wet hair, snagged them on his curls and gave up. "Because I need your help down there." He turned to Rosalina. "Tell them about the monkey."

Ginger cupped her cheeks. "Oh no, was there a monkey down there?" Sometimes Ginger played the ditzy blonde just a little bit too well.

"Not quite." Rosalina resisted pointing out that if there had been a monkey on board the *Flying Seahorse*, there would be absolutely nothing left of it by now. Fortunately, that would be the same for any human bodies that may have gone down with the ship. Because Rosalina absolutely would not be diving on the shipwreck if there was any chance of that.

Rosalina drank a large mouthful of water in an attempt to wash the saltiness from her tongue and cleared her throat. "There's an unusual gold statue positioned just inside the hole in the shipwreck. It looks like it's been placed there on purpose, as if guarding the doorway." She smacked further negative thoughts down. It wasn't like her to be a pessimist.

Maybe the Incident was playing on her mind more than she realized. Being negative wasn't in her repertoire, and just the hint of that shift in her personality made her hate Nox all over again. Nox was dead. And that alone should help her move on from The Incident. But maybe it was going to take longer than she'd originally thought.

"Anyway," she said. "The statue has a monkey's head and a strange pot belly. It's big, about three feet high. And the head may be removable, like it's some kind of urn."

"I'm going to need your help lifting it, Jimmy." Archer's eyes glowed at his best mate. "It's bloody heavy. When I tried to lift the head off, the whole thing fell over, but I couldn't right it again."

"How are we going to raise it then?" Jimmy grew serious, his deep frown pulling his graying eyebrows into a straight line.

"Don't worry about that, I have an idea." Archer checked his watch and clicked his fingers. "But first, let's get washed up and hide all this stuff. The doctor's due in less than an hour." Archer reached for Rosalina's hand. "Hey Ginger, I don't suppose you've planned lunch, I'm starving," he said.

Her face lit up and she rubbed her hands together. "Sure have."

She looked thrilled that he'd asked. Maybe Ginger liked having something to do.

Rosalina still found it difficult to have Ginger doing all the cooking on *Evangeline* though. For three years the professional galley had been her domain but now that Archer needed her to do all the diving, she barely found the energy to create any of her favorite meals. Or the basic ones for that matter. Not that she didn't appreciate bringing priceless treasures up from ocean. With a bit of luck, the doctor would give Jimmy the go-ahead to get back in the water. Hopefully then things would return to normal.

Archer led Rosalina to the Hamilton Suite, shut the door behind him and made his way to the restroom where he adjusted the shower taps to hot. He then offered for her to go first. She didn't argue and slipped out of her bikini and into the cascade. A warm shower after scuba diving was always a luxurious reward. As she attempted to detangle her hair, her mind drifted to Archer's reaction to the pearls. Something had troubled him.

I have to get to the bottom of it.

She reached for the soap. "Hey babe, would you like me to wash your back?"

A heartbeat later, he was in there with her.

He wriggled his eyebrows. "Only 'cause you asked so nicely."

Slipping his arms around her waist, he drew her in for a kiss. Even this simple touch from him set her heart racing. His warm hands on her body was just one of the pleasures she'd missed when they were separated. Thankfully, fate brought them back together.

She debated whether or not to bring up the pearls. Wave after wave of uncertainty tormented her decision. But the more she thought about it, the more she couldn't let it go. He promised never to keep secrets from her again.

She didn't like to think of this as a test, but maybe it was.

"Hey babe." She leaned her back against his warm body and let her head fall against his shoulder. As she had hoped, he wrapped his arms around her, just beneath her breasts.

"Yes." His breath was hot on her cheek.

Archer's hand rode up to cup her breast in his palm and it was her cue to speak before things got carried away. "Honey, when I handed you those pearls you looked so sad. Why?"

He stiffened and his hand dropped away. Rosalina spun to face him. She placed her palm on his chest, directly over the unusual gold necklace that he'd worn every day since his father died. The muscles beneath her fingers were as hard as the look in his eyes. "Tell me, babe. Something flashed into your mind. What was it?"

His eyes shifted to her, yet he'd slipped from reality. She'd seen this look before. He was about to reveal something very sad. If he was willing to let it go.

The finger of gold around his neck was the key to finding the Calimala treasure.

Finding the treasure was the key to unlocking Archer's tragic childhood.

Occasionally, something triggered another flashback and Rosalina believed she was the key to coaxing those memories from him. Some of these flashbacks were horrific and had rocked her to her core. Some, however, were delightful and although they were few and far between, it was unearthing those ones. . . those magical childhood memories that he'd buried from his past with all the other misery, that made this process all worth it.

Archer reached for the soap and avoiding her gaze, he rolled the citrus scented bar around in his palms until a thick lather oozed from his fingers. Rosalina waited and could practically see the debate raging in his mind.

Archer closed his eyes and cleared his throat. "The day before Dad died, he took me shopping with him to buy Mom's birthday present. We were at Santorini, I think." His eyes rolled beneath his closed eyelids and Rosalina imagined he was visualizing that day.

"Dad had a knack for finding the best things at the cheapest prices. We hired two donkeys and went down one of those cobblestone streets. It was so steep I thought I was going to fall off and Dad's donkey did so many shits on the way down, the poor thing must've been bursting under his weight. God, we laughed about that." Archer smiled; only briefly, and he opened his eyes, but he stared at a spot over her head, his eyes unmoving, maybe seeing something deep in his memory.

"We stopped at this tiny alley. Hundreds of copper pots, pans and cooking utensils of every kind hung from the trellis-lined alleyway. The walls were loaded with everything from clothes to fishing gear. It smelled dusty and old and I loved it. Everywhere you looked there was something interesting." He touched his lathered hands to her shoulder and teased the foam over her skin. "I don't know how Dad found these places, but everywhere we went, it was like he'd been there a dozen times before."

For the umpteenth time, Rosalina wished she'd been fortunate to have met Wade.

Archer ran his soapy hand up and down her arm and his eyes followed the movement. "We stopped halfway along the alley to climb a set of stairs. At the top was a dusty little jewelry shop. You'd never even know it was there. How the guy attracted any business I have no idea."

Rosalina smiled. Archer was a great businessman, and obviously even as an eleven-year-old child he could recognize shortcomings in marketing.

"But in saying that, it was obvious the business had been there a very long time. So maybe he didn't need or want to advertise. The right people knew where to find him. My Dad included. We spent so long in that shop. I remember complaining because I was hungry. But Dad was painfully methodical, analyzing almost every pearl necklace. Not once did he ask the price."

Archer's shoulder sagged, as if heavy with the weight of the story, and her stomach twisted as she dreaded what he was about to say. "It took forever. When he finally chose one, the guy behind the counter made a big show of wrapping it up in gold decorated paper and a white ribbon."

He blinked several times then his eyes turned to her. Her breath caught in her throat at the sadness in his coffee-colored eyes. "That was the last time I saw that necklace. He never did get a chance to give it to Mom."

"Oh Archer." Rosalina stepped forward and wrapped her arms around his wet body. She clung to him, flesh to flesh. The steady flow of warm water cascading down his back was both a soothing lullaby and a dramatic contrast to the storm brewing inside his chest.

If only she could take that memory and give it a more deserving ending. But it could never be. . . instead they could only dream of how a gift like that, chosen with the greatest care and detail, would have been received.

Chapter Seven

Archer was preparing to drop *Evangeline's* anchor at Anafi's small marina when Ginger spotted the helicopter coming in low over the horizon.

Archer squinted at the sun-drenched clouds, searching for the chopper. "He's early." So far, every visit from the doctor had them waiting at least half an hour. It'd become the norm for him to be delayed for one medical reason or another. But to be early, that was different. As it neared though, Archer's gut clenched. The chopper was different, smaller in size and rounder in body.

An avalanche of paranoia hit him as he snatched the binoculars and ran to the upper deck.

Maintaining cover behind the wall, he peered through his binoculars at the helicopter. When he saw the man behind the glass dome with his chiseled face and silver hair, a name hissed from his throat. "Ignatius Montpellier."

Son of a bitch! Just when they'd hit the jackpot, that bastard shows up.

His hatred for the man bubbled to the surface like toxic gas. The last time he'd seen him, the thief had snatched a piece of ancient treasure right out from Archer's grasp. At the depth they'd been diving and the way Iggy had shot to the surface, it should've killed him. It was only because Archer had nearly died from decompression sickness once before that he'd halted his chase.

Ignatius was crazy. His continual taunts over the years had only fueled Archer's disdain for the man.

If he ever got his hands on Iggy, he had no intention of holding back.

His appearance was their worst nightmare.

Although Archer wasn't surprised to see him.

The commotion over The Incident had the media all over them, so it was only a matter of time before Iggy found out.

Jimmy's going to blow a gasket if he doesn't get to dive for the treasure he's been dreaming of since Archer asked him to captain Evangeline *from Australia.*

Archer's gut boiled when Iggy gave a salute.

Who is he signaling to? It certainly wasn't him.

The helicopter kicked up the sea spray as it roared past.

Archer raced to the front cabin and bumped into Rosalina. Her hand was over her mouth but her fearful eyes said it all. She knew who it was too. Ignatius had been shadowing Archer's treasure hunts for a decade.

Many moons ago, Archer's father and Ignatius had been friends. Photos of the two of them together had once hung on the walls of his father's boat. Archer could still remember the anger drilled onto his father's face when he'd snatched those frames down and smashed them. Iggy's name was only spoken with seething after that.

Rosalina had heard enough stories to be as concerned about him resurfacing as Archer was.

The other worrying addition was the helicopter. It indicated Ignatius was doing well financially, and that wasn't good either.

A crazy treasure hunter with a blatant disregard for others and funds to burn was a dangerous mix.

"He saluted us," Archer said through gritted teeth. "Who's out there?"

Rosalina's eyebrows drilled together. "Ginger ran out to wave at him."

"Why? Does she know him?" He clenched his jaw as horrifying thoughts tumbled into focus. He knew so little about Ginger. But even as he played out several nasty scenarios, he wanted to deny they could be true. Ginger didn't seem like a deceitful person.

Rosalina blinked up at him. "I guess she thought it was the doctor."

Jimmy stepped into the room. "I thought it was the doc too."

"I wish it was." His gut twisted. "This changes everything." The chopper was just a faint throb in the distance when Archer strode from the room to get Ginger and Alessandro. They needed to hear what he had to say.

Ginger was standing at the railing, shielding her eyes against the sun as she looked up to the sky.

"What're you doing?" he strode toward her.

"What? I—" She backed away her eyes wide. "I thought it was the doctor."

Her fearful look had Archer easing back. He suddenly felt terrible for suspecting her of any form of conspiracy.

Archer shook his head as he imagined Iggy getting a kick out of the bikini-clad Ginger's friendly welcome. "Okay, come inside guys. I need to tell you who that was."

By the time they were all seated, Archer's seething had simmered down enough that he was able to consider their options. "The bastard in that helicopter was Ignatius Montpellier."

"Who?" everyone but Rosalina asked.

"Ignatius Montpellier. Treasure hunter. Ruthless idiot. He'd do anything to get his hands on treasure. He did it to Dad, he's done it to me. The last time I saw him he stole an ancient sword right out my hands. And he damn well nearly killed himself getting away from me. Wish he had."

"Was the sword valuable?" Ginger's eyes lit up.

Archer frowned. Clearly, she missed the point. "Not sure," he said. "I never saw it again. The point is Iggy's crazy."

"Do you think he knows about the *Seahorse*?" Jimmy jabbed his stubby finger at the table top.

"It doesn't matter. He must've seen us on the news and he's obviously curious about what we're doing."

"*Non bene.*" Alessandro squeezed his palms to his temples. "You think he'll go after the treasure?"

"Without a doubt." Archer drove his fingers through his hair; they snagged on his curls and he pushed harder.

"If he thinks he can just fly on over here and get his hands on our treasure, he'll have to get through me first." Jimmy banged his fist.

Ignatius was never one to sneak around. His flyby was a message. He wanted Archer to know he was here. The likes of Jimmy was barely a ripple in the rich bastard's grand plans. But Archer had no intention of putting Jimmy near danger ever again. Or any of them for that matter.

"Let's hope it doesn't come to that." Archer pulled a chair and sat down. "This means we need to hurry now. My guess is he's getting a boat and dive crew together as we speak. First thing we need to do is moor *Evangeline* away from the dive site. We don't need to pinpoint it for him. We were just lucky we were at the marina and not right over *The Seahorse* when he found us."

"But this's our site," Alessandro blurted. His scowl matching Jimmy's.

"Actually, it's not." Archer shook his head. "We haven't legally laid claim to it."

"Well, let's do it!" Alessandro said.

"It's not that easy Alex. Things like that take time. As soon as we lodge a claim, every man and his dog will be in here digging, right up to the day we get that piece of paper in our hands. By then, the whole lot may be gone. What we need to do is beat them to it."

"Well, where the hell is that damn doctor? We got things to do." Jimmy's face was awash with sweat, even with the yacht's efficient air-conditioning.

"Hey Jimmy, you need to calm down before the doc arrives. Don't want your heart rate setting his alarms off."

"Come on, Jimmy." Rosalina stood and placed her hand under his arm to help him stand. "How about you splash some cool water on your face?"

As if on cue, the regular beat of a rotor blade sounded off the port side. Archer glanced out to see the chopper making its approach. It was the doctor this time. Within ten minutes the helicopter had landed on *Evangeline's* helipad and Jimmy greeted him with a charming grin. After small pleasantries, he set about examining both Jimmy and Alessandro's wounds. Doctor Tallaharis was an intense bore of a man who conducted his exam with nothing more than a few indecipherable moans. Waiting for the final result was excruciating, and Archer had no idea how Jimmy was keeping his cool.

Finally, the doctor put his pen down. "Looks like you're healing very well. I think--"

"So, I'm good to scuba dive. Right, Doc?" Jimmy blurted.

The doctor eased back on his chair, and devoid of any emotion he squinted at Jimmy. He then cleared his throat. "I don't think it matters what I say. You've already made up your mind."

Jimmy's mouth gaped, as if deliberating a response.

The doctor was right. After Iggy's appearance everything had changed and Archer was certain nothing short of tying him down would stop Jimmy from getting back in the water.

"Yes Doc. You're right," Archer stepped forward.

The doctor turned to him and the look in his eyes had shifted from concern to resignation.

"He's a stubborn bugger." Archer put his hand on Jimmy's shoulder and tried to squeeze the corded muscle dominating it. The man was built like a rock. "I'm not sure we can hold him back much longer. So, that said, what should we do to make sure he doesn't do any damage?"

It took some convincing, but eventually the doctor softened. He handed out strict instructions, along with a series of prescriptions and fresh bandages. By the time he was back aboard the helicopter and heading toward Athens for the last time, Jimmy was already messing around with his dive gear, preparing for his first dive in nine weeks.

Archer moored *Evangeline* two hundred yards from the *Flying Seahorse* wreck and before he'd even dropped anchor, Jimmy was at the crane lowering the tender. The small boat was crammed full with their dive gear, leaving little room for four people. It was a frustrating waste of time having to motor to the dive site, but it was necessary.

Although she hadn't said it, Archer could tell Rosalina was pleased not to be diving. It wouldn't be quite the same without her, but on the other hand he was dying to show Jimmy what they'd found down there.

When they'd met a decade or so ago, Jimmy had been wallowing in a world of self-pity and anger over his messy divorce. Not only had he lost his wife to a younger man, he'd also lost all his funds in the fight. His work at the wharf was an unpredictable mix of long hours or nothing at all and Jimmy's spare time was spent drinking, pressing weights and beating Archer at their favorite card game. . . canasta.

But from the moment Archer taught Jimmy how to dive, all that changed. He didn't give up the rum or the card playing, but once he'd experienced the pure tranquility of the ocean, Jimmy was a convert. Any chance he could, Jimmy would take a dive with Archer.

It took nearly half an hour to get to the dive site. It was time they didn't have.

Jimmy was slipping into his gear well before Ginger dropped the anchor overboard.

Rosalina looked a knockout in the cotton shirt she was wearing today. The blue fabric accentuated her stunning cornflower blue eyes. He especially appreciated that a few buttons were undone, showing the swell of her cleavage above her string bikini. If they were alone, it would be impossible not to touch her velvet skin. Maybe later tonight he could satisfy the burning fire that threatened to embarrass him at any moment.

"Be back soon, baby." Archer clutched Rosalina's cheeks and gave her a brief kiss. She wrapped her arms around him and whispered, "You take care of him."

Normally Rosalina would be whispering to Jimmy to keep an eye out for Archer. He'd overheard her do it many times. Now it was reversed. Not that she needed to say it, Archer would watch Jimmy like an overprotective parent. He didn't want any more dive incidents on his hands.

Archer checked Jimmy's gear in the pre-dive safety check. "Here we go, mate. Ready."

Jimmy's smile was that of a hyperactive child.

The best way to get from the small boat into the water was to flip backwards. Archer wasn't sure if Jimmy would be able to, but the tough nut gave a quick salute and flipped overboard with the agility of a teenager. Archer laughed at the look of pure joy on Jimmy's face when he resurfaced.

"Guess I better catch up." Archer nodded at the ladies, then he too flipped into the crystal-clear Mediterranean Sea.

He joined Jimmy and the two of them sank below the surface. Behind them they unfolded a length of rope, their lifeline to Rosalina and Ginger. Their plan was simple: the girls would tug on the rope if something wasn't right. But if everything went to plan, then the rope would assist them in raising whatever they find to the surface.

Archer also carried Rosalina's buoyancy vest and tank. He was hoping his idea would work, otherwise they'd have a whole other issue to deal with. Jimmy was carrying a large crate and apparently, he had every intention of filling it to the brim with treasure. Archer could only dream it'd be that easy. Maybe luck would be on their side this time.

Visibility was excellent. The water temperature was a pleasant seventy-five degrees and he was grateful he'd resisted wearing his shorty wetsuit.

Jimmy was fluid in the water. For a big man, recovering from serious injuries, he was as elegant as a dolphin. A butch dolphin maybe. The weightlessness helped.

Archer led the way, making a beeline straight for the coral fan. Its intense tangerine color was easy to spot in the distance. He tugged the fan aside and with their flashlights switched on, he gestured for Jimmy to pass through the gap first. The rope snaked a trail behind him as he too swam through the hole into the ancient boat hull. To think this wreck has been in this very position, hidden from the world for seven hundred years, was mind-boggling. It was a wonder any of it was still intact.

The first stop was the monkey statue. Archer tugged on Jimmy's fin to divert his attention to the side of the entrance where the statue lay on its side. His flashlight brought out the warm glow of the gold. But rather than taking in its beauty, Archer watched for Jimmy's reaction.

A puff of bubbles exploded from Jimmy's regulator and despite his full mouth, "fuck me," was loud and clear.

Jimmy knelt beside the statue and placed his hands on the gold, as if drawing power from the precious metal. Archer cruised up alongside and offered to shake Jimmy's hand.

It felt good to be sharing this with him. Especially as he'd nearly lost his good friend trying to find this treasure.

Together they lifted the monkey statue upright. Archer pointed out the groove in the monkey neck and Jimmy's exaggerated nod indicated he understood what it meant. He couldn't wait to get the monkey up top and see what it was harboring in its big belly. He tugged the second buoyancy vest forward and sat the tank upright in the sand.

Jimmy undid the clips on the vest and helped Archer attach Rosalina's tank to the statue. Together they pulled the straps tight. Once it was attached, Archer indicated for Jimmy to help him roll the monkey forward onto its belly. Archer crossed his fingers as he inflated the vest. With each pump of air, the buoyancy vest swelled and he watched for the moment the statue lifted off the sand. It was beautiful to witness. Just as planned, the gold statue eased off the ground and hovered in the air like an act in a magic show.

Jimmy's attempt at a slamming high five was bollixed by the water and he missed Archer's outstretched hand altogether. They both laughed, releasing precious bubbles from their tanks. It was worth it; seeing Jimmy this happy made this moment all the more special.

Confident his idea worked, Archer deflated the vest and lowered the monkey statue back to the sand. They'd re-inflate when it was time to surface.

Wringing his hands, he turned to the rest of the wreck. It was time to explore. For Jimmy's sake, Archer shone his flashlight on the wooden planks on the side wall.

Archer couldn't imagine any of the vessels he'd come into contact with surviving as long as the *Flying Seahorse* had. Archer had been around boats most of his life. His first though, had been his father's classic gentleman's cruiser. She had a steel hull, was richly decorated with teak elements and chrome finishing, and his father's unabashed doting taught Archer what it meant to love a boat. He wondered what happened to the *Dancing Princess*.

The name of his father's boat tumbled from nowhere and Archer made a connection that he'd never made before. His Dad had named the boat after Archer's mother. For years she'd taught ballroom dancing. Archer made a mental note to ask her what happened to the *Dancing Princess*. The Conrad Cabin cruiser had been his father's pride and joy and as far as Archer could remember, it was the only boat he'd ever owned. Maybe someone had been looking after her all these years.

Jimmy headed toward the middle of the domed area with apparent purpose. If Archer didn't know any better, he'd believe Jimmy had some divine knowledge of the wreck layout.

No sooner had Jimmy eased to his knees on the sandy floor when Archer heard him cheering. Jimmy's hands were filled with gold coins.

Seeing the look on Jimmy's face, lit up with pure excitement, reminded Archer of his father grinning through his mouthpiece like that.

But his gut wrenched.

It was also the last couple of minutes of his father's life.

Chapter Eight

Nox was living in hell and the two men with their sick grins and bulging eyes were the grim reapers. The weapon in their hands, the bowed saw with its jagged teeth and dulled metal, was their scythe.

He wanted to run, but the thought of moving terrified him.

He tried to scream but his throat burned. The sound that did release was nothing more than a terrified moan.

The men were talking, but their language was foreign and their voices were strange.

These two men were not normal. Everything from their disheveled appearance, their foul stench and their lack of communication, led Nox to believe they hadn't lived a normal life.

One of the men had a jagged scar that ran from his eye socket over his cheek and disappeared into the thickness of his beard. The raised pink defect was in brutal contrast to the rest of his sunburned face.

The second man's beard was shorter; the bluntness of its shape made it look like it had been hacked off.

But other than those two anomalies, everything else about them was identical. They had to be twins.

A bottle was shoved in Nox's face. Water! He reached for it, desperate to quench his barren throat. But the second he drew the bottle near, the pungent odor struck him like a snakebite.

They're trying to poison me! He lurched backwards but searing pain shot up his back. He gasping for air. He clawed at the table.

The man thrust the bottle at him again. The vapors alone made his eyes water. He snapped his face away. "No!" The scream tore from his throat and hurt so much he had to force himself to swallow. His tongue was as dry as cracked leather, brittle enough that it may actually snap off.

A harsh grating sound came from Scar Face's throat. Nox glared at him.

Is he laughing?

The second man joined in and between the two of them they cackled like a pack of hyenas in a feeding frenzy. Scar Face snatched the bottle and took a large swig. Through his frizzy beard, his Adam's apple bobbed up and down with each mouthful.

His twin yanked the bottle from Scar Face before he finished, spilling it over his beard and shoulder. A scuffle erupted between them with yelling and punching.

Nox stared in horror.

The crazy twins fell to the floor and the fight continued with swinging fists and rabid groaning.

Nox searched the room, desperate for something he could use as a weapon. One of the rubies in his ring, his poison ring, caught a beam of sunlight penetrating a gap in the wall. It was the briefest of encounters yet the result was dazzling. He twisted the antique around with his thumb. Since he'd found it decades ago, it had always provided some form of comfort. Knowing that he could use the poison powder whenever he wanted was incredibly powerful. This was his chance.

The bottle with the pungent liquid was within reach. He grabbed it. The stench, as powerful as peroxide, stung at his nostrils. With one eye on the fools on the ground, still beating the hell out of each other, he flipped the lid on his jeweled ring. Careful not to lose any of the precious powder, he drew it closer to look inside the tiny well.

But what he saw clawed away the last piece of his sanity. It was empty. Every last grain of his mushroom poison was gone.

A scream tore from his throat. Loud and painful.

When he opened his eyes, Scar Face was right there. The twin's eyes bulged; the whites were a hideous shade of yellow. His teeth were crooked and the color of mustard. His rancid breath was a mixture of rotten teeth and potent liquor.

Was this the man who was going to kill me?

Nox couldn't stand it any longer. The pain, the fear, the unknown, it was all too much. He reached for the bottle and, forcing past the vicious odor, he took giant swallows.

It stung his tongue, stung his throat and clawed at his insides.

He paused, gasping for breath, swallowing back the vile concoction.

The brothers laughed again. But Nox didn't care. His only hope was that the poison worked quickly. All he wanted, was to end this living hell.

Nox tipped the bottle up again and gulped down every last drop. The dryness in his mouth changed from barren wasteland to a strange new sensation, nothing. It was as if he'd been anesthetized. He couldn't tell if his tongue was moving. He turned his attention to his hand. With all the concentration he could assemble he wriggled his fingers. As he blinked away the blurriness, the room began to spin. He couldn't control his eyes.

An incredible weightlessness took control, like floating on a cloud. He could no longer feel the lower half of his body. The pain subsided and became nothing more than a dull ache. He closed his eyes and absorbed the peacefulness.

The last sound he heard before he slipping into a wonderful, pain-free blackness was the sharp rasp of a saw on metal.

Nox drifted. Floating on an endless sea and staring up at the bluest sky he'd ever seen. Fluffy white clouds cruised overhead. He floated past islands covered in thick green vegetation and dotted with brilliant white rocks. The water was warm, lapping at his sides and lulling him to sleep.

He dreamed of treasure, so vast and valuable that it took mighty ships to carry the entire haul. Images flashed through his mind with tickertape craziness. He saw gold, silver, coins and jewels. He saw rats, blood, rotting flesh and wooden crosses. He saw fancy yachts, blonde women in bikinis and fish tanks filled with mushrooms.

And a cat. A silver-gray Chartreux. The name Shadow came to mind. The cat's teeth sawed back and forward, crushing a writhing rodent between his jaws.

Soon there was nothing but a bloody mess.

Nox snapped his eyes open and stared into darkness so black he wondered if he were alive. His body was on fire. Burning up with furnace intensity. He knew he was indeed alive when his sweat dribbled from his arm pit and trickled down his chest, like his life was oozing out of him.

As he blinked into the darkness, shapes began to appear. Slithers of light filtered in through jagged slits in the walls and it showed just how poorly constructed the building was.

Was it a full moon outside providing the limited light?

His eyes adjusted, allowing him to make out his surroundings.

The shabby construction of the building was just the beginning. Everything he looked at appeared to be homemade. And not by someone with any skills. The ladder was made of gnarly wood and rope. As were the chairs and table. The wood he lay on, maybe a table of some sort, wasn't smooth by any means. He ran his fingers over the dozens, maybe hundreds, of dents in the wood. It must be used for chopping. The grooves could be ax marks.

The image of that curved saw with its jagged teeth and dulled metal slammed into his mind. With trembling fingers, Nox reached down to his stomach. His breath caught in his throat. He ran his hand over the area where the spear had been.

Fighting a wave of panic, he looked down. The rod was gone.

Strips of cloth with threaded edges and varying widths was wrapped around his body. But a dark stain was seeping from beneath. It was blood. His blood.

"Help!" he screamed. But nothing came out of his mouth.

He tried again, but it wasn't any more than a pathetic moan. He heard breathing. Ragged strained breathing. It took him a while to realize it was his own.

What's happening to me?

Pain riddled his body. . . from his cracked lips to the pulsing agony down his legs.

Am I being punished?

Maybe, as a Brother of the St Apostoli Church who didn't believe in God, he deserved to be punished.

But this was crazy. He couldn't cope with the agony much longer.

He twisted the bulky antique around his middle finger. He had no choice; he couldn't kill himself. But even if he had his powder, did he really think he could end his life, after all he'd been through?

The ring was an important link. It reminded him where he came from, even if he didn't know where he was now, or how he arrived here. Most of all, the ring represented a vast treasure. His treasure. Thoughts of that treasure were the only thing keeping him alive.

It was the only thing he believed in.

Not God. Not prayer.

Neither of them ever helped him before.

His situation was very similar to when he was ten years old and locked in that cupboard. Alone, in the dark, trapped and scared.

This was another test. God was yet again making him prove he didn't need him, that he was a survivor. He'd been to hell and back many times. What he needed to do now was focus on surviving this new living hell.

He was still on his side and the ache in his shoulder was nothing more than a physical cramp. He'd been lying on his side for a long time. Days at least, maybe weeks. Resting hard up against the cold rough wood, it was a wonder he hadn't seized altogether. He brought his fingers to his temples and tried to massage away a throbbing headache.

Water was his first priority. His headache would be the result of severe dehydration. In researching the effects of ingesting his poisonous mushrooms he'd learned just how cruel severe dehydration was. And if he didn't get water soon, he was heading down the path from where there was no return.

Now that the spear was gone, he should be able to move.

At least, that's what he wanted to believe. It took a few moments to psyche himself up. To prepare, he sucked in deep breaths, as if readying for battle.

Then, with clenched jaw and brute determination, he pushed up from the table.

Chapter Nine

Archer and Jimmy disappeared below the surface for the second time that day and the water was so clear Rosalina was able to follow their descent for a full two minutes before they vanished into obscurity. She checked her watch and set her alarm for fifty minutes time. That's when she'd return with the small boat and prepare for the men to resurface.

With a flick of a switch, she started the engine and motored toward the sandy Anafi shore. The diver-below buoy bobbed in the water, waving the marker flag in her wake. Directly above her, the sun was fireball white and it reflected off a piece of treasure that had slipped out from under the tarpaulin.

"Hey Ginger, can you push that back in please?"

Since their visit from Ignatius, they'd all become paranoid. And with good reason. She couldn't imagine what Archer, or Jimmy would do if Iggy managed to get hold of any of this treasure.

Just trying to estimate the value of what they'd found so far was breathtaking. The monkey statue alone had to be priceless. It had been a mammoth effort to raise it. For starters, it weighed so much it was impossible to lift it into the little motorboat, even with the four of them helping. In the end they had to tow it very slowly back to *Evangeline*.

It was problematic not having the yacht at the dive site and everything was taking a whole lot longer. It was time they couldn't afford to waste. But both Jimmy and Archer had become obsessed with continuing the treasure hunting like a stealth mission.

Once they'd towed the statue to *Evangeline,* Archer used the crane to lift the monkey statue onto the dive deck. The entire operation took hours but seeing that golden statue glowing in the afternoon sunlight had been magical. As per doctor's orders, Archer flatly refused to let Jimmy or Alessandro lift it. So, between Archer, Ginger and Rosalina, the three of them juggled the statue up the stairs and into the saloon.

The statue now took pride of place at the foot of the bar. It looked like it meant to be there. . . an exquisite piece designed specifically for that spot. After the statue was in position, they'd devoured a quick snack of her homemade macadamia and salted caramel friands, and then they set off again. Except for Alessandro. He'd remained aboard *Evangeline,* and was probably trying to work out how to open the monkey statue right now.

"We're coming up to a rock on your left." Ginger pointed the mound out.

It was barely visible beneath the surface but hitting it would have them sinking to the bottom in seconds, especially with what they had onboard.

Once they were past the line of rocks that formed a natural marina for the secluded beach, Rosalina headed straight for the shore.

Ginger jumped off as the boat crunched on the coarse sand and pulled on a rope in an attempt to drag it further ashore. Rosalina climbed over the side too, and even with both of them pulling, they were unable to move the boat any further forward.

Once Rosalina was certain the boat was secured, she set about putting up the beach umbrella and laid a few towels beneath it, while Ginger reapplied sunscreen to her face and hands.

"Think we could have a look at what they found?" Ginger grinned while rubbing cream on her nose.

Rosalina glanced at her watch, forty minutes to go. "I don't see why not, as long as we keep them under cover."

Ginger rubbed her hands together in a move Rosalina had seen Alessandro do dozens of times. It was funny to see her copying his mannerisms. Since Ginger and Alessandro met, they'd become inseparable. With Alessandro being an old flame, a very old flame, Rosalina had thought it would be awkward watching their attraction blossom, but she was honestly pleased for him. He was a good man who deserved to find love and she'd never seen him as smitten with any woman, like he was with Ginger.

Rosalina followed Ginger back to the boat and together they peered under the tarpaulin. The items were jumbled together as if they'd been tossed aboard with little care. It wasn't the right thing to do and they all knew it. But at the moment, speed was more important than fastidious-ness. Once these pieces were aboard *Evangeline*, Alessandro would quickly have them photographed, cataloged and secured in a more deserving facility.

Ginger reached for a chest with a concave lid and by the way she struggled, it was heavy.

"Hang on." Rosalina moved around the boat to help her lift it out. She placed her hand beneath the chest and was surprised by the cold-ness of the metal. Together they crab walked with the chest between them up the beach to the waiting umbrella.

"Can't wait to see what's in here." Ginger giggled like a teenage girl.

"Me neither." The little heart shaped box Rosalina had found with the pearls had belonged to Maria Maridonna Verdelanda, the wife of a rich nobleman. Alessandro was able to establish that she'd died during the plague of 1348, as did her husband and four children. Rosalina wondered if any family members survived the plague, maybe her parents or siblings. It was hard to imagine entire families being wiped out by such a relentless disease.

Her heart squeezed. She missed her Nonna terribly and made a mental note to ring her before dinner tonight. Just the thought of talking to the woman who'd raised her, made her smile, even though Nonna would probably be mad that Rosalina hadn't made contact in over a week. She'd already lost five years with Nonna when she was in Australia and it wasn't until she returned that she realized just how frail her grandmother had become. Guilt curled in her chest. Nonna was getting old and now was the time she should be with her. Especially now that Filippo was giving her such a hard time. The title of 'black sheep in the family' really rang true with her youngest brother. Since he turned twenty-one, his fiery personality hit a whole new level, and with liquor in his system he was even worse. It was stress Nonna didn't need.

Hopefully, now that time was against them, this treasure hunt would be over quickly and Rosalina would be back home very soon.

She adjusted her stance so she could lower the chest carefully onto the towels. The chest was the size and shape of a shoebox, except for the curved lid. Each side was decorated in intricate carvings etched into the metal and surprisingly, like most of the pieces discovered so far, only small bubbles of corrosion were evident. She sat down on the towel and tucked her feet up to her side.

If Rosalina had to guess she'd say the box was made of silver. There were a couple of belt-like loops secured in rows over the entire box. Their purpose slotted into her mind and she clicked her fingers. "I bet these once contained leather straps that held the box together."

"Oh yeah." Ginger ran her fingers over them.

The leather would have long ago disintegrated in the salty water. Rosalina placed her hands on the lid and tried to raise it upward. But it refused to budge. Ginger scrambled to her feet to help.

"It's moving," Ginger squealed. "Pull harder."

The lid flipped off and both Rosalina and Ginger went sprawling. The lid flung from their hands, but thankfully it landed on a towel. Rosalina retrieved it and sat on her knees to take a look inside the box. The sound of the waves rolling into the shore evaporated into oblivion as Rosalina admired the precious contents.

With a breath trapped in her throat, she reached inside the chest and drew out the first item her fingers touched. It was the most beautiful piece of jewelry she'd ever seen. A gold bracelet, with large rectangular cut emerald stones. Each gemstone was centered within a gold disk that was decorated with scalloped edges. It was in immaculate condition. And heavy. She tried to imagine the woman who would have worn it. She must have been quite a big lady to wear such a large piece, and she probably would've had the perfect outfit to wear with it. A smile touched her lips as she recalled that her Nonna always had a unique set of jewelry to match every dress. It was one of the things she was fastidious about.

Ginger held up another bracelet. This one was a series of miniature gold plaques; each one depicted a different image, as if the bracelet told a story. Rosalina recognized one of the symbols. It was an eagle with its talons gripping a bolt of cloth. This was the Arte di Calimala insignia used to represent the wealthy cloth finishers' guild.

"Alessandro will love that piece." Actually, he was excited about every piece. With the ancient diary as his guide, so far, he'd been able to match the descriptions detailed in those lists with the real items. It was like putting the pieces of a puzzle together. A vast, valuable puzzle.

"Don't you think it's weird having your ex-boyfriend around?"

Ginger's comment was a bolt from nowhere. Rosalina turned to her and caught the jealousy in her eyes. The only person she'd been worried about was Archer. She never even contemplated that Ginger might see it as odd. "Well, to be honest," she finally said. "Alessandro and I are still good friends."

"But you had sex with him."

Her words were a slap to the face.

Rosalina tugged her hair behind her ear as she tried to formulate a response. She let out a huge sigh. "Alessandro and I had one night together. It was a very long time ago when we were at uni. We were drunk and it was a mistake. We should never have done it."

Ginger shrugged. "Yeah. That's what he told me too." She said it so flippantly, like she was gossiping about someone else, Rosalina couldn't decide if her question was a test to assess if Alessandro had told her the truth or she didn't trust Rosalina with Alessandro. Either way, it was awkward.

"I see the way he looks at you," Ginger said, "I know there's still something there."

For over a decade Rosalina had been trying to break her spell over Alessandro. His eyes for her always had a passionate yearning. And although it broke her heart to see him that way, she could never find a way to relinquish that hold. Until Ginger stepped into their lives. For the first time since that one fateful night, Alessandro's yearning had shifted. "To be honest, Ginger, I think his eyes are for you," she finally said.

"Really." Her smile lit up her face. "Do you think so?"

"Yes. . . yes I do."

Ginger continued smiling as she reached back into the jewel box. Rosalina assumed the conversation was over. She hoped so. She wasn't keen on any form of confrontation; conflict resolution was more her preference.

As they removed the pieces one by one, it was evident that whoever owned this jewelry was not only very wealthy, she also had impeccable taste. There were nine pieces in total: four bracelets, three brooches, and two necklaces. Each one unique, beautiful, well made and obviously incredibly valuable. Rosalina wondered if this belonged to one of the founding guild member's wives. They were the elite members of Florence, after all.

Rosalina checked her watch and couldn't believe forty minutes had passed. "Oh wow, it's time to go."

A familiar noise cast a steady beat over the water and raised the hairs on the back of her neck. A helicopter.

"Shit! Quick, get this on the boat." She scrambled to her feet, flinging sand everywhere.

Based on Ginger's panic, she must've heard the chopper too. In a matter of seconds, they had the chest back on the boat and hidden beneath the tarpaulin. But even as she scanned the protective sheet, ensuring none of the valuable haul was visible, she knew it was pointless. It was obvious they were hiding something and if her hunch about who was in the helicopter was right, then he'd have no trouble figuring out what.

She scanned the horizon and spotted the helicopter low over the water, heading straight toward them. The size and shape of the chopper left no doubt it was Ignatius Montpellier. *How did he find them?*

A horrifying thought shot through her like a poisonous dart. *Shit!*

She jumped into the boat. "Leave the umbrella. Push us off. Quick." Rosalina couldn't risk waiting another second. She had to get the divers up and return to *Evangeline* now. *What if that bastard had hurt Alessandro or Helen to find out where they were?* He'd do it too. Rosalina resisted voicing her thoughts. Ginger would become hysterical with the idea of anything happening to Alessandro again.

As they pushed off from the beach, the helicopter slowed down. Within a few thumping beats it hovered directly above. The downward draft kicked up water and pelted them like bullets. She switched off the engine and crumbled into a ball, desperate to get away from the painful onslaught. With the chopper this close, the spray was as hard at ice cubes. Her back took the full brunt of every pellet.

When the assault eased, she assumed he'd either moved higher or drifted away and Rosalina turned her face and managed to look up into the cockpit. Ignatius grinned at her with a smugness that made her hate him even more. He tilted the helicopter and scooted away as quickly as he came.

An angry heatwave flushed through her. *Bloody hell!*

Time was against them. They had to alert the divers and get to Evangeline. Now!

"Ginger! Are you okay?"

"Yeah. But shit that hurt. What an asshole!"

"Hang on." Rosalina kicked the engine into gear and headed toward the diver-below marker buoy. *Did Iggy see it?* Maybe he hadn't. The way in which he came, hugging the shoreline, meant he was a good fifty yards away from the flagged marker. With a bit of luck, he missed it. The divers appeared on the surface and she accelerated toward them.

"Did you see him?" Ginger yelled as soon as the men were within earshot.

"Who?" Archer clutched onto the side of the boat as it pulled up alongside him.

"Iggy. He just belted us with his helicopter spray."

Archer's eyes shot to Rosalina and she blinked back tears. She felt like a failure.

"Are you okay?" His concern made her chin dimple.

Unable to speak, she simply nodded.

"Tell me exactly what happened." Archer hooked his net bag, loaded full with riches, onto the side of the boat and then he helped Jimmy do the same.

Ginger dropped the ladder over the back of the boat, and as Jimmy climbed aboard, she told them what Iggy did.

"Do you think he saw us?" Jimmy clenched his jaw.

"I don't know." Rosalina explained what direction the helicopter came in from. "There's a possibility he missed you."

"How did he find us?" Ginger asked the question.

"Oh Jesus! Sit down." Archer slammed the boat into gear.

"What? What's wrong?" Ginger's eyes bulged with panic.

"Mom and Alessandro." It was all Archer said, and her shocked expression confirmed it was enough.

They clung onto the side of the boat as Archer thrust it to maximum speed and headed toward *Evangeline*.

Rosalina's heart was in her throat as she imagined what horrible things Iggy could've done. Their plan was completely foolish.

They should never have left them alone on the yacht.

This was a disaster that was just waiting to happen.

Chapter Ten

Alessandro sat on the deck with his legs splayed out like a discarded doll. He stared at a splatter of blood that lined the floor near his bare feet. A few spots dotted his ankle and the urge to wipe it away was unrelenting, but the thought of moving made his head pound. He blinked, trying to cast the fog from his brain, and the excruciating thud behind his eyes made it impossible to think of anything but the thump, thump, thump.

He rolled to his hands and knees. A drop of blood fell from his forehead and splattered to the polished timber. His legs wobbled.

Collapsing back against the wall, he panted like a man running a marathon.

There was nothing else to do but wait.

Wait for the psychotic Ignatius Montpellier to come back and finish him off.

Wait for Archer and the others to return.

His mind shifted from one question to another and not one of them was pleasant. But the possibility that Ignatius was still on board, hiding and waiting to attack everyone else, sliced through every other thought.

I have to warn them.

Fear spiked in his belly. Nausea wobbled up his throat. He shoved off the floor again. His head spun. His arms trembled. He crumbled backward.

Propped against the wood paneling, he swallowed back bitter bile and listened for sounds. The helicopter. The returning tender. His friends. Anything to show signs of life. But the only interruption to the peace was a couple of seagulls fighting over something as they swooped and dived overhead.

I need to warn everyone. But the strength of his resolve couldn't compete with the weakness in his limbs. He was completely useless.

The same feeling of utter helplessness had engulfed him when Rosalina was abducted by Nox. It was the first time he'd experienced absolute despair. The thought of that madman touching Rosalina, had exposed an emotion that he'd never thought possible. The desire for revenge. He'd would've done anything to save her.

Two things happened during rescuing Rosalina from that crypt. The first was that Alessandro truly understood how much he loved Rosalina. The second was that he saw just how much she loved Archer. Whilst his aching heart crumbled to pieces to let her go, it was gratifying to see how happy she was in Archer's arms.

There was one decent thing that came out of her capture; finding the ancient diary. The fact that Archer's pendant had opened that secret door in the tomb was a miracle. No, it was more than a miracle. . . it was destiny. No other word could describe it. The circumstances that led to that moment were otherwise beyond comprehension and Alessandro would be forever grateful to have shared that special moment with Rosalina. Along with this treasure hunt.

Every time he held an ancient piece of treasure in his hands it was like holding a newborn baby. Each one was unique, precious and irreplaceable. But the whole lot may be gone. Ignatius would have taken it all.

Alessandro had researched Ignatius after Archer had spoken of him. The man was an enigma who swooped in on cash strapped private vendors wanting to offload valuable treasures. He had an abundance of funds and no regard for the rightful place for any antiquities. . . in museums.

Based on that information, they would never see any of the Calimala treasures they'd unearthed so far ever again.

A distant hum floated over the water. Fighting his thumping headache, he tuned into it. Closing his eyes amplified the pounding. He opened them instead and stared at a spot of blood on his shin. The noise was developing, growing closer.

Yes! It's the tender. The noise abruptly stopped and silence engulfed him.

"Help." His voice was a feeble whisper. His eyes burned and welled up. He closed them and placed his hands over his face in an attempt to block out all light.

"Alex. Alex, where are you?" Terror lacerated Rosalina's cries. She must have seen the helicopter and knew he'd been in danger.

"I'm here." He called out but his brain and tongue were poles apart. He counted the throbbing beat behind his eyes, waiting for her to find him.

"Here he is!" Rosalina materialized at his side. "Hey, are you okay?"

Opening his eyes, he squinted against the glare. Rosalina was right there before him. Her beautiful blue eyes were stricken with panic.

"It's okay, Alex. It's me, Rosa." Her voice trembled. When she touched his arm, he was taken back to that night when they were young lovers. When nothing else mattered but exploring her glorious body with all the time in the world. He groaned at the ill-timed thought. That distant memory was a long, long way from where they were now.

"I'm here, Alex." Ginger's angelic voice, twisted with concern, tugged him back to the present and added guilt to his mounting woes. He mentally slapped himself for thinking of Rosalina when his affections were for Ginger.

She crawled to him and touched her hand on his thigh. "Oh my God." She reached up and he closed his eyes as she gently drew his hair back from his forehead and winced. "Jesus."

Alessandro blinked his eyes open and stared at his hands. Blood had dribbled between his fingers like ugly tattoos. He reached to where Ginger's gaze remained and ran his fingers over a lump that'd formed over his eyebrow. The gash was open; bloody and sickening.

"*Il bastardo mi ha colpito.*" He hadn't seen what Ignatius had hit him with, but the shattered pieces of pottery were all around his feet. The ancient ceramic urn, still adorned with intricate patterns, was probably priceless. Ignatius would have known that. Clearly, he didn't care. If this was his way of making a statement, then it was loud and clear.

Archer and Jimmy burst onto the deck. "Is he all right?" Archer's voice was a cocktail of concern and authority.

"Iggy hit him with one of the Calimala pots." Ginger's eyes glistened with tears.

Alessandro leaned into her palm as she cupped his cheek.

"This cut looks deep, baby. You may need stitches."

"*Per favore*, no more stitches." Alessandro was surprised by the quiver in his voice.

"Come on, babe." Ginger eased her arm around Alessandro's back. "Let's get you inside and see how bad this cut is."

"Did the bastard take the lot?" Jimmy barked the question.

"Let's see to Alex first and then we'll have a look." Archer appeared calm, but Alessandro knew he'd be boiling with anger.

Rosalina pushed to stand, and with her hand on Archer's chest she looked up at him. "Is your mom okay?"

Alessandro's heart twisted into knots. He hadn't even considered Helen during the attack. The knots tightened as he searched Archer's face, waiting for his answer.

"She's fine. Looks like she slept through it. Just as well. . ." Archer clenched his jaw until his lip trembled.

Alessandro deflated. *Thank God.* He would never forgive himself if something had happened to Helen.

"Let's get Alex inside and see to that wound." Archer put his hand under Alessandro's armpits and helped him to stand. His knees trembled as he was drawn to his feet.

With Archer on one side and Ginger on the other, Alessandro was propped up between the two of them, led to the saloon and eased onto a lounge.

"I'll get the first-aid kit." Rosalina raced toward the galley.

"Aaah, shit." Jimmy slapped his hand on the kitchen counter so hard it sounded like a cracking whip. "Looks like he's taken fucking everything."

"Maybe not everything," Alessandro said. "Look in the cupboards.

When I heard that helicopter, I tried to hide as many things as I could. I just hope he didn't look in there."

Jimmy bent to open a cupboard, whistled, then he strode over, placed his hands over Alessandro's ears and kissed the top of his head.

"Hey, cut that out." Alessandro winced but couldn't help but smile. "Check the fridge, oven and microwave too."

"I bloody love you, man." Jimmy made short work of the distance from the lounge to the galley. "Genius. You're a dead-set genius."

"I don't think he even saw the monkey statue." Alessandro couldn't believe the statue was still sitting there. "Hidden in plain view and all that."

"Thank God," Archer said.

"I didn't have time to hide everything." Alessandro felt the weight of failure as he tried to mentally tally the relics he didn't save.

Empathy brewed in Rosalina's eyes. "Did you hide the diary, Alessandro?" Rosalina asked.

Alessandro nodded. "Yes. It's in one of the drawers." Of all of them, she knew how much every one of those pieces meant to him. History was his passion. He'd grown up surrounded by it. He made it his life pursuit to teach others the glory of it. And now he was lucky enough to be unveiling history.

Ginger touched a cloth to his forehead and he winced.

"Sorry, babe."

"I can't believe he hit me with a thirteenth century pot." The careless disregard for irreplaceable history was appalling. "*Bastardo*. That pot would've been worth a *fortuna*."

"He doesn't care." Archer hissed the words out with his clenched jaw.

"I did your trick, Rosa, pretended I'd passed out so he couldn't lift me." When Nox had attacked their boat, Rosalina had feigned unconsciousness. She'd been convincing, even Alessandro had thought Nox had knocked her out.

"Jesus, I wonder what he was planning to do?" Ginger dabbed at Alessandro's wound with a feather light touch.

"Probably demand the treasure in exchange for me, like he did to you in Florence Rosalina." The bruise over her eye had long ago vanished but the horrid memories when Nox held her captive in the crypt would probably never fade.

Jimmy was making a mighty racket recovering all the precious pieces from the kitchen cupboards and the sound clattered around Alessandro's battered brain. "Jimmy, *per favore*, be careful."

"Sorry," Jimmy said. "I'm just excited to see all my babies back."

"I hid the most precious pieces first. But I think there were about twenty or thirty items I couldn't hide. Like the pottery." Alessandro hung his head.

"You did a great job, Alex." Archer put his hand on Alessandro's forearm. "I'm sorry we left you alone too. Didn't think that through, did we?" Archer clenched his jaw and his gaze turned to Rosalina's. With a deep frown and slumped shoulders, his body language was a tangle of relief and anger. But his expression quickly shifted to chiseled jaw and steely eyes, and Alessandro wondered what he was thinking now.

"I couldn't believe his audacity when he landed on the roof." Alessandro reached up to touch the lump on his forehead. "How did he know you weren't here?" The second Alessandro threw the question out, he had his answer. *Iggy had been watching them all along.* His met Archer's gaze and a dark shadow crossed his expression.

"He's been spying on us." Archer clenched his fists. "Once we left in the tender, all he had to do was swoop in and pick up the pieces."

"Son of a bitch!" Jimmy's cheeks blazed red. "Thank Christ you hid some Alex. He would've taken the whole lot."

"Fortunately, I'd already photographed everything." Alessandro smiled a lopsided grin, yet it was a bittersweet triumph. "At least we can work out what's missing. Did you find any more?"

Archer clicked his fingers. "We sure did. Come on Jimmy, we better get it aboard and take off before Iggy returns."

"Hang on a minute." Jimmy held up his palms. "What do you mean take off? The way I see it, we need to get back down there before the bastard comes back with the whole shooting match and starts diving himself."

"Hey guys." Rosalina raised her hands. "Let's take this one step at a time. We'll get the pieces up here first, then we'll work out what to do next. Alessandro, are you okay here for a minute?"

"I'm good." He took the folded-up gauze from Ginger and tried to ignore the blood soaked into it. The last time he'd seen his own blood was when it was pooling onto the dive deck after he'd been stabbed. This wound was minuscule in comparison. He reached for Gingers hand. "I'll be okay, *la mia bella*."

She frowned. "What's *la mia bella*?"

He was treated to one of Ginger's beautiful smiles. Not just with her lips, but her eyes too.

He curled a slip of her long blonde hair behind her ear. "It means my beautiful."

Her delightful smile beamed. She cupped his cheeks, leaned forward and kissed him.

She pulled back with her bottom lip between her teeth.

"Go help them, babe. I'll be okay here."

She nodded. "I'll be straight back."

Alessandro was left alone with the remains of the ancient relics and Ginger's lingering scent. . . coconut and peppermint. Ginger was nothing like Rosalina. Which was probably a good thing. To be able to look at another woman with Rosalina in the room was a giant step forward. He had to move on from Rosalina. It was time.

Besides, Ginger was the first woman he'd met in a very long time who had captured his interest so thoroughly. Her naivety was enthralling. Maybe, by pure happenstance, she was the one he'd been waiting for all along.

The entire time they carted the pieces from the boat to the saloon, Jimmy huffed out his reasons why they had to go for another dive today. Rosalina, on the other hand, didn't agree, she wanted to move on.

Occasionally she let that fiery Italian temper of hers surface and a wise man would back down. Jimmy may not be aware of the wrath he was unleashing. It was going to be an interesting couple of hours.

Alessandro had no idea how Jimmy had so much energy. He was supposed to be recovering and relaxing.

Between the four of them, they carted the new haul of valuables up to the saloon and spread the impressive collection across the dining table. Alessandro was on his feet by the time they finished. No pounding headache was going to stop him from viewing these first-hand. The quantity and variety of the items took his breath away.

"Alessandro, have a look at this." Rosalina, standing across the table from him, reached for a silver box.

"Oh, let me." Ginger tugged the box away from Rosalina's outstretched fingers. "You're going to love what's in here."

Alessandro admired the curved lid. The craftsmanship in the design was exquisite. Ginger tugged on the lid and Alessandro felt Rosalina's gaze on him. He glanced over the table at her and a quick smile danced on her lips before she turned her attention to the box.

Alessandro helped Ginger prize the lid off, and she reached in and removed a bracelet.

A breath caught in Alessandro throat. The piece was simply stunning. "The Arte Di Calimala insignia." His eyes met with Rosalina's and her grin was now a full smile, but she tugged on her lower lip as if trying to stop herself. He claimed the bracelet from Ginger and turned it over in his hand. Each one of the little plaques on the bracelet were crafted with a narrative. The bracelet was designed to tell a story. His heart thumped to a whole new beat. He was holding a distinguished piece of history. *"Questo pezzo solo è magnifico."*

Ginger giggled. "I thought you'd be speechless, babe, not talking in tongues."

Alessandro hadn't realized he'd spoken in Italian. "Oh sorry. I was just saying that this is truly magnificent."

"I knew you'd love it."

"Love it! This one piece alone is proof that these valuables are part of the Calimala guild." Alessandro clicked his fingers. "Oh, that reminds me." He glanced from Rosalina to Archer and back again. "I meant to tell you all something. While you were diving, I made an interesting discovery." Alessandro paused and waited for a response from one of them.

"So, spit it out, Galileo." Jimmy had a thing with creative nicknames.

Alessandro shot Jimmy a 'wise-guy' look. "But," he rubbed his chin. "Maybe I should check these pieces first. That way I am certain."

Jimmy groaned and glared at Alessandro. "Really?"

"Perfect." Rosalina ignored Jimmy's melodramatics. "I need a hot shower."

"How long do you need, Alex?" A frown corrugated Archer's forehead.

"Half an hour should be sufficient. I won't be able to check all of them, but with what I'm working on, the pattern should be immediately evident."

"Jesus, Alex, do you have to be so cryptic? Just spit it out." Jimmy was an impatient man.

"I don't blurt things out. I confirm data first."

"Okay you guys, calm down. Half an hour." Archer glanced at the clock in the galley. "Then we'll meet back here." Archer reached for Rosalina's hand and they left the room.

Jimmy spun on his heel and cussing, strode after them.

"What do you think it's worth?" Ginger removed the bracelet from his hands. She nudged it over her delicate fingers onto her wrist and the gold flashed in the saloon's discreet lighting. The bracelet was much too big for Ginger's tiny wrist, in fact, it would be too big for most women. The possibility that the bracelet may have belonged to a man became an idea he rolled around in his mind.

"So?"

He frowned at her. "So, what?"

She huffed. "How much is this worth?"

The question was impossible to answer. An item like this should never be sold. This was a unique piece of Italian history and deserved a place in one of the best museums in Florence or Rome. Alessandro would make sure of that. Ginger looked up at him with big blue expectant eyes.

"It's worth so much, it's literally priceless."

Chapter Eleven

Archer squeezed Rosalina's hand as they made their way towards the Hamilton suite.

Rosalina looked up at him as soon as they were out of earshot. "I can't believe Iggy found us. I'm so sorry."

He frowned. "Why're you sorry? It wasn't your fault."

"We were just sitting on the beach. We should've been hiding."

"Where would you hide? Honey, it was only a matter of time before he found us. Now we just have to figure out how much time we have before he comes back."

Rosalina latched onto his arm, halting their stride. "Arch, I think we should stop this and go home, before someone really gets hurt."

He shunted to a stop. "What? We can't give up now, we've only just started."

"Nothing is worth getting hurt over."

He placed his arm on her shoulder. "Rosa, I need to do this. I have to finish it."

"Finish what?" She glared at him; her clenched jaw amplified her anger. "What your father started all those years ago? That's crazy."

The look in her eyes scared him, he'd seen it before. It was the same look that marred her face when they broke up last time. "My father died because of me--"

"No, Archer. He didn't." She spat the words. "We've been through this." Rosalina shook her head. "Maybe this treasure hunt wasn't the best idea after all."

He eased back, forced his shoulders to relax and inhaled a deep breath. "I can't let this go until I find it all. My father worked on this for years, he deserves the recognition. I want the world to know. . ." He paused and swallowed hard. "Babe, we're this close." He held his thumb and finger slightly apart. "Once we've found it. That's it. The end. I'll take you home. I promise."

Before she could answer, he clutched her to his chest.

But as he listened to her ragged breathing, he wondered if it would ever end.

AFTER A QUICK SHOWER, THEY RETURNED TO THE SALOON AND ARCHER pulled out a chair at the dining table for Rosalina to sit. She smelled divine, all citrus and vanilla. She was addicted to that soap and he was pleased she was.

Archer looked up as his mother walked into the room. It was rare to see her so early in the day and Archer raced over to help her. "Hi Mom, lovely of you to join us."

She nodded. But it was impossible to tell if she'd understood a word he'd said. Archer led her to the table as Rosalina rushed to set another place for her. It would be a nice treat to have his mother sitting with them for lunch, she'd only done it a couple of times since she moved to live on *Evangeline* with them.

Ginger had made a cous cous salad and sweet potato fries to go with the left-over Thai fish cakes Rosalina made last night. As the dishes were handed around, the conversation was stilted. In fact, there was barely any conversation at all. It could be they were just tired and hungry but then again maybe no-one wanted to mention what happened this morning in front of his Mom. It was probably a good idea. He had no idea how his mother would react.

Archer placed a fish cake on Helen's plate. "So, Alex, how about you tell us your new theory?"

The Italian put the food already loaded on his fork into his mouth and chewed quickly. "*Grande* idea." He placed his cutlery down and rubbed his hands together.

They were in for one of Alessandro's dreaded lectures. And as a university professor, he was an expert at dragging out the details.

Even so Archer was sure the lecture would be worth it. Without Alessandro's help in Florence they would never have found the ancient diary that led to the treasure in the first place.

"I thought a visual display would explain my theory better." Alessandro stood and walked toward the portable whiteboard that he must've dragged from the office. He spun it around to reveal a series of A4 sheets of paper tapped to the board.

"So, here are duplicates of the pages in the diary that detail each piece of the Calimala treasure. There are forty-eight pages with a total of 892 items."

"Holy shit Archer, you didn't tell me there were that many pieces." Jimmy's eyes lit up like flashing dollar signs.

"Actually, I hadn't realized there were that many either." Archer stared at the pages and pages of listed treasure. *Could there really be that much?* His mind flipped to a mental picture of what that amount of treasure would look like. He'd found treasure before, small, insignificant finds, especially in comparison to what they were onto now. But this was the treasure that'd been haunting him since he was eleven years old. He reached for the pendant around his neck. This one piece started the hunt for it. His Dad died chasing it. Now it was Archer's job to finish it. And no fool in a helicopter was going to stop him.

Alessandro cleared his throat, attracting Archer's attention again and re-establishing his professor mode. "I have placed the pages in the same order they are in the diary. The first page is here." He pointed to the page taped at the top left-hand corner. "Then second and third." He pointed at each page, going left to right. "The final page is here." The last page was at the bottom right corner.

Archer cut up his mother's fish cake and loaded a portion onto her fork. So far, he hadn't been able to work out if her reluctance to eat was because she wasn't hungry or she couldn't be bothered. Or worse, she just didn't want to be around anymore. He shoved the unpleasant thought aside. Archer liked to think that finding her again after twenty years was destiny. He was meant to save her from her own living hell, and he was determined to do it. Getting her fit and healthy was at the top of his ever-growing agenda.

Alessandro tapped his pen on the whiteboard. "I have successfully identified nearly all of the items you have recovered so far. The descriptions in the diary are detailed and each piece is very unique. But. . ." He held up his index finger and cocked his head. "A distinct pattern has emerged."

Alessandro picked up a sheet of paper. "To date, you have recovered sixty-four pieces. Once I established a match with the description in the diary, I highlighted it in yellow. For example, here's page nineteen." He taped the sheet over the top of the original page nineteen. When he moved away, Archer noticed six highlighted lines on the sheet.

"Here's another." Alessandro taped page after page on the whiteboard. He repeated the process over and over until he had taped up seventeen pages. Then he stopped, turned at them and grinned like he'd found a cure for baldness.

Jimmy pointed his fork at the board. "What about the rest?"

Alessandro cocked his head. "That is exactly my point. There are no others. Every one of the pieces you've recovered from the *Flying Seahorse* are listed in the diary from pages nineteen to thirty-three only. Not one piece from any other page has been discovered yet. You can see them clustered here." He waived his hand over the center of the board.

"Okay professor, it all looks very colorful. But what the hell does it mean?" Jimmy rolled his eyes at Archer. Archer had a bad feeling he knew where this was going.

Alessandro rolled his eyes right back at Jimmy. "What it means is, we need to entertain the possibility that the treasure was divided at one point."

Everyone sat in silence. Jimmy slammed his fist on the table and everyone, including his mother jumped. Her eyes darted to Jimmy and for a second Archer thought he saw a whisper of emotion. He didn't care if it was anger; any kind of reaction from her would be good.

"I don't believe it," Jimmy hissed. "I reckon the whole lot's down there wondering what the hell we're doing up here blabbering, instead of bringing them up."

"The evidence is clear, Archer." Alessandro commanded Archer's attention and he gave it by looking squarely into the Italian's eyes. "I believe more than one ship carried this treasure. You only need to look at the volume--"

"Three ships." Helen's words were barely a whisper yet the conviction in her voice was stunning. It was a statement of fact. She knew what she was talking about and wanted them to know it.

"What did you say, Mom?" Archer wanted her to repeat it, he needed to be sure he'd heard her right.

She sat back, her shoulders rod straight. "Don't you remember, Wade? There were three ships."

Out the corner of his eye, Rosalina covered her mouth. Archer supported that move. To get anything quite so lucid out of his mother was a miracle. But her thinking he was Wade was troubling. He'd already been told he looked like his father, but it was distressing to hear his mother's confusion. He decided to let it slide.

Archer placed his hand over his mother's. "You think there were three ships carrying the treasure, Mom?"

"No."

Archer shook his head. Confused.

Helen turned her palm over and squeezed Archer's hand. She looked up at him. "I *know* there were three ships. The *Flying Seahorse* was one of them."

Alessandro clapped his hands together and rubbed vigorously. "*Te l'avevo detto.*"

Archer had no idea what Alessandro said, but by the look on his face he was obviously gloating. "Do you know anything else about these ships, Mom?"

She slowly shook her head and looked confused by the question. But to Archer's amazement, she started clawing back from whatever world she was tempted to slip into. Her eyes brightened and she looked around the table as if seeing them all for the first time. Her awareness increased and she tucked a slip of hair behind her ear, something he hadn't seen her do since he was a kid. When she looked at him again,

Archer was taken back to a time in his childhood when his mother was perfectly normal. He held his breath as he waited for her to speak.

She blinked several times as if working the words into sentences. "Everything is in the shed."

"Shed?" It was Archer's turn for confusion. "What shed?"

Chapter Twelve

Nox couldn't stand the monotony any more. Every day was an agonizing repeat of the day before. A rooster, so loud it had to be right outside the door, kick-started the twins into gear each morning. They'd roll out of bed, climb down the ladder and without so much as a glance in his direction they'd disappear outside. After a series of noises, he couldn't decipher, they'd return with a bowl of food. It was only out of near starvation that Nox actually ate it. With the consistency of dense porridge and the appearance of soggy cardboard, it was anything but appealing. The taste was as bland as sawdust.

But aware that he needed the sustenance, he'd force down each mouthful with the one and only rationed cup of water he received each morning. But as the days rolled on, he became stronger and movement caused a bearable amount of pain.

It took an enormous amount of effort, but finally, when he was able to climb off the wooden slab he was forced to use as a bed, he dragged his body to the table and sat to eat his food. But even as he sat right there with them, the men made little attempt to communicate with him. It was as if he'd been in their company his whole life and they had absolutely nothing important to discuss.

Not that he could communicate with them anyway.

On the several occasions he'd tried, he couldn't understand a single word they uttered. Even in their company, the isolation was as crippling as his injuries.

Nox recognised their routine. It was like clockwork. After the rooster and the tumble out of bed came the outside work. Then there was the brown slop for breakfast. Next, they'd disappear again and during the course of the day he would see little of them. They'd venture back inside with a cart of firewood for the pot belly stove or to drape dried fish over a series of ropes that hung from the rafters. Late in the day, as the sunlight through the cracks in the walls grew to long spears of light, they'd play a board game and drink their alcoholic brew until one or both of them passed out. Some days, the only change in their routine would be when they took out bundles of tattered clothes. They would return them days later, apparently clean.

There were certain noises that were almost constant. The wind. It came in brilliant gales that forced through the gaps in the walls with a howl or a whistle. Sometimes he thought he heard waves crashing against the shore. But there was also a strange popping or clicking noise that he'd given up trying to figure out. When there was silence, which happened on the odd occasion, Nox wondered where in the hell he could be that would produce such a complete absence of sound.

Time drifted along like the boring sermon's Father Benedici used to perform in the church on Sundays. Nox desperately wanted to see beyond the four walls that had contained him for weeks.

Or was it months?

He was being driven crazy. Too many unanswered questions bombarded his waking thoughts. It was time to get some answers. Today he would go out that door, even if he had to crawl on his hands and knees.

While the twins were outside, Nox scoured the shack for something to use as shoes. He had no idea where his were, and he'd never seen either of the men wearing any. A pile of rags to the side of the ladder was his only option. He'd wrap them around his feet.

The torn-up rag that had been wrapped around his body was bloody and disgusting and barbaric. It was time to remove it. *How long it had been on there?*

He unravelled the knot and as he unwound the bandage, he gagged at the vile stench. *Is that my own flesh? Is it rotten?*

Every loop around his body revealed a bloodstain slightly larger than the last. The final thread of tattered cloth, the part that actually touched his skin, refused to release. Blood and God knows what else held it in place. He had to yank it off.

A cold sweat smothered his forehead.

A million invisible spiders crawled up his neck.

He swallowed the lump in his throat, sucking in a mouthful of air, grabbed a handful of the bandage, clenched his teeth, and yanked. A scream burst from his lips. Tears spilled from his eyes. Nausea shot up his throat. His legs buckled and he clutched the table just managing to remain standing.

Footsteps crunched on the gravel. They were coming.

It was impossible to hide what he'd done. Nox stared at the door; his body stiff with dread.

The door opened and Scar Face stepped into the room. His yellow eyes fell on the bloodied bandage, then he looked at Nox. A frown drilled across his forehead, then he turned and walked back through the door.

Next second a gray cat scampered into the room.

"Shadow?" The name tumbled from Nox's lips. *My cat.* His beloved Chartreux stray that had become his one and only true companion, had found him. The cat's tail weaved its hypnotic magic as it curled slowly from side to side. Shadow sashayed around the tiny room. Soon the feline weaved his way around Nox's legs, as he'd done many times before. Ignoring the sting blazing from his wound, he bent over and ran his hand along Shadow's back. His fur was coarser than he remembered and his ribs were protruding. Shadow wasn't the picture of health Nox usually had him in.

Standing again, Nox glanced down at his wound. Fresh blood dribbled from his pale skin, but other than that, it was just a crusty black scab, no bigger than a coin. A wave of relief flushed through him.

He would survive.

No. . . he was going to do more than that. Once he escaped from here, wherever here was, nothing would stop him from getting his hands on the Calimala treasure that was rightfully his.

It was his only certainty.

Using his bloody bandage, he secured the rags in place over his feet.

With each flick of the disgusting strips around his foot he had to shove the cat aside and fight both head spins and nausea. It took an eternity, but the final result was comfortable and practical.

All he had to do now was be patient.

Once the twins had finished outside, they would return indoors. And like every other day so far, they should play a board game that involved a couple of dice and twenty-four discs of two different colors. During the course of the game they would guzzle copious amounts of the liquor that reeked like poison. Their conversation, if you could call it that, was sporadic. Sometimes several games were played without a word spoken by either of them. The only certainty was the winner would gulp back whatever was in the brown bottle and then they'd start again. Often, before the blackness of night consumed the hut the brothers would pass out at the table.

Sometime during the night, each of them would make their way up to the loft and that's where they'd stay until the rooster started its morning wakeup call.

Nox had no intention of being here to listen to that damn rooster any more.

Nox stood and tested his new shoes. He paced the room, testing them out, and scoped the place for any other items he should take with him. Near the pot belly stove, he plucked several long strips of dried fish off the dangling rope and as he chewed on the rubberized salty flesh, he realized he needed at least one more thing, water.

The men had been very strict in their rationing of one cup of water per day. At first Nox had thought it was their cruel joke, but as the days rolled on, he began to wonder if they were rationing it because water really was scarce. The reasons for the latter conjured up a landslide of questions over where the hell he could be.

He would know soon enough.

Nox did the rounds of the building; chewing on the salty fish and sharing it with the ever-eager Shadow. The door creaked open and the men ventured inside with arms full of wood that they tossed into the corner. They each tugged a couple of slabs of fish from the over-hanging ropes and settled in opposite each other at the table. Nox remained seated on his wooden table nearby. Neither man glanced at him. The board game was produced, as was the bottle and the afternoon ritual began.

Scar Face won the first and second rounds but Short Beard won the next three. Their bulging eyes started drooping. Their hand movements deteriorated to slow motion. Four more rounds were played before Scar Face stood and, without a word, made his way up the homemade ladder and disappeared. Short Beard plonked his head onto his playing discs and began snoring almost immediately.

Nox didn't waste a second. He tugged a handful of dried fish from the rafters, shoved them down his top, opened the door and stepped into fresh air.

The area right outside the door was a scrap yard with all manner of junk piled on top of each other. Bottles. . . lots of plastic bottles, dirty, moldy, with lids and without, were piled higher than his shoulders. There was fishing gear, scraps of metal and other bits and pieces he couldn't decipher. Beyond that was nothing but sheer cliff face, rising up from the junk like a giant edifice. A path wove its way through the mayhem and Nox squeezed his way through it.

The end of the path met with the side of the building and Nox finally understood what produced the never-ending popping noises that nearly drove him crazy. Chickens. Dozens of them. Black, brown and white, big and small. They scattered in all directions as he strode towards them. His mouth salivated at the thought of eating one. But it would never be. . . he didn't have the time and even if he did, he didn't have the strength to catch it.

But his eyes bulged at a row of boxes nestled low against the wall. He scurried towards them and as he silently prayed, he dropped to his knees and looked inside. Two eggs stood out from the twigs as if they were made of gold. Nox reached for them. Ever so carefully, he cracked the first shell on the side of the wooden box and gulped down the raw egg without even thinking. It was disgusting and divinely delicious at the same time. He repeated it with the second egg, and with the chickens milling around him pecking at the ground, Nox took a moment to savor the food in his belly.

He needed to keep moving, there was no telling how much daylight he had left. Using the nesting boxes for support, he climbed to his feet again and continued heading toward the sun. He walked onto a grassy knoll, and with the sun on his face and the wind in his hair, the sense of freedom was overwhelming.

But when he walked to the edge of the clearing and looked down, his newfound freedom evaporated. Below him was nothing but cliff face. Beyond that was vast ocean, as far as he could see. He did a slow three-sixty degree turn and saw nothing but rocks and ocean.

Not a single sign of civilization other than the decrepit building he'd just escaped from.

Chapter Thirteen

The wind whipped up the bluff, threading its way from the Mediterranean Sea to take its dying breath as a low whistle through the cracks in the broken weatherboards of the isolated storage shed. Rosalina could still taste the salt in the air despite the distance the breeze must've drifted up from the ocean. She tried to ignore the cobwebs that'd failed against the breeze and dangled from the abandoned shed's gutters in tightly corded knots.

Rosalina twisted her clammy hands together as Archer turned the key in the lock of the abandoned shed. His fingers trembled, drunk with nervous anticipation, or maybe dread. The decision to come here hadn't been a difficult one. The last couple of days had been intense. Discretion was no longer required as it was obvious Iggy was watching them. So, with *Evangeline* moored right on top of the *Flying Seahorse*, they had extracted the precious items from the ancient wreck, literally by the bucket load.

With each treasured piece in the fresh haul examined, Alessandro's highlighter had marked off every nearly item listed on the middle pages of the ancient manifest.

For Rosalina though, every piece they marked off took her one step closer to going home to her grandmother.

But ever since Archer's mother told him about the storage shed,

Archer had driven everyone crazy with his obsession about it. When the last two dives produced nothing, Archer declared the treasure hunt over and Rosalina breathed a sigh of relief. By that night he'd pulled up anchor and set a course for Patmos Island, and in particular Zoodochos Pigi, the ancient nunnery where he found his mother.

Now that she was here with Archer and Helen, the act of actually opening the door; the vault to a dead man's life, had her pulse pounding in her neck like a battle drum.

Helen's boney knuckles bulged as she clutched Rosalina's arm. Yet she seemed remarkable calm.

The key turned with surprising ease, considering it hadn't been used in nearly twenty years. The roller door, however, was another story. Archer's bulging muscles strained to lift it. Rosalina reached for the door to help and its coldness struck her as a warning. But she shoved the thought aside, and with bent knees, she strained to lift it with him. It was an eternity before whatever trapped it in place finally released, and with every inch it raised the metal screamed in protest, matching the silent screams in Rosalina's mind.

Archer gave it one final shove and the door whipped up to the top. Sunlight filtered into the darkened space, creating an equal amount of light and dark shadows. It was the musty smell, that of a long-vacated tomb, that had her hesitating to step into the room. But she forced herself to break down exactly what it was. The building was nothing more than a rusty old shed that never saw the light of day or be refreshed by the wind off the bluff it was situated on.

Yet even with the rational thoughts forging through her brain, she still stalled at the doorway. They all did. It was as if each of them was waiting for the other to move. Rosalina hoped either Archer or Helen would enter first. The things contained in these walls once belonged to Archer's father and she wondered if Helen could even recall what she'd stored here. It's possible that the darkness that consumed her mind now, may have already affected her then.

It wasn't until Archer made the first step that Rosalina realized she'd been holding her breath. Forcing herself to calm down, she released it as a slow and steady stream. Helen's pale blue eyes stared blankly around the shed's contents.

Has her mind slipped back to the time when she had packed them up?

A time when the life she'd known fractured into a million pieces, destined to never fall back into place. Rosalina reached for Helen's hand and guided her into the dimness.

The room was crammed full with dozens and dozens of randomly sized cardboard boxes. Each box was unique in either its size or the words branded across the exterior. Only one box stood out from the others. Not because it looked unique in any way, but because of its position in the room. It was all alone, several feet from the rest, as if it had been shoved under the door as an afterthought.

Archer walked over, crouched down and reached for the lone box. He placed his hand on the lid and paused. Rosalina waited; she had no intention of pushing him through this. It was hard enough as it was.

Finally, he rolled his shoulders and leaned over to peel off the strip of yellowed tape that sealed the box. The sound, like fingernails scratching down a blackboard, rained shivers down Rosalina's back. The released tape curled into a perfect spiral pattern onto the concrete floor. Archer folded back the flaps of the box and froze. Neither Rosalina nor Helen moved.

Rosalina's breath trapped in her throat.

Archer sat rigid, staring unblinking for a long excruciating pause.

At last he reached into the box.

Slowly, as if mesmerized, Archer lifted something from the box. Rosalina's stomach lurched at the realization of what it was.

Helen gasped, covered her eyes with the palms of her hands and turned her back. Rosalina embraced her and pulled her to her chest. But she didn't take her eyes from Archer.

He was frozen.

The item in his hands was once a life saving device. But the shredded buoyancy vest, almost ruined beyond recognition, was now a shocking reminder of how Archer's father died. Rosalina tried to suppress mental images of Archer witnessing his father being attacked by a shark, but it was impossible.

Razor sharp teeth. Swirling blood. A young boy in agony.

Helen shifted, launching Rosalina back to the present.

Archer had never forgiven himself for what happened that day, now after seeing this, she wondered if he ever would.

Archer's shoulders sagged as if the adrenalin that'd been keeping them rigid dissipated. He dropped the shredded fabric into the box, folded the flaps back over and kicked the box aside. The speed with which it flew across the concrete highlighted both the force of his kick and how lightweight the box must be.

Archer turned to her and a twisted smile inched across his face. But he didn't say anything.

Rosalina was unable to utter a single word either.

Chapter Fourteen

Nox made a conscious effort to slow his racing heartbeat by doing another, more methodical, scope of his surroundings. To his right was a path. He walked toward it. But it was nothing more than a goat track. He traced it through the scrappy weeds and brown grass until it disappeared. Down below, far in the distance, was a sandy beach.

As he walked along the track, he scanned the horizon, but with each step, hope sunk deeper. He didn't see a single boat despite the enormous expanse of ocean before him. Not one.

He arrived at a fork in the path. One continued on down toward the beach, but as he scanned along the other side, a flash of white snagged his attention. A couple more steps revealed it as the top of a building. His heart raced with both excitement and exhaustion as he climbed up the steep cliff toward it.

The building became more visible with each step. It was a lighthouse.

As the slope leveled out, Nox increased his pace, alternating his glances from the rugged path to the building in the distance. But it wasn't long before his hopes of finding civilization, let alone help, were crushed. The building was crumbling. A giant chunk of the tower was missing, as if it had imploded in on itself. Nox continued toward it, though no longer with the sense of drive that had empowered his steps moments ago.

Stepping onto the bluff allowed him a view of the entire tower. Even at this distance of three-hundred or so feet, the peeling white paint, rust stains and decaying cement dominated the structure. The base of the tower was a small square building. It too appeared close to collapsing. The lighthouse looked long ago deserted but he couldn't stop walking toward it. At the very least, the top of the tower would offer the highest view around, and hopefully help him find a way from this desolation.

Nox reached the building. All the windows and doors were gone. Gaping square holes marked their existence. *This was probably where the twins found the wood they'd recycled into their shabby furniture.* Nox stepped over the threshold and into a small empty room. The dominating feature was a spiral staircase with stairs that fanned out from the central core like a splayed deck of cards.

The building was dying. Piece by piece it was crumbling to the ground. The entire far wall looked to be held together by an imposing vine that had long ago died. What was left of it snaked its way along the white blocks like dark veins.

Nox ventured toward the stairs and looked up the tower. It was only because a large chunk of the tower had collapsed that he could see the sky. To figure out where he was, he had to climb to the top. It didn't look safe, but it didn't even enter his mind that he shouldn't do it.

Nox placed his cloth-covered foot on the first step and tested it with his weight. It seemed solid. With a clenched jaw and the tension in his stomach piercing his wounds, he climbed the stairs with the speed of an elderly arthritic man.

Recognizing that the central concrete core was the only thing holding the staircase together, he hugged it as he made his way up. Old paint and dry moss caked his hands in white and dirty green dust.

The place smelled of sea salt and urine. The stench reminded him of the toilets at the orphanage that he'd been forced to clean hundreds of times as a child.

The punishment was meant to break him.

During his childhood he'd suffered at the hands of cruel tormentors who'd found enjoyment in his misery.

During his adolescence he'd suffered repeated punishment from his elders because he wouldn't yield to their narrow-minded ways.

In his adulthood he'd suffered from being ostracized and ridiculed because of his body odor disease.

Nox knew what it was like to suffer. But he also knew what it was like to be a survivor. What he was suffering now was a minor setback.

It will take more than this to break me!

He passed through the ceiling of the small room and entered the tower. As he climbed higher, he caught glimpses of the dark blue ocean through the small square holes that dotted the tower.

Round and around he went, higher and higher.

Crawling on his hands and knees he grew dizzy with exhaustion but kept on regardless. . . driven by hope. Hope that the view from the top would show him some form of civilization. Hope that he'd be rescued from the nightmare he'd somehow floated into.

At last the top was within view. A large section of the tower was missing, as if it had been slammed with a colossal wrecking ball. It felt like he'd been crawling for hours and when he reached the highest step and saw the sun melting into the horizon, he wondered if he had been. He sat with his back against the central core and stared open-mouthed at the vastness beyond him.

There was nothing but blue ocean and sky. No buildings, no people, no boats. No rescue.

Nothing.

Nox tugged his knees to his chest.

Tears of frustration tumbled down his cheeks, just like they'd done when he was a child.

Chapter Fifteen

Archer stretched his back before he bent over to pick up the second last box. Thank Christ it wasn't as heavy as some of the other cartons had been. Jimmy reached for the last one and, by the smile on his face, Jimmy's box was just as light. Together they carried them to the hire truck. The screech of the shed's roller door confirmed Rosalina had shut it. Knowing her, she'd put the padlock into place and lock it again. Not that she needed to, Archer had no intention of returning to the shed ever again.

As Archer walked past the whitewashed walls of Zoodochos Pigi Nunnery, he caught movement in a window. It would be Mother Maria. The frail old nun was an innocent bystander in this mess and he didn't blame her or any of the other nuns for what happened over two decades ago. But they still felt responsible. He decided to go back and say his goodbyes once he'd loaded these last two boxes.

"That it then?" Jimmy barked.

"Thank God."

Jimmy slammed the door of the rental truck shut.

It'd been a long day carting all the boxes from the shed to the truck and they weren't anywhere near finished yet. Every one of these boxes now needed to be loaded onto *Evangeline*. That'll be just as time consuming, especially considering where she was moored. Being such a large super-yacht did have its disadvantages.

The tender will travel a crap load of miles to get these boxes from shore to *Evangeline*. At least it's a good workout. Since he'd left Australia nine months ago, Archer hadn't had a decent training session. But his muscles were gonna be hell come tomorrow.

Rosalina arrived at his side and he turned to her. *How can she could look so damned good after the day they'd had?* He entwined her fingers within his. "I'm going to say goodbye to Mother Maria. Want to come?"

"Of course." Her smile lit up her pale blue eyes. It wasn't until his recent visit to Rosalina's hometown in Italy that he'd realized how unique her eyes were. Every other full-blooded Italian he'd met was of the dark iris kind. Hers were special, just like everything else about her. She did, however, possess the heavy dark lashes, typical of Italians.

Archer turned to Jimmy. "Back in ten minutes." He banged on the side of the truck. It resonated with a surprisingly empty sound, considering it was crammed full.

"I'll wait right here then." Jimmy laughed a hoarse throaty laugh that highlighted his years of cigarette abuse. Archer appreciated him finally giving up the nicotine. The rum, however, was still the love of Jimmy's life. Archer didn't have a problem with the drinking, he'd seen Jimmy guzzle enough grog to take down an entire football team, yet the tough bastard could still beat him at a game of cards.

Archer tugged on Rosalina's hand, directing her back along the path toward the nunnery. They passed beneath an ancient stone arch and stepped onto the gravel walkway. The low afternoon sun filtered through the vine-riddled trellis, creating an odd stepping stone pattern on the ground. The flowers lining the path no longer had the sickly-sweet smell that had turned his stomach when he was a kid. As they strolled along in silence, his brain shot back to the first time they'd walked along here together. What happened that day changed their lives forever.

For a thirty-three-year-old, he'd seen his share of punishing years. *Life has to get better from here.* He shoved the thought aside. Didn't want to jinx himself. Not that he believed in superstition. Unlike Rosalina. Walking under a ladder, broken mirrors, black cats, think of any superstition and Rosalina most likely believed in it. For such a down to earth woman it was hard to understand how she could entertain such farcical ideas.

Mother Maria would likely be in the kitchen fussing about or preparing a pot of tea. The nuns didn't get many guests to Zoodochos Pigi, but those who did make the journey were treated like royalty.

Nearing the doorway, Archer smelled the familiar aroma of stone-ground bread baking. His mouth watered at the thought and hunger pains snapped at his stomach like rabid dogs. Hopefully she'd also serve some of their freshly harvested honey he'd sampled this morning.

"Mmm, smells good." Rosalina was reading his mind. It was a gift of hers, one that had him shaking his head on many occasions.

They reached the kitchen back door. It was an insignificant entrance in comparison to the grand foyer at the front. Rosalina stepped up the three wooden steps and Archer took the opportunity to cup her well-toned butt cheeks. Although she flicked her hand at him, he imagined she was smiling as much as he was.

He stepped up and his eyes adjusted to the dimmed kitchen lights. Mother Maria was at the counter. Knife in hand, she looked the picture of a master chef, ready to carve her decadent creation. He'd seen this look on Rosalina many times. It was like watching an artist reveal their masterpiece for the very first time.

"Oh, how lovely to see you." Mother Maria acted surprised to their arrival and Archer went along with her little game.

After Rosalina finished her embrace and moved aside, Archer stepped up for his turn.

"We couldn't go without saying goodbye." He offered his hand to her outstretched palms and she clasped it within hers. Her skin was cold and he recalled her once telling him she had circulation problems.

"It's only goodbye. . . for now," she said.

He looked into her hooded smoky-gray eyes; their sorrow confirmed she knew the real truth. He was unlikely to ever return. He couldn't bear to voice it though, so he embellished. "Of course we'll be back. This place is in my bones now."

And that was the truth. When he first saw this ancient building high up on the bluff, it was like the whitewashed walls were clutching him, demanding he visit. It was bizarre. Thankfully he'd acted on that impulse or he would never have found his mother again.

Where is Mom? She had come with them up the hill, but he hadn't seen her since they started carting the boxes from the shed to the truck. "Have you seen Mom?"

Mother Maria lowered her eyes. "I think you'll find her out by your father's grave. She knows she may never be back."

Archer sighed and stepped back to lean against the wooden countertop. He hadn't thought of that. Since his mother arrived at this nunnery, she'd spent most of her life sitting by his father's grave and simply looking out to sea. The sad, grieving world she'd slipped into had a very strong hold on her and so far, Archer hadn't been able to ease her pain. Taking her away from here was a good idea at the time, but now, at the thought of her sitting at the top of the hill, next to the grave of her long-lost love, he wondered if she was capable of ever recovering.

"I've never seen her so happy."

Archer frowned.

"Your mother is positively glowing. She even spoke a few words to me. Whatever you and Rosalina have been doing has changed her life."

Huh, maybe she was improving after all. He caught a glimpse of Rosalina; she was radiating. She was the momentum behind the changes to his mother's life and she had the patience of a saint. Rosalina missed her family, especially her grandmother who she talked about all the time. She wanted to go home. And they will. . . once they found all the treasure. Maybe, in the meantime, having his mother live on *Evangeline* was actually good for both of them.

"Have you time for some bread?" Mother Maria's eyes twinkled. "I have that honey you like."

Archer moved to the other side of the table. "I'd travel half the world to eat your homemade bread with that honey."

"Then maybe this could be the start of a tradition."

He nodded his head. "I think that could be arranged."

Archer pulled out a chair for Rosalina and she sat down. He sat beside her and placed his hand on her knee. Rosalina didn't seem to notice. Her eyes followed Mother Maria's every move.

Mother Maria reached up and unhooked a bread board from a bracket dangling from the rafters. Archer scanned all the pots, pans and other cooking equipment hanging from the exposed beams. He followed the line of the timber to where it passed through the wall, which was made of solid stone. Based on the history lesson Alessandro had given him, every one of these stones would've been chosen with painstaking scrutiny and hand laid with meticulous care.

Archer found it interesting to have Alessandro around, even though he was Rosalina's ex. He was both brilliant and comically unworldly at the same time. While Rosalina couldn't wait to travel once she'd graduated from university, Alessandro hadn't ventured at all. His perpetual focus was on architecture, which made it hard for Archer to believe this trip was the professor's first journey from his homeland of Florence. He was practically dribbling over the ancient buildings they'd explored already, and the precious artifacts. Add Ginger to the mix and the Italian professor was having the trip of his lifetime. Alessandro and Ginger were a strange mix, but Archer wasn't complaining. Keeping the professor's fixation off Rosalina was a good thing. While he was confident Rosalina wasn't interested, he wasn't so sure about Alessandro. He'd caught him ogling her many times.

When Mother Maria opened the cast iron oven door; flames blazed away at the back of the dome. He hadn't seen many wood-fired ovens and wondered if this was the reason the bread tasted so damn good. He salivated at the delicious aromas.

Plumes of steam erupted from the bread as Mother Maria cut thick slices. She layered them onto a wooden paddle, added the jar of honey and then placed it onto the table, right in front of Archer. His belly beckoned the food with a grumble.

"Eat."

"If you insist." Archer reached for the slice on top, smothered the honey dipper in the liquid gold and drizzled it over his bread.

The first bite was bloody delicious. Rosalina tore tiny chunks from the bread and savored every little morsel. No doubt she was analyzing why the bread was so tasty and why the honey matched it perfectly.

"Shall we have some wine?" Mother Maria had already tugged a porcelain jug from somewhere and was poised with a chunky wine glass in hand. If Jimmy wasn't waiting at the truck, and Archer didn't have all those boxes to cart over to the yacht, and if he didn't feel so grubby, he would've jumped at the chance to sip wine in this ancient stone-lined kitchen. But it wasn't to be. Not now anyway.

"Mother Maria, you're a tease. Sadly, we can't stay this time. But next time we're here, I promise we'll stay for a feast. Especially if you make this bread."

"Oh, that'd be wonderful," Rosalina said.

Mother Maria sat opposite and grinned, showing off her chipped front tooth. "Let me know when you're coming back, and I'll put on a feast you will never forget."

Rosalina turned to him. Her blue irises drilled into him, begging him to agree.

"If you promise to teach Rosalina how to make this," he waggled his half-eaten slice, "then I promise to bring her back."

Rosalina slapped him on the thigh. "Don't be so bossy."

"It's a deal." Mother Maria clapped.

After Archer had taken his fill of the bread, he said goodbye and hugged Mother Maria to his chest. His head was telling him he wouldn't be back, but his heart was begging for it to be otherwise. When he released her, it took all his might not to wipe the tear from her cheek. He turned, ducked his head to pass through the low arch of the back door and went in search of his mother.

As Mother Maria had suggested, he found her sitting at his father's grave. She sat on the grass, leaning on one hand with her feet tucked up beneath her. The blazing sun in the distance, low on the horizon, was fireball red and presented her as a silhouette. The way she sat, frozen in the moment, made her look as much like a tombstone as the other twenty or so around her. Archer shook his head, trying to cast the wretched thought away as he walked up behind her.

"Hey Mom."

Helen turned to him and a brilliant smile lit up her face. But just a quickly it vanished, replaced instead with a twisted look of distress.

"What is it, Mom?" Archer slid down to her side and reached for her hand.

She strangled his fingers in her grasp. "It's you, Arch." She closed her eyes and breathed in deep. When she opened her eyes again, she stared out over the ocean. "Every time I look at you, I see Wade and my heart leaps for joy. But then. . . then I remember, and I live through his death again. Over and over."

"Oh Mom, I'm so sorry."

She shook her head and turned to him. "It's not your fault." She huffed out a breath. "It's me. I can't let go." She balled her fist. "But I know I'm getting better. Seeing you and Rosalina together reminds me of what Wade and I had. It's beautiful, Archer." She turned back to the sunset. "Beautiful."

Archer sucked through his teeth. He couldn't even begin to imagine what his mother was going through. *How could anyone move on after what happened?* But just having this conversation with her was proof she was improving. "You are getting better, Mom. I know it."

"I know it too." She unfurled her hand and sighed. "One day Wade will just be a memory. But right now, he's still with me."

"Dad will always be in our hearts and minds, Mom, and one day you'll remember him with a smile on your face."

"I hope so Arch. . . because at the moment, it hurts so much."

He tugged her to his chest and as she trembled in his embrace he breathed deeply.

It was a long time before he spoke again. "Are you ready to go now, Mom?"

She nodded and he helped her to stand.

He put his arm around her waist and as they stepped from the grave, Archer said his own silent goodbyes to his father.

Chapter Sixteen

The speed with which night descended caught Nox by surprise. One minute he was watching the sun slip into the horizon. Next minute he was staring at a blanket of stars scattered across the inky black sky. He snapped out of the depression that had him rooted to the spot and pushed to stand. A flickering light in the distance caught his eye. With one hand on the concrete core, he reached up onto his toes. There it was again. He stared at the spot, desperate to see it once more and when the beam flashed around for the third time, he realized what it was. Another lighthouse. But this one was working.

The flashing light was barely a twinkle in the distance. A blaze of frustration streaked through him. The lighthouse was a long way away.

He inched higher, searching for other signs of civilization.

A loud crack shattered the silence. His breath died in his throat.

He fell from the sky.

Nox screamed as he tumbled with giant blocks of concrete. He clawed at the walls. He clawed at the air. Desperate to stop his fall.

A rod of metal reinforcing pierced the center of his hand.

A howl burst from his throat.

He slammed face first into the craggy wall. His nose crunched. Sparks blazed across his eyes. His legs swung back and forward.

He was nailed to the wall like Jesus to the cross.

Nox howled as the full weight of his body dangled from the rod though his right hand. He clawed at the walls searching for purchase.

His right foot touched a small windowsill and he grabbed a toehold. But the pressure off his pierced hand was only a brief reprieve.

For several thumping heartbeats Nox dangled there, completely stunned. Something dribbled down his wrist. It would be blood. But he was too petrified to look.

His mouth faced the wall and with each ragged breath he tasted damp concrete.

He screamed at the heavens.

How much more do I have to suffer?

Haven't I been through enough.

Forcing himself to move, he glanced up at his speared hand. His blood drained.

The blackness of the star-dappled sky failed to mask the metal rod protruding from his right hand like a giant nail. Nox willed his fingers to move and sighed when they did. The bar pointed at the heavens as if mocking his faith.

A strangled laugh burst from his throat at the irony. A Church of St Apostoli Brother, crucified like Jesus before the heavens. *If this wasn't a sign, then what was?*

Razor blades of pain radiated from his hand. He had to move. With his left hand he searched the wall, and found another window up higher. If he could get his feet to it, he'd be able to lift his speared hand free. But to get his feet there he had to dangle his full weight from his pinned hand first.

A plan formed in his mind. But it had nausea bubbling in his stomach.

Nox sucked in a deep breath and forced rage-fueled determination into his trembling legs. It was time.

He dropped his foot off the small ledge. An explosion of pain ripped down his arm.

Fighting a wave of dizziness, he kicked off the lower window and swung his legs in a pendulum trying to reach his foot onto the second, higher windowsill.

But he missed. Screaming with agony and determination he did it again.

His foot reached, but he slipped. The rusted bar tore through his hand further. A torturous howl burst from his throat.

He clamped his jaw, forcing pain and desperation into action. He kicked with the last of his strength, swinging until the agony almost sent him over the edge. It worked! He caught a foothold and pushed up. Using the momentum, he screamed a brutal cry and lunged at the metal rod with his free hand.

He grabbed it just above his pierced hand. But the rod began to bend. "No!" His heart slammed into his chest. He tried to shift his grip. Fear spiked his back.

The rod snapped. Nox plummeted.

His ankle smashed on a concrete step. His elbow hit another. Tumbling over he slammed onto the ground with a sickening crunch. The wind punched out of him. His skull was set to explode. And the metal rod, still imbedded in his hand, reverberated off the concrete so loud it would shatter every bone in his hand.

Nox lay there, stunned beyond moving.

His life flashed before his eyes in fragmented, random memories.

He saw blue crosses, church steeples, and men in dark robes.

He saw mice, mushrooms and little boys who laughed at him with evil glee.

He saw eyes that bulged so big fine spider veins washed over them until the whites were completely red.

And he saw the woman in the bikini with the spear gun. The name Rosalina came to mind. The moment the spear pierced his belly blazed through his memory. He clutched his stomach, reliving the pain all over again.

The last thing Nox saw before his mind slipped into darkness, was his cat Shadow, licking blood off his fingers.

Chapter Seventeen

Archer followed Jimmy along the marina pontoon and was amazed at how his old mate made it look like the box he was carrying was empty. Archer knew that particular box was bloody heavy, but Jimmy handled it with ease. The man was a machine.

The motorboat keeled heavily when Jimmy stepped onto it with the box. Archer was right behind him, and after Jimmy put his box down, he reached up to take Archer's box too.

Archer stepped into the boat and heaved a sigh. That was the last trip from the truck. His exhausted muscles were as useless as over-cooked calamari. And his left knee was throbbing like a bitch. He rarely remembered his scar, usually it didn't bother him at all. But the old wound was caustic misery. It was hard to believe so many boxes had been crammed into such a small shed.

"Thank God that's the last of them." Rosalina was doing her mind reading trick again. He looked up her. She stood on the rickety jetty, legs slightly apart, hands on hips. The end of her ponytail curled over her shoulder and rested upon her cleavage, which unfortunately was hidden beneath her dark t-shirt. *How the hell can she could look so damn gorgeous after that workout?* The pier lights cut a golden glow, adding to her already golden skin. Any more golden and she'd replicate a Greek goddess. He helped her into the boat and with barely any room left for the three of them, Rosalina sat upon his good knee. Exactly where he liked her.

"If I'd known there was going to be that many boxes," Jimmy said. "I would've arm-wrestled Alex for watch duty today." It seemed like days ago that they'd had the discussion over who would go to the shed and who'd stay on *Evangeline*. Ever since Iggy showed up, Archer declared that at least two people had to remain onboard at all times. He'd wanted to put security on *Evangeline*, but Jimmy wouldn't have a bar of it. He was paranoid they'd start snooping around.

Jimmy turned the key to start the motor, the engine rippled to life and they headed toward the rear deck of *Evangeline*. The moon was yet to appear, but with the yachts lights on, she was easy to see. Archer admired her sleek lines. *Evangeline* was still as alluring as the day he'd viewed her in the boat yard nine years ago. He'd never imagined having a boat that big. At just over a hundred and sixty feet, she was about twice the size of what he'd picture himself owning. But once he'd stepped on board her teak-lined decks, he was sold. So much so, he hadn't bothered haggling with the price. The boat broker had thought he was joking when he said he'd take it. It probably didn't help that Archer was only twenty-five, had long hair and was wearing tattered shorts and a singlet at the time. The broker had probably never seen a multimillionaire dressed like that before.

They arrived at *Evangeline* after a few minutes and Alessandro and Ginger appeared on the lower dive deck as they pulled up alongside.

"Hey Romeo, hope you saved some of your energy?" Jimmy called out.

Ginger and Alessandro laughed in unison. When Jimmy had hired Ginger as the on-board chef, it was probably for a little eye candy, and while he certainly got that, he didn't get the girl. Not that he was the jealous type.

Alessandro did a good job of ignoring Jimmy and reached down for the box he was handing up to him. The Italian lurched at the weight, and just when Archer thought he'd topple overboard, he found his balance, strode to the bottom of the stairs and lowered it down.

It was several hours before all the boxes were carted from the truck to the small boat to their new storage place aboard *Evangeline*. Fortunately, one of the two spare bedrooms was big enough to house all the cartons. By the time they'd loaded them all in, the Moreton suite was so full there was barely any room to move.

"I reckon it's time for a beer." Jimmy shoved the last carton onto the top of a tower of boxes.

Archer craved the taste of a cold beer, but his filthy hands changed his mind. Shower first, followed by an icy cold ale. "I hear ya, Jimmy. I'll clean up first. I'll meet you at the bar in twenty or so."

"Don't take too long, you know I don't like to drink alone." Jimmy laughed at his own white lie.

Archer reached for Rosalina and hugged her to his chest. Her hair, still secured in a high ponytail smelled of green apples. "Want me to wash your back?" He glided his hand up the delicate curve of her spine.

"Sounds wonderful."

Archer followed Rosalina's swaying hips towards the Hamilton Suite they shared. The master bedroom never failed to impress, and he was first to admit the room's aesthetic qualities would never have been achieved if Rosalina hadn't taken over redecorating it.

Archer paused at the control panel inside the door and selected a playlist. He was keen for something a little upbeat and chose the Caribbean mix. The drums set the rhythm, and as he watched Rosalina slip out of her clothes his heart accelerated too.

Rosalina looked at him with her usually plump lips drawn into a thin line. "Are you okay?"

He knew she was referring to the boxes. Since he'd removed the shredded buoyancy vest from the box this morning, he'd tried not to think about what other surprises would be inside the other cartons. Every item would represent a part of his father's life in one way or another. The father he'd only known for eleven years was about to come alive through a jumble of random things. Archer wasn't sure he was ready for that.

What he was primed for, however, was his gorgeous Italian woman, completely naked before him. "I couldn't be better." He scooped her up and she giggled as he carried her toward the bathroom.

He sat her on the marble-topped counter, her back to the vanity mirror. Reaching over he adjusted the lighting down a notch. As he stripped out of his filthy clothes, her eyes played over his body. A smile curled at her lips when he flung his underpants aside.

Naked now, he took a moment to turn on the shower, thoroughly wash his hands, then returned his attention back to his beautiful fiancée. He eased her legs apart and slipped his hips between her thighs. Her full breasts nudged his chest, teasing him to attention. As he cupped her face in his hands, their eyes met. He'd never grow tired of how she looked at him. Her eyes told a story, a wonderful, eternally loving story, and he hoped his did the same.

Just being with her reduced him to raw emotions. He wanted her. He needed her. Nothing else existed. She drove away the demon nightmares and made every ounce of his flesh come alive.

She ran her tongue over her lips and snagged the corner with her teeth. Even without lipstick her luscious, full lips were a delicious blush of red. He leaned in to kiss her and when their mouths met her tongue eased out, soft yet probing and he obliged by sucking her tongue into his mouth. She tasted sweet and delicious. He snaked his hand around the fine curve of her neck, drawing her closer. She arched her back, pressing her breasts onto him. His tongue probed deeper and with each of her moans his excitement grew. His body pulsed its own delicious pulse, boosting the furnace already burning inside him. Her hands fell to his hips like she was ready to grab hold, but if he didn't move soon, he'd have to take her right there and then.

With her legs wrapped around his waist, he lifted her off the counter and carried her into the shower. Rosalina drew back from their kiss and her eyes twinkled as he stepped under the warm cascade. She tugged the band from her hair, shook her long dark hair free, and squeezing her legs around his waist she tilted her head back. Rivers of water threaded down her neck and trapped in the valley of her bosom.

Archer lowered her to her feet, so he too could do some exploring. He cupped her magnificent breasts together and lowered his head down to run his tongue along her cleavage, tasting the saltiness of the sea air upon her skin. She rose up on her tippy toes and latched her mouth to his. Her fingers clawed through his hair and she grabbed a handful as her tongue went deep. . . tasting, exploring.

With his foot, he parted her legs and as she nuzzled into his neck, his hand slid over the curves of her body and between her legs. The warmth, the wetness, her movements; it took him on an extraordinary journey.

Her nails clawed his back and with a gasp, she bit into his shoulder as her body quaked against his.

It was a few heartbeats before she relaxed. She pulled back with her bottom lip tugged into her mouth again and a cheeky gleam in her eyes. "Sorry."

She was referring to her bite mark on his shoulder. "I'm not."

He lifted her up to the perfect height and with his hands clasped around her firm butt cheeks, they finished what they'd started. This wasn't slow and sensual. This was driven by a desperate need for one another. It was a raw burning desire.

"Oh Arch." His name whispered off her lips, yet it spoke volumes.

With his fingers digging into her flesh, he sought her mouth, drawing his tongue along her lips and then kissing her. The way she kissed him back convinced him she'd enjoyed the ride as much as he had. He squeezed her to him and her breath tickled his shoulder. Soon he felt the cascading water again, it had vanished into obscurity during their lovemaking. For the umpteenth time he was grateful he'd paid for the extra-large desalination machine or they would've run out of fresh water halfway through.

Sex with Rosalina had always been special, but ever since they came close to death at the hands of a madman, when they made love, it was as if they were sharing their last breath. He was amazed that his love for her could grow more and more every day.

They dressed quickly, he in shorts and a t-shirt and Rosalina slipped into one of her favorite flowing dresses. He noticed the gold loop earrings she chose were the first pair of earrings he'd ever bought her. Rosalina had an extensive earrings collection, though fortunately for him, she never tired of receiving them.

Archer clutched Rosalina's hand, and her skirt danced around their legs as they walked to the bar. As they neared the lounge, Jimmy burst into his throaty rugged laughter and Archer knew what would come next. Years of cigarette abuse had paid its toll and it was impossible for Jimmy to laugh like that without backing it up with a racking cough. Archer tugged Rosalina into a quick embrace while they rode out the horrid noise down the corridor.

Archer was grateful for laughter coming from Jimmy and the others. What he didn't need was everyone to be on tenterhooks. They would be. Each of them knew what happened to his father and they all probably tried to guess what could be in the boxes.

Alessandro, sitting on one of the leather stools at the end of the bar, was whispering something in Ginger's ear that had the Australian blushing. In Alessandro's hand was his new-found signature drink. Thanks to Ginger, he'd taken a shine to Cosmopolitan cocktails. Just the thought of all that cranberry juice made Archer's stomach curdle. Ginger giggled, and with her hand on his leg, made no secret of her affection for him. Alessandro's lopsided grin showed he was enjoying her attention just as much too.

"Bout bloody time, you two." Jimmy raised his half-empty beer bottle toward them.

"Sorry about that," Archer said. "We needed a good scrub." Archer winked at Rosalina and she blushed. She squeezed his hand in a 'don't be rude' gesture. But Archer wasn't fazed. He'd lost her once due to his secretiveness, now that he had her back, there were nothing he needed to hide.

Archer's mother was asleep in the recliner chair. She'd probably sleep for a week after today's stress. He released Rosalina's hand, walked over and scooped up his mother. Rosalina followed him as he carried her to her room. His mother didn't even wake while Rosalina changed her into her nightgown and tucked her into bed. Archer kissed her on the forehead, and as they were about to leave the room, he adjusted the air-conditioning so it wasn't too cool. He turned off the lights and left. He'd check on her again a bit later.

They returned to the saloon and Archer strode straight to the fridge. He'd delayed that cold beer long enough. He grabbed a wine bottle too; Rosalina would want her favorite drop of Chianti as well.

He strolled to table, filled her wine glass and then sat down beside her.

Jimmy was kicking back on one of the lounges with his heavy hoofs up on a footstool. If he wasn't careful, he'd be asleep in no time, and there was no way in hell Archer would be able to carry him to his room. Jimmy'd have to stay where he was for the night. It wouldn't be the first time and certainly wouldn't be the last.

Alessandro and Ginger remained seated at the bar, but the way Alessandro was sucking back the cocktail he was likely to slip off the bar stool very soon. Alessandro was an excellent wine drinker but put a spirit in his hand and he slipped from sophistication to silly pretty darn quickly. One of Jimmy's favorite pastimes was plying the Italian full of scotch and seeing how far he could push him. Alessandro was gutsy though and so far, he hadn't backed down from any of Jimmy's friendly jousting.

"So how do you think we should tackle all that stuff?" Archer said to no one in particular.

Alessandro cleared his throat; professor mode was about to surface. "I think we should catalog everything. Itemize the boxes and list the contents." He nodded with assertiveness. "We should be able to establish some kind of order to it all."

"There may not be any order." Archer shrugged. "Remember, Dad kept everything disorganized on purpose. It was his way of hiding information."

Ginger raised her hand, and Archer stifled a laugh. "Who was he hiding it from?"

"Anybody. Other treasure hunters. Ignatius Montpellier."

"Least it won't be that crazy priest." Jimmy polished off his beer in one swig.

Archer nodded. Unlike Rosalina, Archer and everyone else believed Nox was dead. The crazy priest had gone overboard with a fishing spear through his belly. Nobody would survive a wound like that. And if that didn't kill him, drowning would. Although. . . his body never being found was a mystery. If it had been, a dead priest with a spear through his belly would've made headline news.

Archer shrugged the thoughts away. Maybe the fish ate him. "The only thing we have to worry about now is Alessandro falling off that bar stool." Archer saluted the Italian with his beer.

"I'll drink to that." Jimmy cracked open another stubby from the little stash he had in an ice bucket at his side.

"You guys are hilarious." Alessandro drained his glass in response. "So, Archer. . . your Dad's disorganization was. . . *deliberato*?" His disgust was obvious.

"Yep. His idea was that if ever someone got their hands on his stuff, then they'd have no idea what they were looking at."

"If it's anything like what we witnessed in those books, then his plan works." Jimmy thumbed at the stack of his father's notepads on the dining table.

"It's just a jigsaw puzzle." Alessandro smiled. Prior to joining Archer and Rosalina in their treasure hunt, the most excitement Alessandro had experienced was a flat tire on the *autobahn* with cars whizzing by at a hundred miles an hour. Although Alessandro tells it with humor, Archer had no doubt he was probably wetting his pants at the time.

"And it's our job to put it all together." Rosalina raised her glass.

Archer raised his glass, as did everyone else.

They all made it sound so easy. But for some inexplicable reason, Archer was suddenly gripped with burning doubt.

Chapter Eighteen

Rosalina woke early the next morning embraced in Archer's arms. It was the perfect way to welcome a new day. Two bodies that molded into one, sharing a journey together, sharing a lifetime. She was looking forward to their future. A time when they could look back on what was happening here with a laugh.

Now that Archer's recurring nightmares had all but vanished, nearly everything was perfect. Nearly. The unusual finger of gold was still around his neck, but she no longer considered it his noose. The treasure had become the new albatross. Hopefully that would be off the yacht very soon. Then, and only then, would she feel safe again.

Rosalina slipped out of bed and into the restroom. As she showered, she thought about the treasure and in particular the realization that they may only find one third of it. If Helen hadn't informed them when she did, they could've wasted months off the shores of Anafi looking for items that simply weren't there. And it was time she didn't want to waste. Archer had proposed to her a few months ago and Nonna still hadn't seen her engagement ring. Going home to her family in Italy seemed so much more important now.

She dressed in a floral maxi dress and chose a pair of aquamarine teardrop earrings. Her mind flashed to the moment Archer had given them to her. She'd spotted them earlier in the day at an antique jewelry store in Melbourne. Somehow, he'd managed to slip back to the store, buy them and have them gift-wrapped, all without her knowing. Over dinner he'd made a big fuss about the color of the stone matching her eyes. She glanced in the mirror and made the comparison. It was true, the stone was remarkably similar to her eye color.

She slipped out of the bedroom and her intention was to start preparing breakfast. But as if drawn by ghostly whispers, she was lured to the Moreton room. Her heart thundered as she opened the door, stepped into the room and closed it behind her. The boxes took up the majority of the expensively decorated room, but it was the smell, like old attic furniture, that dominated the space. Each breath laced her tongue with ancient dust. She swallowed it *and* the lump of anxiety sitting heavy in her throat. It was a pity someone hadn't thought to open the windows before they'd loaded up all these boxes, as there was no hope of reaching them now.

As she glanced over the dozens and dozens of boxes, she willed her heartbeat to settle back to normal. But it hit a whole new level when she recognized one box. With the tape missing, the cardboard lid was slightly ajar. Her heart set to explode as she reached for it.

Tears tumbled down her cheeks before she'd even raised the flaps. But her tears weren't for Archer's father. They were for Archer and the terror he'd witnessed all those years ago. She crumbled to the floor, tugged the tattered vest onto her lap, closed her eyes and with a clenched jaw, she couldn't prevent bloody images flooding her mind. With sudden clarity she understood Archer's drive to finish what his father started. They should've done it together. Father and son, side by side, unveiling a slice of history. That precious moment, stolen from them so brutally, needs a better ending. Or else he would forever remember his father by what happened, and not by what could have been.

She jumped when a hand touched her cheek. It was Archer. The look on his face was a tangle of emotions as she rose up, wrapped her arms around him and wept into his chest.

"I'm sorry," she stammered. "I couldn't help it."

"It's okay baby." He wiped her tears with his thumb. "We'll go through all the boxes today. It won't be easy, but I want to do it. I need to." With his finger under her chin, he lifted her face to him. "But I need you to be strong for me."

She looked into his dark eyes; the halo of gold flecks that usually danced around the rim of his irises was gone. Clouded over. Probably with uncertainty. It was something she wasn't accustomed to seeing in her man. Archer was the most decisive person she knew, and that drove his positive attitude. His jaw was squared; he was clenching his teeth, perhaps fighting his own set of tears.

As he wiped her cheek, she sucked on her bottom lip, begging her emotions to settle. Archer was right. He needed to go through all these things and her blubbering away like this was no help. She swallowed the lump in her throat and stepped back. "I'm sorry," she said. "I've had my cry. Now we're looking at the future."

"Exactly. Now give me that."

She released her grip on the buoyancy vest and remained silent as he lowered it back into the box and flipped over the cardboard flaps. He reached for her hand. "I hope you have big plans for breakfast because looking at all these boxes, I think we're in for a long day."

Archer understood her need to cook. It transported her to her happy place. Her form of therapy. Memories of her cooking classes with some of the most prestigious chefs in Italy now seemed like a lifetime ago. In some ways, it was. For so many years all she dreamed about was running her own five-star restaurant. But that was no longer important. She had everything she needed right here on Archer's yacht.

From the moment she stepped into the professionally appointed galley she was in her element. Today's breakfast would be crepes, with bacon, feta and semi-dried tomatoes, topped with a drizzle of maple syrup yoghurt and a scattering of candied walnuts. The sizzling bacon aroma soon had everyone sitting around the dining table. Ginger offered to help and the two of them worked together as if they'd been doing it for years. Although Ginger had no formal cooking training, she certainly had a taste for it. She may look and act like a ditzy blonde teenager sometimes, but her taste buds were very mature.

As usual, it wasn't long before the beautifully presented meal was reduced to plates of scattered crumbs.

Alessandro palmed his chest and closed his eyes as if about to sing to the stars. "*Delizioso, Rosa.*"

When Rosalina blew him a kiss, she felt Ginger's glare.

He seemed oblivious to it though and as he collected the dirty dishes, Ginger stood and, avoiding Rosalina's eyes, she proceeded to help him.

Archer placed his hand on Rosalina's knee. "Yummy, as usual." He swallowed the last of his coffee and stood too. "Might as well get this over and done with." After a quick kiss on her cheek he strode from the room and Rosalina, Jimmy, Alessandro and Ginger shared only a brief glance at each other before they raced after him.

Archer was in the Moreton room with his hands on his hips, as if contemplating where to start. Archer reached for the nearest box, hefted it into his arms and strode out the door. Rosalina avoided the open box and chose a much heavier one instead. Each of the others did the same and they followed in a procession back to the lounge area.

Alessandro placed his box on the floor then raced away. "*Un momento*, I'll get my laptop," he yelled over his shoulder as he disappeared out the doorway.

Rosalina likened them all sitting silently over their boxes to opponents in a chess game, each of them waited for the other to make a move. The moment Alessandro returned and opened his laptop, Archer tore the tape off his box, flung it away and reached inside.

The contents of his box were dozens and dozens of books, journals and newspapers. The collection included reference books, fiction and non-fiction books, all involving treasure of one form or another. The journals ranged from cheap exercise books ideal for a child's schoolbag to leather bound journals with gold trimmed pages more suited to a professional's office. Every one of them contained Wade's scribble. Archer's father's erratic handwriting could be mistaken for the musings of a psychopath.

If Rosalina hadn't seen firsthand how important Wade's notes were, she would have quickly discarded the journals by now. But even with that knowledge, there was no clear pattern to Wade's ramblings. The journals had missing pages, blank pages, glued in pages, pages of handwriting and drawings and not a single date or notation of any chronological order to guide them. Just flicking through one of them was exhausting, let alone the dozens that now lay on the plush carpet before them.

Under Alessandro's expert guidance, Ginger placed a sticker on each one of the journals and labeled them according to Alessandro's directive. The first two boxes required a full hour to catalog.

"This's going to take a friggin' week to get through." Jimmy said what everybody had to be thinking.

"You're not kidding." Archer rolled his head from side to side. "What's in your box Rosa?"

Rosalina tore off the tape and folded back the lid to reveal newspapers. Some of them were complete editions but most were just a single page folded in a manner that left no obvious article being highlighted. She examined one of the papers, front and back, but couldn't work out why Wade had bothered to save it. It turned out many of them were like that and Rosalina mulled over the idea that maybe most of the items in these boxes were just a clever diversion from the real, important things.

Last time Wade's cryptic clues had helped them discover the Calimala treasure. But looking at the dozens of items removed from just two boxes, Rosalina was already daunted by the prospect of having to analyze everything. They may never find the rest of the treasure.

Alessandro on the other hand, obviously didn't share her concern. He was jittery with childish glee. After spending most of his life doing research in universities and museums, this was probably the type of day he'd only ever dreamed about.

Ever since Helen mentioned the storage shed and what it contained, Rosalina believed it was simply a matter of putting the clues together to find the rest of the treasure. But now that she'd seen the lengths Wade went to, to disguise his findings, they may not be any closer to discovering anything. Not anytime soon anyway. And it was time she didn't want to waste.

The niggling feeling that Nonna needed her just wouldn't go away.

Wade's success as a treasure hunter was undoubted. During the course of his short life he'd discovered three significant hoards of missing treasure. And countless smaller ones. Some said he was just lucky. But dragging his wife and son all over the world chasing the elusive gold and jewels can't have been an easy decision. Her eyes darted to Archer as an abrupt realization hit her like a blow to the chest; her future may be exactly the same.

Can I really spend the rest of my life chasing elusive gold?

It was a question she'd never considered. The Archer she'd fallen in love with was a businessman, running his exclusive yacht charter for rich clients with mountains of cash. Treasure hunting had been a hobby. Now, treasure hunting had become his obsession.

She studied him as he flicked through the pages of a leather journal and couldn't quite read his expression. There was a touch of excitement there with a half-smile on his lips, but a frown also rippled his forehead. One thing was certain, he was completely engrossed in finding the hidden clues in the books that lay before him.

Archer tossed the notebook to the floor. "You know Dad didn't just follow one treasure. There's probably clues to dozens of missing treasures here."

Rosalina jostled for comprehension. Looking for the clues to one treasure was hard enough but compiling the clues to more than one would be mammoth.

"Why couldn't he have just written GPS co-ordinates?" Jimmy's bushy eyebrows dragged together.

"I told you," Archer said, "he was paranoid about his research getting into the hands of the wrong people."

"I have to admit, I have some trepidation about our situation." Alessandro rolled his chair back from his laptop. "More than one helicopter has been watching us since. . . The Incident. Maybe it would be timely to move away from here for a while, before other people find out what we have on board."

Rosalina was pleased to hear she wasn't the only one desperate to leave this location.

"I hear ya, Alex." Jimmy's frown deepened even further. "If I see another one of those damn news helicopters hoverin' around I just may shoot it down myself. Pesky bloody reporters." He made a pistol shape with his fingers and pointed toward the sky.

"There's not much chance of getting away from them. Not when the crazy priest is still missing and not while we're still in Greek waters." Archer shook his head.

"Maybe it's time to move on then." Jimmy shrugged and tore the tape off the box nearest him. "Ha, no wonder this box was so light. It's only got one thing in it." He lifted a globe from the cardboard, placed it on the table and flicked it with his thumb.

As it spun around a ray of sunlight caught on something on the globe. "What's that?" Rosalina stood and walked toward Jimmy. She spun the globe slowly in her hands until she pinpointed the source of the reflection. A small star, no bigger than a peppercorn was stuck on the M of the words Solomon Islands. "Hey Archer, have you ever been to the Solomon Islands?"

Archer scrunched up his face. "Not that I know of."

"I bet them damn helicopters won't go chasing us there." Jimmy eyeballed the globe.

"If it's true that only one third of the treasure is here, then maybe our time here is over anyway," Archer said. "And it makes sense to forget about the Calimala treasure for a while. At least until all the hype cools down."

Rosalina sat in stunned silence. *Did I hear that right? Could he really forget this treasure for a while?* She chewed on the inside of her lip, waiting for the conversation to unfold.

"But before we jump to any rash decisions," Archer continued, "let's keep going through these things and see if we can piece a plan together."

"Sure thing boss." Jimmy stood and strode from the room. His heavy footfalls were a clear indication that being holed up in the lounge room was making him antsy. He preferred the outdoors. His weather-hardened skin was a testament to that.

Rosalina understood Jimmy's impatience. She rolled her shoulders and tilted her head from side to side, trying to loosen the muscles in her neck as she watched Ginger tear the tape off another box. Ginger reached in and the item she removed made Rosalina freeze. The parcel was exactly as Archer had described it. The box was no bigger than Ginger's palm and wrapped in gold decorated paper and a white ribbon. Ginger went to tug on the ribbon.

"Wait!" Rosalina had said it much louder than she intended and everyone looked at her. But she turned to Archer and when his eyes fell on the box, and he looked like he was about to implode, she knew her assumption was correct.

"What's wrong?" A startled look rippled across Ginger's face. She thought she was in trouble.

Archer looked petrified to move. Rosalina had to do something.

"May I have that, Ginger?" She held out her hand and Ginger handed it over like it was a grenade.

"Archer was just telling me about this the other day," Rosalina said. "It was meant to be a present for his mom, but. . . unfortunately Wade never had the chance to give it to her." Rosalina deliberately kept an upbeat tone in her voice as she placed it on the table and tried not to look at Archer.

"What else is in there, Ginger?"

Ginger blinked at Rosalina a few times, as if suspicious of her reasoning, and Rosalina silently begged her to carry on. Thankfully Ginger reached back into the box and as she removed the items one by one, Rosalina hoped the little present would be forgotten.

Except by Archer, that is.

She wished for Archer to give the necklace to his mother and tell the story of how Wade had bought it for her. Although it was incredibly tragic that he hadn't given it to her, the amount of effort Wade went to in selecting the necklace showed just how much he loved her. A moment like that should never be kept secret. And Archer should have learned his lesson about keeping secrets.

By mid-afternoon they'd opened and cataloged about three quarters of the boxes. But with each box they opened, everyone was becoming more disheartened.

As it had turned out, the first three boxes were probably the most organized of the lot. Most of the other boxes were a jumble of random things. Everything from chopsticks to a silver Gigliato coin.

Alessandro turned the coin over in his fingers. "Did you know this coin was made from pure silver?" He cleared his throat. "It dates back to the thirteenth century and Charles II of Anjou Naples is depicted on the face. See here." He pointed to the coin. "I am *certo* this will be a piece from the Calimala treasure." He nodded as he flipped it over.

Rosalina rolled Alessandro's information around in her mind as she scanned the eclectic collection spread out across the floor. Her eyes snagged on the chopsticks. While the coin was an exciting find, they certainly were not. Why on earth anyone would go to the trouble of keeping chopsticks was beyond reasoning. Rosalina gathered one off the floor to look at the writing on the side. It didn't look professional; in fact, if she hadn't seen the engraving tool removed from one of the other boxes, she wouldn't have been the least bit curious. She squinted as she tried to make out the lettering. An idea hit her, "Hey I don't suppose anyone can read Japanese?"

Ginger shot her hand up and Rosalina smothered a laugh.

"I can speak and read Japanese."

"Really?" Now that was a surprise. Not for the first time, Rosalina wondered if there was much more to Ginger than she was letting on. Ginger's ditsy personality did a good job of covering many layers of an intriguing woman? She'd been living on the yacht with her for a few months yet Rosalina barely knew anything about her.

Ginger seemed a little nervous as she knotted her hair around her hand. "When I was growing up, my family housed Japanese students. We needed the money." She shrugged. "After years and years of sitting at the table with a Japanese boy or girl who I couldn't understand, I decided to learn the language."

Alessandro puffed his chest out with obvious pride. "Fabulous, do you think you can read this?" She handed over the wooden chopstick.

"It looks like *Awa Maru*."

"Bless you." Jimmy laughed at his own joke.

Ginger curled her lip up at Jimmy. "Very funny. I bet I'm right. Look up *Awa Maru* please, Alessandro."

Alessandro's fingers danced over the keyboard and seconds later his eyebrows shot up. "According to Google, the *Awa Maru* was a Japanese ocean liner built between 1941 and 1943."

"There you go. I told you I knew Japanese." Ginger and Alessandro exchanged a glance that made Rosalina smile.

"What else does it say, Alex?" Archer leaned forward.

Alessandro's eyes travelled to the laptop screen again and it was a long moment before he finally spoke. "This is very interesting."

"What?" Jimmy barked.

"The ship was built for passenger service but was requisitioned by the Japanese Navy during the war. In 1945 she was employed as a Red Cross relief ship and carried supplies for the American and Allied POW's held in Japanese custody."

"Here we go with the detailed history lessons." Jimmy grumbled and Rosalina shot him a warning glance.

Alessandro cocked his head. "Would you like me to continue?"

Jimmy was as impatient as Alessandro was fastidious and they were each as childish as each other when it came to being annoying.

Jimmy rolled his eyes. "Of course."

"You will enjoy this history lesson. I promise. Once the *Awa Maru* delivered the supplies at Singapore, she took on hundreds of stranded merchant marines, military personnel, diplomats and civilians. In addition to this, she reportedly carried billions of dollars' worth of treasure."

Jimmy sat forward with a long whistle. "Now that's what I'm talkin' about."

"Here we go. So, what happened?" Archer winked at Rosalina and she noticed the familiar glint in his eye. Archer was born into treasure hunting and it was times like this. . . and she'd seen a few, that made her aware of just how important it was to him. When he was like this, it was impossible not to get caught up in the excitement.

"Hold onto your ponies. There's more. And it is really *interessante!*" Alessandro's eyes twinkled. "Through the years it had been rumored that the ship carried the fossil remains of Peking Man."

"Who's a peeking man?" Jimmy screwed his face with the question.

Alessandro huffed. "Peking Man. . . as in China's Peking Man. It's considered to be one of the oldest known fossils. Around 500,000 years old. They were found in a cave in 1927. They're priceless."

"That's bizarre." Rosalina cocked her head. "How or why would those fossils be on a Japanese war ship?"

"Apparently they were packed up to be sent to America for safe-keeping until the end of the war. But they vanished en-route to Northern China, the theory is, as the bones went missing at the same time the *Awa Maru* sank, then the skulls could have been on board."

"The *Awa Maru* sank?" Rosalina shook her head in confusion.

"Oh yes, it was very tragic. She left Singapore on March 28, 1945. But three days later, an American submarine captain thought she was a destroyer and torpedoed her. Interestingly, of the two thousand and four people on board, there was only one survivor. He was the

Captain's steward and that was the third time the poor man had been the sole survivor of a torpedoed ship."

Jimmy huffed. "That's one lucky bastard."

"So, hang on a minute," Rosalina said. "Surely a Red Cross ship would have notified the Americans of where they were going?"

"*Precisamente*, but according to the captain of the submarine, the *Awa Maru* was some distance from her designated route." Alessandro ran his hand through his thick hair. "In spite of all this, the captain was still court-martialed."

"Let's go back to the treasure," Jimmy smiled like a man who'd just inherited a million.

"*Bene.*" Alessandro guided the mouse in his hand as everyone waited in silence. "None of this has ever been confirmed, however the *Awa Maru* was reportedly carrying forty tons of gold, twelve tons of platinum, 150,000 carats of diamonds and other less important materials."

"That's enough." Jimmy laughed and Ginger giggled with him.

Archer eased further forward on his chair, the look on his face, darkened eyes, pursed lips and gathered brows, was nothing short of intense concentration. He pressed his fingers together until his knuckles bulged white. "But they know where the boat sank, so surely there would've been salvage attempts."

"*Precisamente*," Alessandro said again. "In 1980 China made the biggest salvage effort in history on a single ship. They consequently found the wreck, but it took them five years to declare that it contained no treasure."

Jimmy slapped his palm on the table and Rosalina jumped. "Well where the hell did it go?"

It was only because everyone was completely silent that Rosalina noticed Helen walk into the room. She stood to assist her to a chair.

Archer raced to his mother's side as well and helped her to sit down. "Hey Mom, did you have a good sleep?"

Helen blinked several times at Archer. Her eyes were clouded over with confusion and her mouth fell open as if she was about to say something. But then slowly, as Helen looked around the room, she seemed to be taking everything in and Rosalina thought she was clawing back from whatever haven she was tempted to crawl into. It occurred to Rosalina that going through these boxes in front of her wasn't the right thing to do.

"Maybe we should finish up for today," Rosalina said.

"No." Helen slapped her palm on the table.

Rosalina blinked at her. Helen had never been this assertive.

Archer crouched at his mother's side. "We're going through Dad's boxes, Mom."

"I can see that."

Rosalina was surprised at the confidence in her voice. Helen appeared angry that Archer had pointed out the obvious.

Archer frowned at Rosalina, and unsure what to do, Rosalina just shrugged. She hoped Archer didn't bring up the pearl necklace. That was a moment he should share with her in private.

"Are you okay with that, Mom?"

"Yes." Her voice was still a brittle whisper, as if it hurt to talk.

Archer baulked, possibly unsure of what to do next.

"Hey, Helen, have you ever heard of the *Awa Maru*?" Ginger broke the silence and Rosalina glared at her. Ginger's eyes turned to her and then bulged as she mouthed 'what'. Clearly Ginger had no idea how sensitive Helen was.

"Yes Wade, don't you remember?" Helen gave Archer a cocky grin. But the crooked smile on Archer's face showed his distress. Helen's progress was slow; two steps forward, one step back.

Archer's anguish was like a blazing hazard symbol. He placed his hand over Helen's frail fingers. "What do you remember, *Mom*?" He emphasized the word.

"Japanese war ship."

The gold flecks dazzled around Archer's dark irises.

"That's right. It sank during World War Two."

"Yes."

"What else do you remember?"

Helen frowned and blinked as if forcing her memory to the surface. "Treasure," she finally said.

"That's right. Apparently when she sunk, she was carrying tons of treasure."

"No." She shook her head.

Archer blinked several times. "No, she wasn't carrying treasure?"

"Yes."

Archer looked at the ceiling and let out a sigh as he squeezed his mother's hand. "Mom, do you know if the *Awa Maru* was carrying treasure?"

"Yes, but not when she sunk."

Everyone in the room shifted forward.

Jimmy slammed his hand on the table and everyone jumped. "They offloaded the loot. That's why the *Awa Maru* wasn't on her reported route."

"Correct." Helen's eyes darted around the room as if she was proud of them for working out the answer. "That's why there was no treasure on the wreck." Ever so slowly, the dark shadows that had marred Helen's complexion vanished and a smile lit up her face.

Chapter Nineteen

Nox woke to a bright light shining into his eyes and piercing through his throbbing brain. Excruciating pain radiated from his hand up to his elbow. He blinked his eyes open, pushed up from the cold floor and crawled backwards so he could lean against a wall. It was several long, agonizing breaths before he'd conjured up the courage to take a look at his right hand.

His stomach wrenched.

His hand was barely recognizable, swollen to twice its size. Most of his skin had turned a ghastly purple and the rusted rod, with its corrugated surface and sharp point, threaded through the middle of his palm like a giant nail.

He fought dizziness. He swallowed back the urge to throw up.

He could not believe he'd been speared. Again.

With each movement, every muscle screamed. Just lifting his hand took great effort. While he stared unblinking at a small weed that had found its way through a crack in the floor, his fingers explored the lump at the back of his skull. It was the size of an egg and he winced each time he touched it. But he couldn't resist and as he examined one injury to the next, he kept returning to the lump, trying to come to grips with just how big it was.

He looked up toward the top of the tower. The dark blue sky was still dotted with the odd star.

Jesus! He could believe how far he had fallen. At least two stories.

Ironically, bouncing off the stairs and being pinned to the wall had actually broken his fall. If he'd fallen straight from the top, he'd be dead. From what he could tell, other than the trauma to his hand, and the lump on his head, he was fairly unscathed. Given the distance he'd plummeted, it was a miracle he could move at all.

With the sun's morning rays piercing the cracks in the building like laser beams and lumps of shattered concrete plastering the moss-covered concrete floor, it would be easy to believe he'd woken up on a strange planet.

He'd be happier with that.

Anything but this island with the weird twins and no avenue for escape.

The island was as foreign as any strange planet would be.

He rose to his feet and, with his arm across his chest and holding his hand upwards in an attempt to ease the throbbing, he stepped from this alien world and walked toward another.

Chapter Twenty

Archer glanced at the time and wasn't surprised to see it was two o'clock in the morning. Thankfully, it wasn't a nightmare that woke him. For decades, visions of his father's shark attack had hijacked his dreams.

Huh, I haven't had that nightmare since we found the treasure.

His thoughts bounced to the therapist he'd visited about the nightmares in his early twenties. She was right after all. She'd told him that all he needed to do was find the key. It was almost comical that the key had been around his neck all along. He reached for the pendant and ran his thumb along the raised letters. The true irony was that the necklace both started and ended all that horror.

Rosalina rolled away from him and he took the opportunity to slip out of bed. He pulled on his favorite pair of track pants and made his way to the galley. Switching on the lights he squinted against the glare and headed for the coffee machine. After a minute or so of staring into the fridge, he reached for the last piece of Rosalina's homemade apple pie and then lavished it with a good dollop of her creamy custard. With coffee and food in his hands, he wandered to the lounge area.

The room looked like it'd ridden out a tornado. Almost every inch of the carpet was scattered with items removed from the cardboard boxes. He chuckled. Because the way the room now, covered in his father's paraphernalia, was exactly the chaos he'd remembered on his Dad's boat.

Archer took a mouthful of apple pie and reached for one of his father's notebooks. After a quick flick through, he decided to start at the beginning and study it more thoroughly. The cover was devoid of any notations whatsoever. In fact, they were all like that. . . put the thirty or so books together and they were practically identical. It was just the curled corners and general wear and tear that differentiated them in any way.

He flipped open to the first page. The inside cover had four countries listed: Brazil, Guam, Singapore and Egypt. Archer reached for another book, it had four completely different countries listed. Unsure if it meant anything, he checked the inside covers of several other books and discovered two more with Singapore listed as the third country. He set his coffee mug aside as his mind began to race with the notion that he may have stumbled upon something.

He cleared the table except for the three books with the matching country. Now, with them laid out side by side, he turned the pages in sequence. Page by page he turned, scrutinizing every note, picture, scribble and otherwise random mark, but nothing else stood out. Finally, at the middle of the book, where the staples that keep the book together were exposed, there was something. All three books had a number with a circle around it. The numbers in these books were 7, 11 and 24.

Archer reached for another book and opened it to the middle. It too had a number in a circle. Number 19. With his mind skipping into overdrive, he reached for book after book. It seemed like hours before he had all thirty-four books laid out in sequence. Eight books were missing. As he rubbed his hands together, he admired his handiwork. But his elation over the discovery quickly dissipated as it became apparent he had no idea fucking idea what the numbers meant.

"Hey babe."

Rosalina was tying her silk robe around her waist as she sidled up to him. He wrapped his arms around her and from this height he was able to kiss the swell of her breasts. It was a lovely morning delight. Rosalina giggled, cupped his cheeks and kissed the top of his head.

"What time did you wake up?" She slipped into the chair beside him and scanned the books laid out on the table.

"About two, but I promise it wasn't a nightmare. I just couldn't sleep."

She reached for his coffee mug and took a sip. "Ewww. It's cold." She pulled a face and plonked the mug down. "I'll make us a fresh pot. So, what have you been doing all morning?"

She walked from him and the sight of her luscious curves beneath the silk triggered an immediate stirring in his loins as he pictured her beautiful body beneath the fine fabric. But there was no point acting on that desire, Rosalina had seen what he'd been doing and she wouldn't let up until he filled her in. She was like a fisherman with a hooked line when she thought he was keeping secrets. And rightly so. He'd never keep a secret from her again.

Maybe if he could summarize this quickly he could entice her back to the bedroom. "I've found a pattern to Dad's scrapbooks."

"Really? What is it?" Her eyes dazzled as she frowned at him.

"For starters, each of the books has four countries listed in the front. I'm not quite sure what it means. But then I found every one of the notebooks had a number written in the center pages, right between the staples."

As she walked back holding two steaming mugs, her robe slinked slightly lower on her breasts with each step. If she'd had a few more steps to take, he was certain her nipple would've been revealed. The throbbing in his groin became a full-blown jackhammer.

As she placed the coffee before him, he smelled both the potent coffee aroma and the delicious citrus and vanilla scent lingering on her skin. Archer couldn't hold back any longer. He stood, leaned over, scooped her into his arms, and without any real plan he headed for the upper deck.

She grinned at him. "Where are we going?"

Her breast was exposed now and Archer watched as her nipple peaked. "I think it's time we explored the upper deck again."

A smile curled at her lips and she whispered a throaty, "Okay."

He climbed the stairs and stepped into the early dawn. It was still at least two hours until the sun came up, but the sundeck wasn't shrouded in complete darkness. Just a hint of glow from the full moon glistened off the fine drops of overnight dew. He lowered her onto one of the sun lounges, and to his pleasure her gown glided sideways. Her breast, buxom and exquisite, was completely exposed. Archer lowered to his knees and savored her nipple. Sucking the delicate bud into his mouth, he slowly ran his tongue around and around. Her fingers combed through his hair driving tingling sensations across his scalp.

He undid the bow at her waist and the lilac-colored silk fell away to reveal all of her. Her skin was heavenly in this light and her white underpants, with the sheer lace, barely hid her small dark patch of hair. *So damn sexy.*

His body throbbed to an erotic beat. He turned his attention to her lips. They were slightly apart and when she glided her tongue along her bottom lip it sent him into overdrive. Archer stood and undid the knot on his track pants so fast he nearly pulled the drawstring all the way out. He slipped them off and stood before Rosalina naked.

Watching the desire and delight in her eyes as they scanned up his flesh shot him to heaven and back.

He lowered her back on the chair and helped her wriggle out of lace underwear. Naked now, he guided her legs apart and devoured her with his gaze. She seemed happy to let him relish her like that. Just looking at her gorgeous body had his blood running riot. The swell of her breasts rose up and down with every breath she took.

Archer knelt down and leaned over to kiss her. Their lips met, their tongues danced and he tasted toothpaste and coffee as he glided his fingers over her firm stomach and down between her legs.

He found her hot zone and she clawed at the lounge fabric. Grabbing his hair, she pulled his lips to hers. A deep moan tumbled from her throat and she writhed beneath him.

When her eyes re-opened, they were fiery with passion.

She pushed up from the sun lounge "Your turn."

He didn't need to be asked twice. He flipped onto the lounge and Rosalina stood over him, naked and glorious for the whole world to see. Her eyes were drawn to his, digging deep into his mind, taking his mind and body on a delicious journey. She slowly lowered herself onto him.

Her hair fell forward cascading over her breasts so her nipples flashed like a game of peek-a-boo.

Sound obliterated. Sensations intensified.

With each delicious movement, she took him further into the stratosphere. He couldn't hold back a second more. His fingers dug into the flesh at her hips and she took him to another world.

Rosalina cried out and fell to his chest panting. He clutched her there, running kisses over her hair until she pulled back to look down at him. "What was that all about?" She was smiling as she said it.

"You. Just you. You turn me on." That was an understatement.

She smiled and curled a strand of hair behind her ear. Rosalina, his beautiful Italian fiancée, truly was oblivious to how incredible she was.

"Come on." She climbed to her feet. "We better get dressed before someone catches us out here."

Archer wriggled his eyebrows, but a low thumping beat in the distance made his euphoria nosedive. He jumped up, grabbed Rosalina's hand and urged her back under the covered area. "Quick, get inside."

Tt was a helicopter and it was coming toward them.

As the distinct thudding grew, so did his thumping heartbeat. He gripped the railing and peered into the pre-dawn sky. But saw nothing. He tried to convince himself it could be anyone, but his instincts told him exactly who it was. Trusting his instincts was the smart thing to do.

He turned to Rosalina, her eyes were wide and darting.

"Rosa! Listen to me." He clutched her cheeks, drawing her attention to him. "Get Jimmy up, tell him to meet me back here. Then get Alex and Ginger and go to Mom's room. Stay there until I get you. Understand?"

Archer kissed her forehead and turned her shoulders toward the stairs.

But she spun toward him. "I think I should stay. You know I can handle it."

He wrapped his arms around her body and although he tried to portray calmness by kissing her gently and smoothing down her hair, every part of him was screaming with urgency. Trouble was on the way. "Please! Just do as I ask." He nudged her toward the stairs.

Before she stepped down, she looked back. "Be careful, babe."

"Always."

To his relief she disappeared down the stairs. Archer turned his attention back to the chopper. He still couldn't see it but was fully aware the pilot would be able to see their boat. *Evangeline* was impossible to miss. Archer tugged his track pants on, shoved the loose drawstring inside the elastic and sunk back against the wall to scan the horizon. Several stars still dotted the sky, but the radiance on the horizon confirmed sunrise wasn't too far away.

His gut told him it was Ignatius in the helicopter.

Iggy would have chosen this time of the day for a reason. The glow from the rising sun meant the chopper didn't need spotlights to land. This also made it harder for Archer to see it. The chopper wasn't approaching at a breakneck speed, maybe trying to pretend it was a tourist chopper out for a pre-dawn flight. For a fleeting second, he considered that may indeed be an option. But as quickly as he thought it, he dismissed it.

Archer did a mental check of what was within grabbing distance that could serve as a weapon. The sundeck was exactly that. Fancy sun lounges with matching side tables dotted the area exposed to the elements. The other half was under cover and was furnished with a custom-built semicircular lounge with a glass-topped table centered in the middle. Directly above the covered area, linked only by a narrow set of steps, was the helipad.

Archer made a snap decision. He flipped over a deck chair, and with all the force he could muster he slammed his foot into the evenly spaced wooden slats. The noise was much louder than he anticipated, but he kicked at the slats once more anyway.

Jimmy strode onto the deck rustling his gray chest hairs with his scratching. "What's up, boss?"

Archer pointed over the rail. "Chopper coming in and I've got a bad feeling about it."

Jimmy's eyes shot open, blasting away the last of his sleep. "Fuck. What d'ya want me to do?"

Archer tugged one of the slats free and handed the makeshift weapon to Jimmy. "Just do what you always do. . . back me up. But no macho stuff, I don't want you getting injured again."

"It'd be worth it. Can you see it?"

"Not yet." He guided Jimmy into the covered area and they ducked down between the lounges and the center table. He stared at the plank

in his hand and, as he pondered the foolishness of his plan, he listened
to a combination of the rotor blades and Jimmy's heavy breathing. If it
wasn't so serious it would be comical. Two grown men, both with their
shirts off, hiding between white leather lounges and a glass-topped
coffee table. Jokes aside, having his mate there made Archer feel a hell
of a lot better.

As much as he wanted to get up and look for the source of the
thumping noise, it would be a foolish move. Bunkering down was the
smart thing to do, but it was downright frustrating just sitting there.
Waiting.

"What d'ya think his plan is?"

Archer turned his head toward Jimmy, but he was hidden behind
the center table. "My guess is he thought he'd just land aboard and
catch us all by surprise." It was a miracle Archer had been awake at
this early hour, especially as he no longer had the nightmares. And to
have been on the upper deck when he heard the chopper was nothing
but a freak coincidence.

"What? By himself?"

Jimmy had a good point. How many men were on the chopper?
Taking into account the size of the chopper, other than Iggy, it could fit
three more people, max. "No more than four."

"Four! Against the two of us. Lucky we've got these planks then."
Jimmy was a cracker at sarcasm.

Archer realized how foolhardy his counterattack was, but they had
the element of surprise on their side. "He assumes we're asleep. When
we jump, they'll have no idea what hit them."

The chopper was almost right on them now. In a split second, it
was hovering right over the covered area, above where they were
hiding. But as quickly as it arrived, it was off again. Barely three
seconds, he guessed. Archer frowned, and as he considered that maybe
he and Jimmy had been spotted, footsteps stomped on the helipad
above.

The hairs on the back of his neck bristled as he tried to calculate
how many men had been offloaded. Two. At least that's what he
hoped. Neither man would be Iggy. Iggy hired men to do his dirty
work. That insight put fear into Archer's veins. Iggy had money. The
kind of money that could buy the right type of man for any particular

job. Nasty, snaky or otherwise. What he didn't know was what their mission actually was. And that's what he intended to find out.

Archer's plan: catch the bad guys. Make them talk.

He needed to know what the hell Iggy was up to.

He couldn't believe Rosalina was in potential danger yet again. He allowed that notion to drive his fury. With his fingers squeezed around the plank he waited. Fortunately, the men would need to climb down the ladder one by one. That gave Archer the edge. But if he pounced too early, the second man would have the upper hand. If he moved too late, the first man would have the advantage. He clenched down on his jaw and his stomach contorted with hatred.

Everything moved in slow motion yet sounds amplified. Jimmy's breathing was rough and restless. Small waves, whipped up from the chopper blades, lapped against the sides of *Evangeline*. The intruder's shoes squeaked against the smooth white paint on the steps down from the helipad. The only other sound was his own heart, pounding like a bombing raid in his ears.

A pair of feet, clad in black boots, appeared on the stairs. A leather strap was around the man's ankle. If it was similar to the one Archer had, it secured his dive knife at the ankle, or maybe it was a gun. And that wasn't good. Soon, the rest of the black-clad body was revealed. The man was built, clearly working out was his obsession. Archer almost crumbled with complete inadequacy.

The man was halfway down the stairs.

Archer braced to tackle him. The stranger jumped down the last two steps, and the second pair of feet appeared on the steps. The first man stepped aside and scanned the area with the awareness of a jungle cat. With his back turned away from Archer, he looked toward the stairs that lead down to the lower deck. It was exactly what Archer had hoped.

The second man was halfway down. *Six steps to go. Five. Four. Three.*

Archer lunged. Swinging the plank as he ran at the first man. The guy turned but was too late, taking the full brunt of the wood across the back of his shoulders. He crumbled to the floor with a howl.

Archer turned to grab the second man's foot. He missed. A heavy boot slammed into the side of his head. The blow was fast and hard. Pain ripped across his temple. Blood pooled on his tongue.

Ignoring the pain, he wrapped his arms around both legs and dropped his full weight in an attempt to pull the man from the ladder. It didn't work. The asshole snatched one leg free and stomped on Archer's shoulder. The force was a sledgehammer. Archer howled as he crumbled to the floor.

Jimmy stormed across the deck and drove his elbow into the neck of the first man. The attacker released a muffled cry and Jimmy punched him in his nose. Jimmy could handle himself.

Archer turned his attention to the second attacker.

The thug scurried up the ladder and was gone in a flash.

Ignoring the pain in this shoulder and neck, Archer grabbed the plank of wood and raced after him. He paused at the top step, peering out to ensure he wouldn't get a kick in the teeth. The black-clad man was on the far side of the helipad. Archer had him. There was nowhere to go from there. Except down of course, and it was a fair distance to the water. A fall from this deck could break a rib or two.

The man turned; fists balled, jaw clenched, fierce dark eyes.

Archer was in for a fight.

He clutched the plank and held it over his shoulder like a baseball bat. He may not win in a punch up with this guy, but maybe, just maybe, the plank of wood gave him a fighting chance.

"What do you want?" Archer rocked side to side on his haunches, ready to duck either way if needed.

The man didn't answer. Instead he stepped towards Archer.

"Ignatius sent you in to do his dirty work? He's a coward like that."

The man halted. His eyes narrowed. But other than that, he didn't portray the fear of a trapped man. If anything, he presented as the opposite. A man on a mission.

The attacker's stance changed; right shoulder dropped, weight onto his front foot. Archer had seen the move before, hell, he'd used it himself a few times. Growing up in an orphanage had taught him a trick or two about fighting.

The brute charged like a raging bull.

The distance across the helipad was barely six strides. He made it in four.

Archer planted his feet and forged all his anger into smacking the wood across the thug's head. Archer swung. The wood smashed into two as it cracked against the man's skull. But he didn't break stride. Archer twisted his body and took the full brunt of the attack side on.

He was airborne.

They'd gone overboard.

He braced for impact and they were a tangle of arms and legs when they hit the water. Wind punched out of him. Stinging pain ripped up his bare back.

Archer gulped for air.

But swallowed mouthfuls of water instead.

Chapter Twenty-One

The sun was high off the horizon when Nox limped out of the crumbling lighthouse. He soon spotted the rustic cottage he had escaped from the day before. Smoke was billowing from a pipe on the far side of the building and it looked more like a comfortable refuge than the ramshackle hut it was. The twins obviously weren't distressed by his disappearance. Maybe, fully aware that he couldn't go anywhere, they were just waiting for him to step back through their door. That would be the smart thing to do, given that his mouth was bone dry and his hand was a bloody mess.

But he couldn't do it. Not yet. He was driven. Driven by the need to get off the island. Driven by hunger to eat something other than dried fish and cardboard slop. Driven by a yearning to have his multiple wounds properly attended to. And the greatest drive of all. . . justice. The Calimala treasure was his. He'd lived a lifetime of hell waiting to get his hands on it and he would never stop looking for it.

But first he needed water. Even a dirty puddle would do.

The decrepit lighthouse was centered atop a large grassy knoll. He skirted the building scouring for a drop of moisture. Swallowing hurt. Everything hurt.

He stumbled across a water tank. Its buckled-in top, rusted corrugated sides and precarious angle offered little hope of it containing anything potable. But he was desperate. A tap was jutting from the curved edge. He hobbled to it.

Using his left hand was awkward enough, but the tap, bubbled with corrosion and crusted in what looked like sea salt, wouldn't budge. Nox clenched his jaw and put everything he had into twisting it. But when the fingers he had wrapped around the corroded metal ached as much as his clenched jaw, he gave up. He slammed his palm on the tank in frustration and a hollow rumble emanated from the rusted metal. It hadn't even occurred to him that the tank may be empty. He thumped the metal again and the same hollow rumble released. When he tapped on the lowest rung of corrugated iron, the sound was different, deeper. Starting at the bottom, he tapped on the rungs and when the sound changed to a higher pitch, he was convinced that there was indeed water inside. The tank was at least one-third full.

With a new sense of purpose, he searched for a way to make the tap work. A chunk of concrete nestled against the wall caught his eye. He grabbed it and with all the strength he could muster, smashed it onto the tap. The concrete shattered to pieces but the tap moved.

Water! Brown shitty-colored water spewed from the faucet and splashed over his cloth-covered feet. He cupped his good hand and lapped at the liquid. It tasted of dirt and rust; regardless, he gulped it down. He resisted the urge to wash the blood from his right hand. He chose not to look at it at all. The pain rippling down his arm was enough of a reminder.

With a full stomach and gasping for breath, he leaned back against the wall and took a moment to scan his surroundings. He pushed off from the wall and walked toward the cliff.

When he could walk no further, he stopped at the very edge and looked down. Enormous waves rolled in and crashed against the jagged rocks below. The breeze, carrying a fine mist of salty water, sprinkled his face. As he wiped the dampness from his cheeks he looked out toward the empty horizon. In the very far distance the sky met the ocean, blue against blue. The sun, now sitting high off the water, cast a white stripe across the ocean like it was dividing the world in half.

He walked along the precipice, on the brink of life and certain death, alternating his glances from the jagged edge, to the rocks below, to the vast beyond. The edge of his existence was right here.

It would be so easy to end it all. End the pain. End the hunger.

Time meant nothing as he cradled his speared hand to his chest and placed one foot in front of the other. The sun continued its steady arc above but the view below didn't change.

As the realization set in that he really was stranded on an island, his stomach started twisting into painful knots. The speed with which it came frightened him. He doubled over in agony and fell to the ground, slamming the metal rod in his hand.

Pain exploded up his arm. He howled in agony.

As he stared at the fresh blood oozing from pierced palm he threw up.

Over and over he heaved, spewing rust-colored water onto the spindly grass.

When he had nothing more to give, Nox rolled to a sitting position on the barren hilltop, wiped his mouth with the back of his good hand and sucked in deep breaths.

It took a huge effort to examine his pierced hand again. When he did, what he saw. . . the fresh blood, the dried blood, the purple swelling, the hideous wound. . . made him fight a fresh wave of nausea.

It was impossible to believe he was looking at his own hand. But the fact that he could still wriggle his fingers made him believe that once the rusted rod was removed, his hand would be perfectly normal again. This belief cemented his conviction that he was the chosen one. After all he'd been through already, it was a wonder he was still breathing. It seemed nothing could stop him from fulfilling his destiny to find what was rightfully his, the Calimala treasure.

From where he sat, he couldn't see the twins hut, the steep slope ensured it was hidden from his view. But the smoke billowing up from his left gave away its location. He searched the vast ocean around him, looking with half-hearted hope for signs of civilization. It was impossible to recall where the working lighthouse was. After he'd climbed the spiral steps, he'd lost all sense of direction, and even if he wanted to it would be impossible to climb up there again now.

As he breathed in, salty air laced his tongue; the opposite of what he needed. If Nox wasn't thirsty beyond belief, he would've sat in this very position until the sun went down and the elusive lighthouse showed him the way again. But he couldn't ignore the burning in his throat any more.

Without any other options, he clambered to his feet, careful not to jar his hand, and after a few wobbly steps, he found his pace and set a course for the smoke stream. He walked over the rise and the hut came into view. Something down in the ocean caught his eye. He squinted against the blazing sun reflecting off the water.

His heart leapt to his throat. A boat. A very small boat. But it was heading away from the island. Nox ran toward it. The incline was so steep he risked toppling forward, yet he kept up his pace.

Shielding the sun with his hand, he searched for the boat again. Two people were in it. With a jolt he recognized who they were. The twins. Their frizzy, red hair flapping in the wind was as obvious as giant crosses.

"Hey. Wait. Wait for me." His voice was a pathetic croak.

Nox ran faster, waving his good hand and screaming to them. But it was futile. The boat continued to motor further and further away. Nox lost his footing and cried out as he fell to his hands and knees.

He screamed in agony as the metal rod punched almost all the way through his palm.

Blood oozed in a fresh stream.

Driven by pure rage, Nox did the unthinkable. He grabbed the metal with his left hand and, before he changed his mind, he splayed his fingers on his right hand, clamped his jaw and pulled.

As the bar sliced through his palm it made a sickening sucking noise. Nox howled as the final jagged edges passed through. With the pole free, the hole in his palm closed up quickly, filling up with blood and mangled flesh.

Clawing at his failing strength, Nox flung the rod in the direction of the disappearing boat, now barely visible. The metal bar tumbled, end over end, and vanished over the cliff. He didn't hear it land.

His world tilted and twirled out of control. He fell back on the rocks. The sun was a furnace that penetrated his face. Listening to his ragged breathing, he squeezed his thumbs to his temples and fumed over his stupidity.

Of course the twins had a boat!
Why didn't I think of that?

That's how they'd found me.

The memory flashed with vivid clarity, especially the agony from the fishing spear as they manhandled him onto their boat like a dead dolphin.

It was an eternity, before he sat up and glanced out to sea again. The boat was barely a speck in the distance. He looked for something to mark the direction they were heading. He faced the boat and squared out his shoulders. Over his right shoulder was the sun, but without any sense of time, he had no idea how to mark its position. Directly behind him was the decrepit lighthouse. To his left, nestled against the cliff was the cabin. The only other landmark was the beach, a long way down below.

The ugly twins will be back. He would be ready for them.

First, he needed food and water. He climbed to his feet and strode along the steep cliff toward the cabin. Teetering on the edge of delirium, he stopped at the chicken boxes and scooped out three eggs. One by one he cracked them open and gulped down the slimy sustenance.

Clambering around the outside of the cabin, he searched around for the water holding. It had to be a tank of some sort. He found it on the far side of the cabin and shook his head in disbelief. Now he understood why he was rationed to just one cup of water each day; the tank was barely bigger than a wine barrel. Adamant today would be his last day on this island, he turned on the tap and drank as much as his belly could hold.

Gritting his teeth, he guided his bloody hand beneath the flow.

A scream tore from his throat and he snatched it out. Nausea wobbled in his stomach as he studied the bloody pool on the floor. "Do it."

Gripping his wrist, he clenched his jaw and eased his hand back into the water.

The agony tipped him into hell. Stars darted across his eyes as fire crawled over his skin. But he fought the insanity until the wound was nothing more than an angry red circle in the middle of his palm.

Nox turned off the tap and went into the cabin in search of something he could use as a bandage. Shadow was sitting on the table. Of course, now he knew it wasn't *his* Shadow at all. He went to the cat and smoothed the fur along the feline's back. It purred and leaned into him.

It was comforting to know he had at least one friend. He tugged a couple of strips of dried fish from the dangling ropes, fed one to the cat, and chewed on one himself.

After a handful of the dried fish, he forced down a plate of the cardboard slop. When he couldn't fit in another mouthful, he sat back and belched. This was the best he'd felt in a very long time. The wounds, hunger pains and dehydration no longer crushed his sanity. His body was savoring a brief reprieve from the painful injuries that had been his constant companion since he woke up on the bizarre island.

He ran his good hand over his scalp, assessing the agonizing walnut-sized lump at the back of his head, and was surprised by the length of his hair. At least two inches long. For as long as he could remember he'd been shaving his head. He couldn't begin to imagine what he looked like with hair. *I've been on this island longer than I'd thought. Could it be months?*

He had no intention of spending even one more night.

Nox found a cotton plaid shirt in a pile of clothes in the corner and he tore it into strips to wrap around his hand. With a desire to get out of the filthy clothes he'd worn since the day he'd woken up with the spear through his torso, he removed his shirt and put on a blue t-shirt he found in the pile. It was a bit tight, but it was clean. The exchange made him feel better still.

The twins owned very little. Certainly nothing of value. After the brief search around the downstairs room, he dragged himself up the ladder to explore the loft area. Growing up in an orphanage, he'd witnessed his share of messy living conditions, but these brothers kept their belongings in chaos. Apparently, their clothes also served as their bed. Just the thought of looking through the mess made him cringe.

He was about to retrace his steps down the ladder, when he spied a book wedged into a crack in the wall. Keeping his head lowered, he crawled towards it and had to dig the book out from the crack. It had obviously been there a long time. When it finally dislodged, it fell open at his knees. In the dimmed light he saw a sketch of a lighthouse on the right-hand side. He lifted the book to read the writing scrawled across the page, but it was in a foreign language and he snapped the book closed. A picture of a lighthouse adorned the front cover. It was an instruction manual for the lighthouse. Maybe the twins had been care-takers of the building. If so, considering the state of disrepair the light-house was in, they'd been living a reclusive life on the island a very long time.

He tossed the book onto the bedding and a slip of paper fluttered out. He reached for it. A number with a pile of zeros caught his eye. It was some form of receipt. As he eased back on his haunches, a scenario ran through his mind. When the lighthouse was decommissioned the twins were paid out. But for whatever reason they deliberately aban-doned modern society and chose to stay here. The next thought hit him like a lightning bolt.

"Did they hide the money here?"

There was only one possible hiding place.

With a new sense of purpose, he dug his good hand into the piles of clothes and flung them aside.

Chapter Twenty-Two

Archer clawed at the water, fighting his way to the surface. But it was pointless. Iggy's thug had a death hold. He couldn't break free. Archer's chest burned. He needed a breath.

Bright sparks blazed across his eyes as he rained punches low and hard at the man's head. Yet the vise didn't release. He squeezed tighter instead. One second a chill raced through Archer's body, the next his chest burned like he'd swallowed molten lava. His ribs were set to crack. Either the resistance of the water was lessening Archer's punches or the man had a head of steel, because he'd didn't react to Archer's barrage one bit.

Archer's attack lost momentum. The twinkling surface faded from view.

He drifted downwards. He needed a new plan. Now.

He went for the man's hair, but found an ear instead and pulled hard. So hard he thought it would rip right off. The man released with a muffled howl.

Archer scrambled for the surface. *Four feet to go. Two.*

But fingers clutched around his ankles and dragged him down. The surface drifted away.

The brute twisted so he was behind Archer; his arms clamped

around Archer's legs. Archer bent down and clawed at his arms. But it was impossible.

Time was running out. Precious bubbles floated upwards.

He needed oxygen.

An idea slammed into his brain. He whipped the drawstring out of his track pants, clutched it over his hands, twisted behind as much as he could and in one swift movement wrapped it around the brute's throat and pulled.

The tips of his fingers bulged red.

His eyes bulged too, as he stared at the surface several yards above.

Sunlight was still some time away, but the twinkling lights from *Evangeline* looked pretty, like hundreds of flickering candles. The blackness around him wafted with the current, sweeping him up in a tide of weightlessness.

A bright light appeared out of nowhere and Archer wished he could swim toward it. But he had nothing to give. All energy was gone. His body was a hollow useless shell.

Rosalina came into focus and he smiled. Her usual morning glow surrounded her and she looked lovely with her hair dancing in the water like it was having a party. She looked more heavenly than ever, like a mermaid.

His last bubble of breath released, and as it drifted downward an incredible sense of euphoria enveloped him. He relaxed completely.

Archer was dying but with Rosalina right there with him, he found peace.

He closed his eyes and let the ocean carry him away.

Chapter Twenty-Three

An almighty splash had Rosalina bolting upright. Disregarding Archer's instructions to stay in Alessandro's room, she raced up to the sundeck. She heard Jimmy before she saw him. His guttural growl was unmistakable. He had one of the attackers pinned to the decking by an elbow to his throat. The man beneath him was swinging fists that failed to connect with Jimmy's head. Both men were growling like angry dogs but the intruder was no match for Jimmy's brute strength.

"Where's Archer?" Her breath burst in and out.

"He went overboard. Go get him." Jimmy eyeballed the starboard side.

Rosalina's legs wobbled like jello as she dashed down the stairs. At the bottom step she slammed into Alessandro.

"What's happened?" The whites of his eyes flared.

"Go help Jimmy on the sundeck, Ginger come with me." Rosalina ran to the back of the boat. A chill raced through her as she yanked open the dive gear cupboard and tossed out the things she needed. With the flick of a switch, she turned on the high-powered flashlight.

"Here," she shoved it into Gingers hands. "Find Archer, he went over the starboard side."

Two seconds later, clutching her fins in one hand and her own personal flashlight in the other, Rosalina took a giant breath and dived into the black water. In record time she tugged her fins on and with her heart pounding in her ears, she shone the light beam in sweeping arcs, searching for the man she loved.

Archer's a strong swimmer. He can swim three miles non-stop and did it regularly just to keep fit. But by the sound of that splash, he hadn't gone in alone, and he hadn't fallen gracefully. He may be winded, or worse, injured. She cast the thought aside as she scanned the flashlight from side to side.

She kicked to the surface for a breath.

"There he is!" Ginger must've been ready to yell out to her. She pointed to a spot several feet to Rosalina's left.

"Shine the light on him." Rosalina kicked her fins and with frantic arms she raced to the pool of light. She sucked in a huge breath and duck dived down.

She saw him.

Her heart thundered. A cocktail of adrenalin and fear raced through her.

He was sinking. His face was turned upwards. His eyes were open as if he was looking right at her, but he showed no emotion; he wasn't actually seeing.

It was like he was in a trance and it terrified the hell out of her.

With almighty kicks, she pushed through the panic that threatened to drown her.

She reached him in seconds, praying for him to hang on. The instant she touched him his eyelids fluttered open, but the whites of his eyes were riddled with red veins.

Rosalina gasped. A large bubble burst from her throat.

Every millisecond counted. Her mind screamed at her to get moving. She did.

She clawed at the thick arms wrapped around Archer's legs and to her surprise they came away freely. She didn't want to look but couldn't help it. The attacker's eyes were wide open as he drifted toward the ocean floor.

Her rescue diver instincts kicked in. She moved around behind Archer, wrapped her arm around his body, directly beneath his armpits, and kicked with all her might to the surface. She counted the seconds, one. . . two. . . three. . . four. Finally, they punched through the surface, but she didn't stop there. She aimed for the rear dive platform.

"There they are," Ginger's squeal was welcome relief.

Archer was heavy, but desperation was a powerful motivator as she dragged his lifeless body through the water.

Ginger splashed into the water and helped her pull Archer toward the dive deck. The instant they reached the platform, Jimmy and Alessandro dragged Archer's limp body from the water. Gasping for breath, Rosalina snapped off her fins and scrambled up the ladder.

"Come on, baby." She dropped to her knees at Archer's side.

His lips were blue. His chest unmoving.

One of his eyes was slightly open, but Rosalina forced herself to ignore it.

She opened his mouth to ensure there were no blockages, then she leaned forward and breathed into Archer's mouth. Her mind was working through the next step in the CPR process, when Ginger fell in beside her, and with her fingers interlocked together she performed compressions like an expert.

"One, two, three. . ." Ginger kept up the count as she pumped a pulse back into Archer's lifeless heart.

"I'm here, baby, come back to me. Come on Archer." Rosalina's heart thundered in her chest as she kept up her own chant. Her eyes darted from Ginger's pounding palms to Archer's unwavering eyes. When Ginger finished her repetitions Rosalina leaned over, placed her mouth over Archer's and breathed life into him again.

With every passing second Rosalina's world crumbled. Life without Archer wouldn't be a life at all. It would just be existing. Her mind flashed to her father. A man who was so full of life and devoted to his wife and children but became a hollowed-out shell when her mother died. The transition was instant. She understood why.

She shoved the ghastly thoughts aside and fought the tears stinging her eyes. Archer would make it. He had to make it. Grit and determination took hold of her. She'd damn well make sure he'd live. She leaned over again, blew air into his lungs and jumped when Archer bucked beneath her.

"He's alive," she squealed as Ginger helped her roll him onto his side. Water spewed from his throat in great gushes, and then he gasped an enormous life-giving breath.

"Thank God." Rosalina pulled his head onto her lap and wept as Archer came back to life in her arms. Tears spilled down her cheeks as his blue lips regained their color. His cheeks began to glow golden and she realized the sun had crested the horizon casting a heavenly aura over the water. It was a precious reminder of just how delicate life was.

The vacuum that had consumed the last few minutes evaporated and every sound became amplified. Archer's breathing was ragged but regular. Ginger sniffled back tears and Alessandro and Jimmy were mumbling sounds of relief.

Rosalina looked over at Ginger. Her wet hair clung to her cheeks in thin strips. Her cheeks were flushed red from exertion and she sniffed as she wiped away tears. When their gaze met, Rosalina saw relief and pride in Ginger's beautiful blue eyes. "Thank you. You were amazing." No amount of words would be enough to thank Ginger properly.

Ginger's chin dimpled and she sucked on her bottom lip, clearly incapable of speaking and Rosalina nodded in understanding.

Rosalina turned her attention back to Archer. He squinted against the sun and blinked several times. When he seemed to have figured out where he was, he looked up at her with eyes riddled with so many red spider veins she was certain he'd have rose-colored vision.

He frowned. "I thought I told you to stay in Alessandro's room." His voice was a ragged croak.

"I'm sorry. . . I thought it was more important to save your life." Rosalina caught a tear tickling her cheek as she looked down his body for other signs of injury.

She did a double take. Archer was naked.

His pants must've come off in the water. Her instant reaction was to cover him, but she barely had the strength to move. Instead she burst out laughing. "You're naked."

"Hey buddy. . . finished nudie sun-baking out here?" Jimmy's laughter was hearty and welcome.

Archer lifted his head to look down his body. "Where are my pants?"

She wiped his wet fringe from his forehead. "You must've lost them in the water."

"Damn it. They were my favorite."

Rosalina's laughter was more out of relief than anything. As she glanced around at the four people she loved, all starting to join in, she made an instant decision that this treasure hunt was over. Well and truly over. They needed to get these valuables off the yacht before someone was killed.

Her mind shunted to the man she'd let float away and the crazy priest she'd speared.

People had already been killed.

Enough was enough. As she wiped a trickle of water off Archer's brow, she was grateful it wasn't any of them.

"Time to put some duds on, dude." Jimmy huffed and turned to climb up the stairs. Archer cupped his hand over his private parts.

Alessandro removed his shirt. "Here, *la mia bella*. You were incredible." He helped the dripping Ginger into the sleeves, wrapped his arm around her waist and guided her to follow Jimmy. Rosalina would be eternally grateful for Ginger's help today and she made a mental note to thank her properly later.

When they were gone, Rosalina helped Archer to stand. With her arm around his waist she directed him to the stairs. He leaned against her for support, but for a man just brought back from the dead, he was surprisingly steady on his feet.

"I told you that Rescue Diver course may save someone one day."

Archer must be feeling better to remind her of that. Rosalina had hated that diver training course. With days in freezing cold water, lugging grown men in pretend states of unconsciousness up the beach, it was her definition of torture. Never in her wildest dreams did she imagine she'd ever need those skills. Now, after bringing Archer back to life, she was grateful that she'd forged through the misery to get her certified training. "Lucky for you I did." They arrived at the base of the stairs. "After you," she said with a grin.

A smirk formed on Archer's lips before he turned and climbed the steps. Rosalina couldn't help herself and enjoyed every step he made upwards.

"I know you're checking out my butt."

"Maybe." She giggled and playfully slapped his behind.

Archer waited for her at the top. "Do you know what happened to the other guy? The last I saw, Jimmy was wrestling him on the upper deck."

"Oh, I don't know." She'd totally forgotten about the other intruder.

"My guess is he's either unconscious or he's tied up somewhere. We better find out."

"You should put some pants on first."

Archer snarled. "I really did love those track pants."

Rosalina strolled into the gym and grabbed two towels from the cupboard. One she wrapped around herself; when she went to drape the other over Archer's shoulders, he pulled her into his chest. He ran his hand over her wet hair as she listened to his heartbeat. It was amazing to hear just how steady his heart was after that trauma.

"I thought you were a mermaid." He kissed her wet hair and his warm breath cascaded over her scalp.

She chuckled and tried to pull back but he gripped onto her tightly. "When I was under the water, I thought it was the end. I saw this light and it transformed into you. You were the most beautiful woman I'd ever seen. You *are* the most beautiful woman, Rosa. What you did to save me was amazing."

"I thought I'd lost you, Arch. I watched that other guy drift away. Dead. You scared the hell out of me. Your eyes were so red. Your lips were blue. You'd stopped breathing." Her shoulders heaved as she sobbed into his chest.

"It's okay, babe. I'm okay." He rested his chin upon her head.

"It's not okay." She pushed back from him. "It's not safe here anymore. We need to get these treasures off *Evangeline* before one of us is killed."

"I know, Rosa. I agree. After we talk to this guy, we'll get a plan."

"I don't want a plan. I want to go. I've had enough. No stupid treasure is worth this."

"I know, babe--"

"You don't know." She thumped him in the chest. "This silly notion that you have to finish what your father started is poisoning your sanity. Your decisions are not rational." Her chin quivered.

"Babe, please." He cupped her cheeks. "It's been a stressful morning." He tugged her to his chest. "Let's make sure everyone is okay and then we'll make some decisions. Okay?"

She sucked in a few shaky breaths as he ran his hand over her hair. "I want a decision today." She pulled back so she could read his expression. "Okay?"

His eyes softened and he curled his hand around behind her neck. "Yes, today."

Hand in hand they walked to find the others. They were in the saloon and looked like they'd been waiting for them. They were a somber looking bunch and she had a horrible feeling they may have overheard her arguing with Archer. She furrowed her brow at the motley crew. The smell of liquor laced the air yet no-one seemed to be drinking. Clearly, they had no idea what to do. And Rosalina didn't blame them. Once again, they'd nearly lost someone they loved. With a crazy man with a helicopter and an abundance of funds who was determined to get his hands on their treasure, reality had slipped into a horror movie. No wonder no-one knew what to do.

"Glad to see you're decent. You were startin' to scare the ladies." Jimmy's cheeky smile deepened the crow's feet lining his eyes.

Archer slapped him on the shoulder. "Yeah funny, Jimmy. What did you do with your guy?"

"He's getting a few rays on the sundeck."

Archer nodded. "Have I got time to put some clothes on before we see what we've caught?"

"Take all the time you want, Alessandro used up nearly an entire roll of gaffer tape tying the asshole to a pole. Right now, he's getting a bird's eye view of that spectacular sunrise."

Rosalina glanced at Alessandro. He was grinning like a man who'd won a fight he didn't expect to win.

"You should have seen us, Rosalina." Alessandro was as excited as a puppy at feeding time. "That creep made it all the way into here, and I just happened to be near the bar when I saw him. Jimmy wasn't far behind. Lucky for me there was a bottle of rum within reaching distance. *Ho rotto sopra la sua testa.*" Alessandro's words were rapid fire and he didn't seem to realize he'd slipped into his native Italian tongue. But it didn't matter. His re-enactment of smashing a bottle over the man's head said it all.

"Broke the bottle too." Jimmy chimed in, shaking his head in mock disappointment. "Shocking waste of rum, if you ask me."

Now she realized what the liquor smell was. She glanced over at the floor by the bar and saw the wet stain on the carpet.

Alessandro palmed his chest. "Are you complaining?"

"No. I'm impressed. You did real good, for a professor." Jimmy held his hand towards Alessandro. "If it wasn't 0700 hours, I'd offer you a drink."

Alessandro accepted the handshake. "*Grazie*. I'll take up your offer after lunch."

Rosalina was shocked to learn how early it was. Her shoulders sagged with the weight of exhaustion. She'd love nothing more than a hot shower and to crawl back into bed. But that wasn't going to happen any time soon.

"How about I get dressed, then Jimmy and I'll go and have a little chat with our new friend while we wait for the police to arrive. Again."

"The police! What do we need them for?" Jimmy's eyes darted to Archer.

It's been four months since the police last stepped aboard, but The Incident felt like it was only weeks ago. It can't look good having yet another madman on board *Evangeline*.

Their story held up last time, but Rosalina doubted they'd get away with it again. This time though, at least they'd caught the attacker, so maybe it would be different after all. Her head was spinning just thinking about it. She needed a shower and coffee and it didn't matter in which order they came.

"Look. Let me get some clothes." Archer placed his hand on Jimmy's shoulder. "Then we'll work on a plan together. Okay?"

"Sure. But don't expect me to be nice to this guy. He had a knife in one ankle holster and a gun in the other, and by the look in his eyes he had every intention of using them."

A gun and a knife. Rosalina gasped. They were so lucky to escape unharmed. He obviously meant business. She was horrified by that thought and looked towards Archer, searching for some sign that he felt the same fear that was coursing through her veins. But he didn't show any sense of dread.

"No Jimmy, I don't expect you to be nice to him." Archer reached for Rosalina's hand and tugged her toward the bedroom suites.

Rosalina waited until they were nearly there before she spoke. "Do you think the thugs would have hurt us?"

"To be honest, babe, I have no idea. And that's why we need to talk to this guy and find out all we can. Hopefully we can figure out what Iggy was trying to do."

"Iggy? Are you certain it was him?"

"Positive. Just before the other guy attacked me, I tried to reason with him. When I mentioned Ignatius, he did a double take. I have no doubt Iggy is behind this."

Archer's eyes shone, but it wasn't with fear, it was something else. Excitement maybe? For a horrifying moment she contemplated that he was actually enjoying this. She dashed that thought aside, certain that she'd misread him. He'd nearly died this morning. It wasn't possible he enjoyed that.

An ache burned in her chest. She wanted to go home. And not just to be with Nonna. She wanted to be in the warmth and comfort of the villa kitchen she grew up in. She wanted to be surrounded by her family. She wanted to feel safe.

And for the first time ever, she questioned whether spending the rest of her life with Archer was what she really wanted.

Chapter Twenty-Four

A rcher had completely forgotten about his dad's books that he'd been analyzing earlier that morning, *and* the discovery he'd made. The books were still scattered all over the dining table and he began packing them up as he waited for Jimmy to resurface.

Alessandro bounded into the saloon like a kid at playtime. Clearly, he was still excited about his earlier bravado. Wielding that rum bottle must've taken some serious backbone. The Italian had shown another side to him that Archer hadn't expected, and once again, Archer wondered if he and Alessandro were destined to meet.

"*Buongiorno*, are you feeling better?"

"Yes. I'm good."

The Italian's bushy eyebrows thumped together. "You don't look fine."

"Gee, thanks."

Ginger stepped into the room. "Hey Archer, how are you?"

"I'm feeling great, thank you." He exaggerated a grin for Alessandro's benefit.

Jimmy lobbed into the room seconds later and flopped into a chair. As Archer had thought, this morning's adrenalin rush had hit him hard. The way he looked, with heavy eyelids and drooping shoulders, it was obvious Jimmy would prefer to crawl back into bed and stay there for the rest of the day.

"Any changes?" Jimmy grunted.

"No. Are you okay?" Archer said.

"Yep. Just bloody unfit. All this cruising around the Greek Islands is making me fat and lazy."

Archer studied his mate. Jimmy was nearly twenty years older than Archer, and even with his recent surgery, he could probably give Archer a run for his money in a wrestling match. But Archer knew it wouldn't matter what he said, Jimmy was hard on himself when it came to his fitness.

Rosalina strolled into the room looking completely refreshed in a long pink maxi dress. "Helen's still sleeping."

"That's good." Archer already knew that as he'd checked in on his mom after he'd changed.

Archer watched Rosalina go straight for the coffee machine and although he'd love a caffeine fix right now, it'd have to wait. He playfully tapped Jimmy on his non-existent belly. "You ready?"

Jimmy grunted. "Ready to beat the answers out of him, you mean? Hell, yes."

Archer knew Jimmy would dive in front of a bullet for him, and he'd do the same for Jimmy. It was a great relief to know Jimmy had his back.

"Has anyone called the police?" Ginger twisted her hands into knots as she asked the question.

Archer clicked his fingers. "Not yet."

"I'll do it." Ginger raised her hand like she was volunteering to taste ice cream.

"Okay, thanks."

When Jimmy stood, his demeanor had changed completely, resonating with a real sense of purpose. "Let's get this over with." He walked out the door and Archer jumped up and dashed after him.

Archer had never interrogated a man before and he assumed Jimmy hadn't either. As he tried to catch up to the striding Jimmy he wondered if they should've devised some kind of good cop, bad cop routine. Although, based on Jimmy's balled fists and audible grunts, he figured Jimmy was keen on the bad cop character. Jimmy radiated some seriously pissed-off vibes. Just before he stepped onto the stairs to the upper deck, Jimmy stopped and turned to eyeball Archer.

"There's somethin' you should know."

Jimmy looked about as uncomfortable as a priest in a brothel and Archer swallowed back the unexpected nerves over what his mate was about to say. "What?"

"I. . ." He cleared his throat. "I screwed up this morning."

"No, you did--"

"Hear me out." Jimmy planted his oversized palm on the wall. "At one point, not long after I heard you go overboard, this guy managed to get the better of me. He actually had me at a point where I couldn't move."

Archer frowned.

"I think he deliberately let me go."

Archer cocked his head. "Why would he do that?"

Jimmy ran his hand through his thinning hair as he shook his head. "First, he had me. And I mean really had me. Second, he had both a knife and a gun in his ankle holsters, but he chose not to use either of them. And finally, he ran inside, when A, he knew there were more people in there and B, there was a greater chance of being trapped. If it were me, I would've stayed on the upper deck. We were just lucky Alessandro hit him over the head when he did. Don't know where he was going, but he sure was keen on gettin' there."

Archer rolled the scenario around in his mind. Eventually he just shook his head. This was an unexpected twist and he had no idea what to make of it. He glanced up at his mate and saw just how much Jimmy was pained by this situation. Jimmy was as steadfast as an old sea dog. His morals were built on dependability, backbone, and loyalty. He would consider the thug getting away from him as a personal defeat. Archer didn't. He was about to say something profound that would mend Jimmy's unfounded thoughts of failure, but he wasn't quick enough. Jimmy turned and stomped up the stairs with heavy footfalls. Archer chased after him.

The morning sun was skimming the horizon when they stepped onto the upper deck. Not a whisper of breeze stirred the air and the ocean was as calm as a bathtub. The man was much bigger than

Archer remembered. He was still standing. Still tied to the pole. Though he couldn't do anything else, even if he wanted to. Alessandro had liberally taped every part of his body to the pole. It looked like a scene from a Wile E. Coyote cartoon and would be comical if it wasn't so serious.

The only thing the intruder could move was his eyes. And his eyes were incensed, full of what Archer read as justification. There was also a hint of arrogance, like he'd done nothing wrong. Archer had seen this look before on a man he'd once hired. It'd taken Archer four weeks to establish that Dave was stealing from him. He didn't want to believe it. He'd liked the guy until that point, and he'd been a good worker. The fact that he had a wife, twin babies and a mortgage was supposed to provide vindication for the theft. The irony was Archer would've gladly given him extra cash if he'd asked. The last Archer had heard, Dave was filleting fish at the markets and pulling double shifts just to get by. Archer cast the idle thought aside. Now was not the time to feel sorry for anyone.

The intruder's glare conveyed something else too. A you-can't-touch-me smugness. Like he knew his rights. It crossed Archer's mind that he was military or police. He wouldn't put it past Ignatius to have either or both on his payroll.

Jimmy ripped the tape off the thug's mouth.

Archer winced at the harsh sound but other than a serious death stare, the prisoner barely flinched. He had a bad feeling brewing in his gut that they were wasting their time. He figured they had at least thirty minutes until the police arrived, unless they came by chopper, in which case it would more likely be ten or fifteen. Either way, time was against them, and by the look on this guy's face no amount of time would be enough.

Jimmy got right in the guy's face. "What's your mission?"

The way he said it had Archer wondering if Jimmy had indeed done something like this before.

The prisoner squared out his jaw and glared in response.

Archer stepped in. "We know Ignatius Montpellier hired you." The man's eyes shot to Archer and he hoped he'd hit a trigger that may make the man talk. "What's he paying you to do? Kill us?"

The man did the slightest of head-shakes but halted as if catching himself out.

"If it wasn't to kill us, what was it? Kidnap? Take the boat? What?"

He glared at Archer, steely defiance blazed across his eyes.

Jimmy's slap came out of nowhere. It startled Archer as much as it startled the thug. The intruder blinked several times and made a point of rolling his tongue around his mouth. He spat on the deck and Archer tried to ignore the bloody mess.

"How much is he paying you?"

"What's your mission?"

"I'll pay you to tell me what Iggy's up to."

"What were you after?"

Between them, Archer and Jimmy fired question after question. But every one was met with silence.

Archer eased back. "The police will be here any minute. We'll have our answers then."

"The police do nothing."

Archer suspected the man's thick accent to be Ukrainian or Russian.

The statement hung in the air and Archer's earlier assumption that Ignatius had law enforcement in his pocket rang true. That wasn't good. Archer studied the man, trying to work out what would make him talk. "Your colleague didn't make it."

Again, nothing.

"Maybe you'll have a little accident too." Jimmy's grin bordered on frightening. "I wonder if you can swim with your hands tied behind your back."

The man's upper lip twitched. "Then it not look like accident."

"We'll tell the police you went crazy after we tied your hands up. You tried to tackle me and went overboard." Jimmy waved a knife before in the prisoner's face. "By the time we find you. . . well, you can guess the rest."

Jimmy flung something to the floor. It was the ankle holster he'd seen on the man earlier. That'd be where the knife came from. Jimmy bent down and slit the tape from the man's ankles to his hip. "It won't look like an accident with all this tape on you, will it?"

Archer couldn't tell if Jimmy was serious or not. He certainly had Archer believing him. "Let me guess," Archer said, before things really got out of hand. "Ignatius promised you a villa in the South of France and a healthy paycheck for the rest of your life."

Recognition crossed the man's face.

"Want to know how I know that?"

He gave a quick nod.

"He's been making that exact same promise for decades. My guess is the men who take him up on it never make it to the South of France."

For the first time, the prisoner's eyes conveyed an element of defeat.

Archer pounced. "Iggy's been pushing people around with his money for too bloody long. You're just another disposable thug, hired to do his dirty work."

"He kill me already."

"Not if you disappear."

Jimmy shot Archer a glare. Archer chose to ignore it.

"Tell us what's going on and I'll let you go. We'll tell the police there was only one attacker."

"That's not a good plan, Arch." Jimmy gripped Archer's bicep.

As Archer tried to ignore Jimmy's comment, he began to wonder if this guy could actually disappear. It's not easy to vanish without a trace. He'd need money. He'd have to let go of friends and family. If he had any. A man in this type of business probably didn't. The man lowered his eyes, maybe stewing over his options.

A very familiar beat confirmed a helicopter was on approach.

"Hear that? The police are about to land above us. You have about two minutes to make up your mind." Archer turned, gave Jimmy a nod, trying to convey that he knew what he was doing.

"It's not a good idea, Arch. He'll go straight back to Iggy."

"And what do you think Iggy will do? He'll torture him to find out what he's told us and then he'll probably toss him out the helicopter at high altitude."

Archer maintained Jimmy's glare. His mate wasn't happy, but he knew his place. Archer was boss and Jimmy would never mess with that.

Jimmy shot a glance at the prisoner and if hatred could kill, those eyes would be heat-seeking missiles. "He deserves everything he gets."

Archer put his hand on Jimmy's shoulder about to speak.

"Okay," the thug bellowed. "I talk now."

Chapter Twenty-Five

Nox found the money. It wasn't hard. The two fools made no effort to hide it. Beneath the multiple layers of clothes they used as bedding were bundles of cash.

He clutched at handful of notes and flicked through the variety of denominations. He'd never seen this much money before. In fact, he'd rarely held any cash at all. As a Brother of the St Apostoli Church, all his food, accommodation and living expenses were provided for. The only times he'd actually had a decent amount of money was when he'd stolen it from the collection box.

As he contemplated just how much was here, he wondered if it was enough to finally get the medical treatment he needed. It had taken him decades to learn how to cope with Trimethylaminuria, the rare disease that caused his excessive body odor.

But now, after the lifetime of ostracizing and ridicule he'd been forced to endure, he wanted more. Money was just the beginning. With the Calimala treasure in his hands and his disease treated, Nox would return to Florence as a new man and take his rightful place at the top of Florence's nobility. That's what he wanted. Respect and power.

Nox pushed most of the clothes over the edge to reveal a canvas of cash. It was impossible to estimate how much was here, but whatever the amount, it was more than enough to help him once he got off the island.

He grabbed a tattered pair of jeans, tied knots at the feet and began stuffing wads of cash into it. The first leg filled quickly and he'd barely made a dent in the money stash. With the second leg he chose the money more carefully, fishing out the higher denominations and placing them meticulously into the pants. It was therapeutic. . . find the note, stuff the leg, find the note, stuff the leg. It seemed like the most constructive thing he'd done in months.

He was back in control of his life.

With the jeans now full, he tore a threadbare shirt into a long thin strip, wove it through the belt loops on the jeans and pulled it together into a tight bunch to seal up the top. The end result looked like he was holding half a man. He laughed aloud and despite his ribs hurting, his head throbbing and his injured hand stinging, he felt good. No, it was better than that. With a sense of purpose back in his life and a plan to escape, it was like he could feel his body healing itself.

He rummaged through the small amount of clothes that were left on the bed and found another pair of pants, tan-colored this time. After repeating the knot tying process, he started stuffing again.

Suddenly, he smelled something that made the hairs on his neck bristle. Smoke. He turned around and gasped at the thick smoke pooling in the cabin's pitched roof. He leaned over the edge of the loft and stared in horror at the blazing piles of clothes he'd tossed over the side of the bed. He'd thrown them right onto the pot belly stove.

"Shit!" He jumped up and slammed his head into the roof. Howling in pain, he dropped to his knees again. Sparks blinded his eyes as he rubbed the opposite side of his head to his earlier injury. Popping sounds, as loud as gunfire, startled him into moving as smoke flooded the loft area. Holding his breath, he crawled to the ladder, looked down and stared in disbelief at the leaping flames, now nearly as high as the loft.

"My money!"

Without a moment to spare, he grabbed fistfuls of cash and shoved them into the tan-colored pants. His eyes stung and blinking away the thick smoke, tears spilled down his checks. A loud bang made him jump and when he looked over his shoulder, he gasped at the flames leaping up the wall. He erupted into a coughing fit and his lungs burned with each caustic breath.

It was the jolt he needed.

He tugged his two pairs of stuffed jeans to the ladder. But when he looked down, he stared at the dancing flames covering the clothes he'd tossed all over the floor. The flames were licked with streaks of blue and Nox suddenly realized why the fire had the ferocity it did. . . that poison the twins guzzled every night was fueling the flames. He'd seen them spill it enough times to know the floor would be saturated with it.

Situated where it is, the cabin must have withstood many seasons of ferocious winds and fierce storms, but it would be no match for this blaze. Nox had only a minute or two to get out of there before the whole thing came crashing down.

The clothes at the base of the ladder were all on fire, as was the floor and two walls. Black smoke spewed from the flaming fabric and pooled in a swirling cloud in the roof space of the cabin. One of the ropes, weighted down with the dried fish, fell from the ceiling, swinging the flaming braid right in front of his face. The rope crashed into the opposite wall and the wooden table it landed on blasted into a fireball.

"Holy hell." Nox snatched a shirt from the pile of clothes and ignoring the sickly body odor imbedded in the fabric, wrapped it around his head to cover his nose and mouth.

He squinted against the smoke, searching for another way down. There wasn't one. It was now or never. He grabbed the tan pants and aiming for the wooden slab he'd been forced to sleep upon, swung them with all the strength he had. But the bundle hit the roof rafters and plummeted straight down onto the inferno and erupted into flames.

"No!" Nox couldn't tear his eyes away as tongues of fire lashed out and reduced his precious money to black smoke.

Not willing to risk his second stash of money, he tucked the padded jeans under his right arm and squeezed it close to his body. He'd need his good hand to get down the ladder. Another loud crash snapped him into action.

He was about to step into the flames of hell. But he had no choice.

Nox sucked in a huge breath, and with only a quick glance towards the door to identify the way to run, he stepped onto the top rung.

He wouldn't say a prayer. He'd given up on that bullshit many years ago.

With clenched teeth he hobbled down the ladder, squeezing his good hand around the wooden ladder rungs so he didn't fall backwards. It was a fine balance between speed and safety and the second his feet touched the flaming clothes he turned. The heat hit him like a sheet of molten glass. Flames lashed out from every direction.

His heart slammed into his chest as he clutched the shirt over his mouth and ran for the door. He yanked it open and at the same moment Shadow came tearing out of the cabin, hair up in shackles and screaming his own terrified wails.

Nox tripped over the feline and fell face first into the junk pile.

His nose hit something hard. Pain exploded behind his already stinging eyes.

Bottles, timber and piles of junk tumbled onto him, burying him beneath the clutter. Dazed and confused he lay there, gasping for air. A loud explosion shattered the silence and Nox dug himself out of the mess and bolted upright. With the stuffed jeans under his arm he stumbled to his feet and wove his way through the junkyard. He didn't stop until he was a decent distance from the cabin.

Gasping for breath, he tugged the shirt from his face, crumbled to the rocky ground and stared at the fiery hell he'd escaped from. Yellow and red flames leapt from the roofline. As he held his hand up to shield his eyes, a brilliant display of fire danced off his ring, bringing the stones to life. As he adjusted the angle of his ring, admiring the glow from within the precious stones, he had a moment of clarity. In spite of everything that had happened, the fact that he was alive, and also blessed with an abundance of money, convinced him that he would, no matter what, fulfill his destiny.

Through the cracks in the walls, the interior of the hut had become white, like some kind of power source was about to explode from its belly. A trickle of liquid oozed down his chin and when he wiped it away, he wasn't surprised it was blood. He'd seen his fair share of it lately and took little notice as he wiped it onto his shirt.

After a while, he lay back on the grass and stared up at the heavens and screamed. "HAVE YOU FINISHED WITH ME YET?"

An almighty crash had him bolt up in time to see the entire cabin implode. Flames, sparks and smoke leapt high into the air. The cabin was engulfed in a huge fireball. The chickens scattered, squawking in their escape and the water tank that he'd gulped from earlier tumbled off its stilts, rolled down the hill and disappeared over the cliff.

Nox ran his dry tongue around his mouth and all he could taste was smoke. With the only water source gone, along with the stash of dried fish, the twins would have no choice but to leave the island with him.

His eyes followed the threads of smoke that caught in the ocean breeze and drifted out to sea. Suddenly he spied a boat down in the water. It was heading towards his island, casting a ribbon of white water in its wake. It had to be the twins. The pace it was traveling was much greater than the speed it had left. They must have seen what he'd done to their cabin.

Nox was thirsty, hungry, and shattered, and his body trembled with both pain and exhaustion. But he had a horrible suspicion he was about to experience another kind of wrath.

Would he have the strength to deal with the crazy twins?

As he glanced at the horizon, he made another shocking discovery. The sun was setting. They didn't have much time before the blackness of night would consume them and they'd be stuck here for another night. He would not spend one more night on this island, not without food, and not with his tongue as dry as the poisonous mushroom powder he used to store in his antique ring.

He eyeballed the boat again and a sense of despair gripped him. He estimated less than ten minutes before the twins hit the shore.

Nox rolled to his feet and searched for something to use as a weapon. A plank of wood, a metal pole, a glass bottle, anything would do.

The piles of junk at the back of the cabin would be a perfect place to start looking, but not only was the heat too intense to get anywhere near it, the rubbish was already dotted with flames. He disregarded that idea. There was nothing else. He gave up and began running down to the beach.

At the top of the cliff, just before the island gave way to jagged rocks, he looked out at the endless stretch of water, hoping one last time to see signs of civilization. But there was nothing. Absolutely nothing but indigo blue ocean and a blood red sunset. With relief he noted the boat was still a good mile or two off shore. Clutching his bandaged hand to his chest, and with the padded jeans beneath his elbow, he ran as fast as his cloth-covered feet could carry him down the rugged path.

The track wound down the steep cliff, cutting back on itself in numerous, sharp hairpin turns. The twins had made some attempt to make the trail easier with several sets of stairs but for the most part, the path was jagged uneven rocks, gravel and clumps of spikey weeds. His cloth shoes were no match for the rough terrain, and not only did it hurt the soles of his feet, he was a hell of a lot slower than he needed to be. *Was this their regular path?* Maybe there was an easier way down. He clenched his good fist at that cruel thought.

Nox was in a race for his life. A race to beat the men to the beach. A race to leave on the boat before sunset. And a race to find water, because right now he couldn't even swallow.

A straight piece of wood lying in the middle of the path caught his eye. When he reached it, he couldn't believe what he was actually seeing. It was the blood soaked, rusty metal reinforcing that he'd yanked from his hand and tossed over the cliff hours ago.

Laughing like a crazy man, he picked up the weapon with his good hand and ran on.

He hit the sand so abruptly, he lost his footing and stumbled to his hands and knees. The padded jeans broke his fall and in a nice twist they also saved him from injuring his hand again. From that position it looked like the small boat was about to hit land. Nox swallowed hard, climbed to his feet and staggered to greet them.

But communication between them so far had been impossible. He needed their help. Nox dropped the stuffed jeans above the waterline and at the ocean's edge he fell to his knees and, like his father had done just before Nox had killed him, Nox placed his hands together and begged.

"Please. Help me." His voice was a rusty croak. He tried to swallow again, forcing down the razor blades.

"Help me."

They waved their fists with angry gestures and yelled at him as if he understood every word they said. The boat speared onto the sand, barely three feet from where Nox was kneeling. Short Beard jumped out and ran straight at Nox. As he leaned over him, he yelled with such ferocity, spittle landed in his fizzy orange beard.

"Help me. Please." Nox willed his eyes to show his desperation. He clutched at Short Beard's wrist and with his injured hand he imitated drinking. "Help me. I need water."

Short Beard fired words that Nox had no hope of understanding and at the same time he was trying to yank his hand free. But Nox wouldn't let go. He used his grip to pull himself up, face to face with Short Beard. "We need to go. Now." Yet it was obvious his pleading was a waste of time.

Short Beard slapped him. Full calloused palm. Right across the cheek.

The pain shot up Nox's battered nose and shrieking he fell to his knees again. As Nox cupped his burning cheek and fresh blood poured from his nose, a rage as hungry as a ferocious predator drove up from within.

He allowed the anger to drive him.

Nox clutched the metal rod in his good hand, and with the speed of a panther he shot up from his knees and whipped the weapon across Short Beard's neck. The ugly twin's hands leapt to his throat as he dropped to the ground face first, like a cadaver.

Nox was as startled as Short Beard must have been.

Did I knock him out? Or is he dead?

Either way, he didn't care. He turned his attention to Scar Face. The look on the twin's face snapped from alarmed to enraged.

Nox hunched down, planted his feet in the sand and waved the metal rod for the standing twin to see. The growl that spewed from Scar Face's throat was unnatural; a wild animal had been unleashed. The twin charged, kicking up sand as he aimed straight for Nox.

Nox had no intention of getting into a wrestling match. Complete exhaustion and a battery of injuries ensured he wasn't fit enough for it. If he was going to make it out of this alive, he'd have to dodge the attack. He waited until the very last second to dive to the side. It worked, and Scar Face tumbled to the sand. But he was up in a flash, his eyes daggers of revenge. His face contorted into fury as he charged again.

Nox's arms trembled as he held the metal rod above his head, ready to whip it across the twin's face. Seconds before impact he brought the pole down, but his aim with his left hand was off and the weapon bounced off Scar Face's shoulder.

His feet were knocked out beneath him and Nox slammed back first onto the sand.

Scar Face jumped on top of him. Smothering him with wild punches.

Nox fought back, using the metal pole as a baton, clobbering Scar Face with as much power as he could harness. But the crazed twin was immune from the blows, taking each hit as if the hardened steel was nothing but a rubber tube. Nox had seen fury like this before and if he didn't get out from under Scar Face, he was going to die.

Scar Face's fist connected with Nox's chin and Nox lashed out, clamping his teeth right into the flesh. The metallic taste of blood flooded his mouth, but Nox clenched harder. Just when he thought he was going to bite off a chunk, Scar Face screamed.

Nox released, spat out the blood, and drove his knee into the twin's groin.

An explosive breath punched from Scar Face's mouth, and this time when he screamed, he also keeled sideways.

Nox rolled to his hands and knees gasping. He could barely move. His body was ready to surrender. His mind wasn't. Panting and fighting waves of delirium, Nox crawled towards the boat. To hell with the twins. The floating body of metal would be his salvation; they can die on this wretched island.

And without food, water and a way to get off, they probably will.

Scar Face was groaning and mumbling something unintelligible behind him. Nox ignored it and focused only on moving his hands and feet, one in front of the other. He waded out and screamed as the sting of salty water lashed out at his wounds. He clenched his teeth and forced himself to keep going. Once he was knee deep, he used the side of the boat to drag himself up and over the side. He fell like a dead man onto the cold metal and the vessel rocked wildly from side to side.

His mind screamed. *Start the engine. Get away while you can.*

Two seats stretched across the width of the boat. It took all his might to drag himself onto the one at the back. Gasping for breath, he took a moment to look over at the twins. Scar Face was leaning over his brother, and Nox thought he heard him sobbing. He blocked the sound as he studied the engine. It wasn't the same as the boat Nox had hired in Athens. This one had a pull start. When the man at the boat yard had shown him this variety, he'd deliberately steered clear of it. It required a good dose of strength to pull the string. Even back then, when he was in full health, he'd resisted that option.

He wrapped his fingers around the handgrip, and as he was about to pull it, he saw Scar Face running at him.

"Ahhh, shit." He tried to swallow, but it was impossible.

It was now or never.

Scar Face hit the water before Nox had time to ready himself. The twin grabbed onto the side of the boat and Nox whipped the string from the motor with brute determination. To his surprise, the engine roared to life and with the twin hanging onto the side, the boat tilted wildly. Nox was forced to grip on with his injured hand as he steered with the other.

The boat was in barely two feet of water and Nox had milliseconds to act before he ran it aground. Ironically, it was Scar Face's weight that helped with the maneuvering and he managed to quickly turn the boat around and head out to sea.

Scar Face's screech was that of a crazy man. His strength was amazing. He held on with one elbow hooked over the side of the boat and tried to swipe at Nox with his other hand.

Nox had had enough. He let go of the motor and the boat bucked with momentum. Nox gripped onto the seat and with rage-driven energy he kicked at Scar Face's head. It took two blows, but finally the ugly twin was gone. Nox turned back to the motor, grabbed the tiller and aimed it away from the island.

He looked back. Scar Face was swimming in his wake, and to his amazement Short Beard was standing at the shoreline. By the way Scar Face had reacted, Nox believed he had killed him. *Pity.* He rolled his eyes at the overreaction and spied the ribbons of smoke flowing from the cabin.

Yes! This would ensure he didn't steer the boat in circles.

He headed the boat in the direction of the drifting smoke and prayed that he hit land before the red sky above him became black.

He settled into the journey and as the loud buzz of the motor became his new companion, his numerous injuries began screaming at him in unison. As he assessed the damage, his purple and swollen hand, the lumps on the back of his head, his painful and swollen nose, his ribs, his back, hell. . . just about everything, he thought about what lay ahead. With his money. . .

"MY MONEY!" Nox stood up so abruptly the boat rocked and he fell forward onto his hands. Pain shot up from his injured palm and he howled at the new onslaught.

"My money." Nox fell to the bottom of the boat, curled into a ball and tears that welled up from deep down released in a gut-wrenching wail.

Chapter Twenty-Six

U nder Archer's rapid questioning, the prisoner reluctantly opened up. But the more he said, the more Archer was convinced it was a practiced speech. Their mission, according to this guy, had been to simply tie them all up and call Iggy to return to *Evangeline* once the job was done. Archer was certain it was bullshit.

Maybe Iggy thought they were an easy target. That would be the only explanation for sending just two men to overpower five of them. Sure, they'd arrived in the darkness of early morning. No doubt Ignatius expected them to be asleep. But to arrive by helicopter seemed ridiculous. Not only because of the noise, but because he'd already taunted them with it. Any fool would know they'd be listening for that sound constantly.

Much to Jimmy's disgust, Archer had promised to let the captured thug go if he told them everything. Jimmy's seething over his plan was distressing to see. But it was necessary. For now. Jimmy knew his place, but his clenched jaw and dagger eyes made it clear he wasn't happy with Archer.

The police helicopter was off the starboard railing and Archer stepped aside to deliberately block the prisoner from their bird's eye view. He shielded his hand against the sun's brilliant glare and tried to peer into the chopper's cockpit. But it was pointless. The darkened glass reflected the fireball, making it impossible to see the number of men concealed within.

The beat of the rotors was a heavy thud as the chopper hovered over the landing pad directly above them.

Jimmy raised his eyebrows at Archer and cocked his head at the prisoner. The pleading in his eyes confirmed he was wondering what the hell Archer was waiting for.

Archer turned his attention to the thug. "I think we've heard enough."

The prisoner raised his chin. "I go now."

The chopper's rotors whipped up a sea spray, casting a fine mist over all of them. Archer shrugged. "I don't think so."

The prisoner's eyes shot to Archer. "We had deal."

"I agree." Archer shrugged. "The deal was, you tell me your mission and I let you go."

The thug gave an exaggerated nod. "I did."

The thumping helicopter was so loud Archer was forced to raise his voice. "What you told me was bullshit!"

Jimmy folded his arms over his chest and grinned at Archer. The worried scowl that had etched his face for the last ten minutes evaporated in a flash.

"I tell truth." The man's pleading elevated.

"You told me lies. Iggy could have put three men in that chopper, yet he offloaded just two." Archer shoved two fingers in the man's face. "Two. . . to overcome five people."

The prisoner wrestled against his constraints. "I only do as told."

"Not good enough."

Archer snatched a strip of loose tape off the thug's leg and pressed it over his mouth. The anger in the prisoner's clenched jaw matched his burning death stare.

Archer stepped back, collected the knife ankle holster from the floor and the other holster that still contained the gun, and turned his back on the man. As he heard the chopper's skids touch down on the helicopter pad above, he raised one of the cushion seats and tossed the leather straps and weapons into the concealed storage compartment.

Jimmy sidled up beside him. "You old dog, you." He playfully thumped Archer in the ribs.

"What?" Archer grinned at his mate.

"The old good cop, bad cop routine. You really had me going."

"Needed to get you as angry as I could."

"You bloody well did that. After these guys go, I'm gonna need a good dose of rum to settle my nerves back to normal."

"I hear ya buddy. I hear ya."

Archer stepped onto the stairs leading up to the helipad and looked up at the spinning rotors. Wind whipped his hair across his face and as Archer brushed it aside, he made a mental note to get a haircut, he was well overdue. As the rotors began to slow down, two sets of black leather boots with thick soles emerged from the helicopter.

Archer stepped back from the handrail, deciding to stay where he was and let the police come down to him instead.

He watched them descend the stairs with a sense of déjà vu. It was hard to believe he'd experienced nearly the exact same scenario just an hour or so earlier. So much had happened since then. Archer's gaze flicked from one officer to the next. While one was tall and gangly, the other was stout and sporting a barrel-like stomach. Both were dressed in police uniform and both surveyed the scene around Archer with darting accusatory eyes.

The barrel-shaped officer was showing signs of exertion and Archer was already wondering how he would get back up the stairs, especially with a prisoner in tow. The officer extended his hand. "Mr. Mahoney, I assume." His Greek accent was strong but decipherable.

"Correct. Please call me Archer, and this's Jimmy." Something about his first impression of the officers made Archer refrain from revealing Jimmy's surname. Maybe it was the way they flanked him, closing in on his personal space, but it suddenly seemed important to give them as little information as possible.

The police could see the taped-up prisoner, yet neither of them moved in his direction. Archer stepped back and opened his palm, guiding the men to him.

"Here's one of the attackers."

The tall one cocked his head at Archer. "Where's the other man?"

The hairs on Archer's neck bristled and the still morning air wasn't to blame. The way he'd said "man" made it obvious he knew there were two. If he'd said men, or if he'd actually questioned how many, it would be different. But he knew there was only one other man. Archer looked squarely into his eyes and when the officer's glare shifted to his partner, Archer spoke. "The other guy attacked me and we went overboard. He didn't make it."

"Where is he?"

Archer shrugged. "Out there somewhere. My guess is he drowned."

The two officers shot rapid fire words at each other in another language. Presumably Greek. The gangly one pulled a phone from his pocket, punched in a number and moved to the far end of the deck to speak into his phone privately. The other officer seemed content to wait until he was finished.

The officer ended his call and slipped the phone into his pocket as he walked back to them. "The divers are on their way. Is there somewhere we can talk?" he said.

"Yes. Here." Archer had no intention of inviting them any further into *Evangeline*.

"Right. How about you tell us what happened?"

Archer guided the two officers to sit and then he and Jimmy did the same. He began telling details of the day's events, but the two officers hit them with their own set of intense questions and matched it with idle note taking.

When Archer had mentioned Ignatius as the likely perpetrator, they wrote the name down. But the way they did it, in a doodle-like manner rather than as if it were an important name in a serious crime, confirmed they had no intention of acting upon it.

In fact, their whole casual-like discussion seemed fake. It may've been the look that crossed between them, or it may've been the fact that they didn't clarify how Archer knew it was Iggy. Either way, he was certain, reporting this to the police was a complete waste of time.

As the questions progressed, they centered more on why the attackers were targeting *Evangeline* rather than extracting details of the actual attack. They were fishing for information, and with every passing question Archer clammed up that little bit more. Jimmy hadn't said one word since he'd sat down, but one look at him was enough to know he had exactly the same vibes about this pair.

A commotion erupted from a lower deck at the back of the boat and the policemen jumped up from their seats, strode to the railing and looked down.

Archer cleared his throat to attract Jimmy's attention. "They didn't ask any questions about Iggy."

"Nope." He hissed through his clenched jaw. "What d'ya think it means?"

"It means they know exactly who he is, but they have no plans of doing one fucking thing about it."

Jimmy huffed. "Just say the word and I'll rip this guy's arm off and beat the two of them over the head with it."

Archer glanced at the prisoner. He was still tied up with silver tape. The police were here to take him away, yet he looked as comfortable as if he'd stepped aboard for a drink. He wasn't worried enough for a man in his situation.

Before Archer was tempted with Jimmy's farcical offer, he strode towards the railing. Below them, nestled against the dive deck, was a police-issued rubber craft. Archer counted four men, all clad in black wetsuits, all in various stages of preparation to dive overboard. Archer used the distraction to gather his thoughts. The fact that there were six officers here was as disturbing as if they hadn't turned up at all. If they truly intended to find the drowned intruder, there'd be a dozen men and a couple of choppers in the air. Like they had when Nox went overboard.

Right from the moment the police set foot on the boat, Archer had felt like someone was still pulling all the strings. Now even more so.

Archer watched as one by one the police divers flopped backwards into the water, and after a brief safety check they each vanished below the surface. As he pondered how long it would take for the body to be found, his mind flashed to the crazy priest. His body had never resurfaced. Maybe this one was destined for the same fate, and maybe the ocean current won't be entirely to blame.

The officer with the barrel belly spun on his heel and took in Archer with his dark accusatory eyes. "May we search your boat?"

Archer's mind snapped to attention. "No."

The officer cocked his head. "Are you hiding something?"

"This is my home and without a search warrant, there's no need to go beyond this upper deck."

The two officers glanced at each other and the tall one's Adam's apple bobbed up and down. "Why do you think you've been attacked again?" he said.

"I have no idea. People see a yacht like this and assume we have bundles of money stashed aboard."

"Do you?"

Archer pushed back on the railing. "I told you who our attacker was, Ignatius Montpellier. Ask him what this's all about."

"We will. Is there anyone else aboard?" The officer turned his attention to the prisoner.

"I'm sure you know the answer to that." With impeccable timing, Rosalina stepped onto the upper deck. Archer clamped his teeth, trying to contain his frustration. He let out a calming breath. "Officer. . ." It occurred to Archer that neither man had properly introduced themselves. "May I see your badges please?"

The barrel belly one smiled in a way that indicated he was itching for someone to ask him that. He reached inside his jacket and produced a leather billfold that he flicked toward Archer. Archer inhaled the smell of fresh leather as he read and memorized the name.

"Officer Nikolaos, this is Rosalina. She resuscitated me after the other guy tried to drown me."

Nikolaos nodded in her direction. "Did you see the other attacker?"

She glanced at Archer, obviously seeking his advice.

"They're looking for his body now," Archer said.

Rosalina blinked a few times. "Yes, I saw him. But only briefly. He. . . um. . . I think he drowned."

"I was just lucky Rosalina found me when she did. Or you'd be looking for two bodies."

A fresh round of commotion erupted from the dive deck and all five of them moved to the railing to look below. Two divers had popped above the water and then, as they watched, a body floated to the surface. Rosalina gasped and turned away. The face on the body was ghostly pale, stained with dark blue around his eyes and mouth. From this distance he looked much smaller than Archer remembered him. Nothing like the raging bull that'd tackled him overboard.

After a series of squeaking noises, the police divers launched the body over the side of the rubber boat and it flopped into the bottom of the craft like the soggy corpse it was. They quickly had it covered in a black plastic sheet.

Archer turned to Nikolaos. "Are you going to question this guy?" Rather than turn to the prisoner, Archer trained his eyes on Nikolaos. As the officer paused with obvious indecision, Archer remembered his earlier promise to Rosalina to get out of Greece soon.

It was time to do that.

He wanted the police off his yacht and if it meant helping them do so, he would. "Come on, Jimmy, let's get this guy untied so they can take him away for questioning."

Jimmy didn't hesitate to following Archer's lead.

"Rosa, you can head back downstairs. You don't need to see this."

"Okay." Her face relaxed, showing relief at his directive.

He watched her leave before he and Jimmy began tearing off strips of tape that attached the prisoner to the pole.

"Leave the tape on his mouth. And hands," Archer said and Jimmy smirked in response.

Strangely, the police held back and just watched, cementing Archer's belief that these guys weren't police at all. Once he was released, Jimmy wrapped his enormous hand around the thug's bicep and shoved him toward the officers.

Nikolaos reached for the prisoner and yanked the tape off his mouth. "What's your name?"

After a brief pause in which nobody spoke, including the thug, the officer directed the prisoner toward the stairs. The lanky policeman climbed the stairs first, followed by the thug.

"So, I guess you'll be in touch," Archer called out as Nikolaos stepped onto the first rung.

"Yes. We'll contact you soon."

"Like hell you will." Jimmy read Archer's mind.

In a matter of minutes, the helicopter roared to life and with a cyclonic blast it lifted off. Archer stood at the railing and tracked its departure until it was barely a blip in the distance.

Jimmy touched his shoulder. "Time to get out of here, boss."

"Agreed."

Chapter Twenty-Seven

The transition from dusk to dark was swift, as if a giant blanket had been tossed over the world. One minute Nox was steering the little boat towards the ever-decreasing smoke threads, the next minute all he could see were thousands of stars sprinkling the blackness.

Other than the twinkling stars above, there were no lights anywhere, and the moon failed to show itself too.

Once again Nox was in an alien world.

Was the working lighthouse an illusion?

Maybe he was so desperate to see civilization that he'd concocted the whole flashing light image.

Nox was driving into and surrounded by complete blackness. He eased back on the throttle, aware that he could crash into something. The engine noise was the only constant and filled the void around him like an angry drone. But as much as he didn't want to do it, he was forced to turn off the engine altogether. Just the thought of ending up in the water again was enough to convince him it was too dangerous to carry on.

The silence that engulfed him was tremendous. Nothing but small waves tickling the sides of the boat, along with his own ragged breathing. With his bruised ribs and smoke-infused lungs, it was wonder he could breathe at all.

For a long time, he stared into the black beyond. Sheer exhaustion, and the sound of the lapping waves, soon began to weigh in on him. He was powerless to fight it and caught his head nodding onto his chest several times before he admitted defeat. Nox crawled between the two seats, wriggled around to get comfortable and tried not to think about the endless possibilities of what could happen.

There was some small comfort. At least the boat offered a modicum of security.

But he'd done everything he could possibly do and once again he was in the hands of fate. Somehow, he was comfortable with that thought.

In light of everything that had happened, the fact that he was still alive was nothing short of a miracle.

He was not going to be die. Not yet anyway.

Nox blinked against the glare and it took all his might to raise his arm to shield his eyes. It was some time before he realized it was the sun. He'd slept right through the night, or maybe it was two or possibly more. A sharp scraping noise startled him. It reminded him of the one and only time he'd had his teeth checked. The sadistic dentist had actually smiled at Nox's fear over the contraption grinding his teeth. The sound and the pain were one of the worst experiences of his life, and even though it had been thirty years ago, the memory guaranteed he never went to a dentist again.

The scraping noise was louder this time and with it the boat tilted over slightly. Nox shoved himself up and gasped. Every muscle in his body strained against the movement. His eyes blurred with the pain and he blinked back tears. The boat tilted again, forcing Nox to hang on. The sea spray on his face was cold and refreshing and helped snap him out of his daze.

Nox saw the next wave coming and as he braced for it, he eased up onto his knees and leaned over the seat. The waved crashed over the side and wet his legs and cloth-covered feet. He moved over as far as he could and when he looked around, he couldn't believe his eyes. Two little kids were standing side by side and staring at him from barely three feet away. They wore matching denim overalls, but that's where the similarities ended. One had blond hair, some of which danced across his eyes in the breeze, the other child had curly dark hair that scattered in all directions.

Certain he was hallucinating, Nox blinked a few times.

The blond-haired child took a bite of something. An apple maybe. Nox rolled his tongue around his mouth, it was solid, foreign and as useless as hardened leather, incapable of producing moisture.

Whatever that boy was eating, Nox wanted it. He reached out. As he watched the little boy take another bite, he imagined the moisture, the sweetness, and a groan released from his throat.

The boy took an apprehensive step forward and handed over the apple. Nox floated in a hazy dream as he reached for it. He took an enormous bite and felt the sting as his cracked lips split even further. Despite mingling with his blood, the apple was sweet and delicious. With the eyes of both children watching his every move, he devoured the whole fruit, core and all, in a matter of seconds.

The boat continued to rock back and forth, caught in the shallow waves rolling into shore. With every roll of momentum, the bottom of the boat protested with a scrape of metal on shoal. Nox glanced out to the ocean and the abundance of blue made him grateful that he'd hit land so quickly.

He could've floated for days. He'd be dead from dehydration if he had.

A person materialized behind the boys, high up on a cliff. "τι τα αγόρια κάνουν?"

Although Nox couldn't understand a single word the person said, the accusatory tone was unmistakable. A sense of déjà vu gripped him. Could this really be happening again? The curly haired boy turned and yelled something over his shoulder.

Nox had no idea what he'd said, but he no longer cared. Just to be on dry land, and to have food in his belly was satisfaction enough.

He summoned his energy, braced himself on the side of the boat and attempted to stand. But his legs crumbled beneath him and he fell back onto the seat. Even though he must have slept for hours, he was physically and mentally exhausted. The sun's hot rays were a warm embrace on his face and he considered closing his eyes and falling back to sleep.

In a surreal dream, he allowed himself to be swept up. It took a while for him to realize he was in a woman's arms. Her bosoms were enormous and he had no choice but to snuggle into their soft mounds as she eased him out of the boat, carried him a few steps and then lowered him onto the gravelly sand.

He looked up at her, and with the sun radiating behind her she looked like the angel in the painting he'd viewed almost every day of his life in the church hall. Nox wondered if he'd died and woken up in heaven. But he was quick to realize that was impossible; after what he'd done in his life, he was destined for hell. Besides, the pain rippling through his body convinced him he had to be alive.

The woman spoke to him and her touch on his forehead was as gentle as flower petals.

"Water," Nox's voice was barely a croak but he motioned *drink* with his hand and she nodded.

"*Si, Si.*" She spoke to the children and then the dark-haired one dashed off somewhere out of view.

Nox closed his eyes and either through exhaustion or relief, he drifted in and out of awareness. One minute he was walking along wedged between the woman and her two children. Next minute he was gulping down mouthfuls of cool water, then chomping his way through thick slices of warm bread smothered in bittersweet lemon butter. Finally, he was lying on a bed that enveloped him in its soft cushioning.

As the muscles in his body unravelled, he stared at the three faces hovering over him. After the ugly twins this trio were delightful. The woman was cherubic in her features with pudgy cheeks, plum-colored lips that were permanently pouting and a mop of curly dark hair that she'd tucked in behind her unadorned ears. The two children were boys and both had inherited their mother's plump cheeks and they smiled with mischievous grins.

To Nox's relief they all looked friendly.

Before long he allowed his heavy eyelids to close and he succumbed to exhausted sleep.

A BEAUTIFUL ANGELIC VOICE PERMEATED NOX'S DREAMS TAKING HIM TO a place of safety, free from pain, free from angst. Free. A long-forgotten childhood scene rattled from his memory banks. He saw himself sitting at a table decorated in a red and white checkered cloth. A bunch of white flowers in a crystal vase were in the middle. There was a woman beyond the flowers, her back was to him. She was humming a tune he didn't recognize. He had a fork in his hand, clearly ready to eat. A small child ran up to the woman and she wrapped him up into her arms and swung him around with obvious glee.

The child giggled. The woman laughed. Nox waited.

It was a long time before their spinning stopped. But when they did, neither of them glanced in his direction. Neither of them even seemed aware that he was there. Until the woman grabbed two steaming bowls off the counter. She shot a belittling sneer in Nox's direction and strode from the room as if she couldn't wait to get out of there.

Nox was left behind. Alone and hungry.

The beautiful singing grew louder and it dragged Nox from the ugly childhood memory. He resisted opening his eyes for fear the comforts he was relishing would evaporate as fast as a dream. Nox could smell her too. She smelled of cinnamon and butter and flowers that reminded him of the night jasmine that blossomed at the back of his church every summer.

Why didn't she flee from him like everyone else did? Maybe he was so relaxed that his body odor was insignificant. But he knew that wouldn't be the case. He couldn't remember the last time he'd had a shower, and he'd been wearing the same pants since the morning he was shot with the spear gun. Was that weeks ago? Months even? It was impossible to calculate. He didn't want to think of it. He wanted to stay right where he was, on the soft bed, listening to her beautiful voice, smelling her sweet perfume. Avoiding the reality, he was destined to slam back into.

She touched his arm with cotton wool tenderness, barely applying any pressure, yet the sensation sent shockwaves through him.

Nobody touched him like this. Ever.

Not knowing what to do, and not wanting the bliss to end, he kept his eyes shut and expected her to scurry away at any second.

But instead, the most incredible thing happened. She began to undress him. With meticulous care she wove his arms in through the t-shirt he'd stolen from the twins and lifted it up and over his head. When she winced, he could only assume she'd seen one of his many wounds.

His hand maybe. His stomach. His bruised hip or ankle.

It didn't matter, all of them must look grotesque. The bruising would be black and swollen while his scabbing would still be covered in dried blood. Even he didn't want to look at them.

He heard a trickling sound and seconds later she touched his chest with a sponge soaked in warm water. Her singing resumed as she swept the sponge in soothing arcs across his bare chest.

Nox had slipped into heaven.

The sponge bath continued down his chest to his stomach and her singing only stopped when she glided the sponge around his wound.

She squeezed out the liquid and when he heard her footsteps, he peeked out just in time to see her disappear from the room. She was a large woman with her hips nearly as wide as the door. She tinkering about in the room next door. A tap was turned on and moments later she walked toward him again. He closed his eyes and concentrated on calming his breathing down.

The sponge bath continued down his arms and when she held his palm in her hand it was the most tender moment of his life. She played the sponge around and over his wound in such a way that he barely felt it at all. Once again, she stepped from the room to change the water, humming to herself during the whole process and returning once more.

When he felt her presence beside him, the humming stopped, and to his horror he felt her touching the button on his pants. The instant he heard the zipper, sweat trickled from his armpits. His condition was about to ruin his new-found bliss.

Once she smelled him, it would all be over.

She gently tugged his pants off, rolling them down over his knees. He wanted the bath, God yes, it was heavenly to feel clean again. He wanted to be cared for, he wanted to be nursed back to health. But what he wasn't prepared for was the arousal that sprung to life as she removed his pants from his ankles. His groin began to throb in a sensation he hadn't felt in a very long time.

Without pause she quickly removed his underpants and her singing resumed as she squeezed the water from the sponge and began bathing his feet. The stirring in his loins was stimulation overload and it took all his might to keep his eyes shut and to remain completely still.

It had been decades since he'd felt such delicious sensations. He could pinpoint that exact moment. He'd been seventeen at the time. The young woman who instigated his arousal had long slender legs, breasts like delicate buds, and skin as pure as fresh cream. Sofia was her name. From the instant she'd held his hand, his penis had bounced to life. She had captured him in her spell and he'd fallen for it.

If he'd had his senses about him, he would have questioned her motives. Nobody ever looked at him, let alone a young beautiful woman. He'd seen her having sex with other boys, courtesy of one of the many peepholes he'd discovered in the ancient church corridors. So, he was led to believe that he was just another conquest.

This girl, this beautiful blonde-haired girl, just liked to have sex.

She had him naked in no time and he'd willingly agreed to be tied up. The promise of having her do to him what he'd seen her do to the other boys was too much. She even touched him, down there, and at the time, he'd been confused by the look on her face. It was more curiosity than seduction. She'd stepped back from him and her gazed skipped over his body to settle on his erection. When she said, "I'm ready, are you?" Nox just about exploded right there and then. And he would have, if two boys hadn't tumbled into the room laughing and ogling. At him.

Sofia almost looked sad at what she'd done. Almost. If she'd been even slightly repentant, Nox may have let her live. But she'd gone along with those boys and their embarrassing jeers. It was another one of his life lessons that taught him a whole lot more about himself than his tormentors. Nox learned to remove himself from the persecution. He suffered through their torturous humiliation with seemingly no emotion.

But what they couldn't see was the putrid loathing festering inside him.

His tormentors were going to suffer greatly for what they did to him.

A moist sponge touched his inner thigh and Nox was wrenched free from the horrible nightmare he'd slipped into.

She parted his legs.

His heartbeat thundered in his ears.

His penis rose to attention.

Nox had never felt a mother's touch. Or a lover. This was the closest he'd ever come to either. He'd never believe a woman's touch could affect him like this.

Her humming stopped and he pictured her staring at his groin. The one and only time a female had seen him at full erection, she had scorned him. But this woman was the opposite. Her pause was only for the briefest of moments. She recommenced humming and Nox thought it was louder, and more joyous.

Could it be that this woman found him appealing?

As much as he found the thought ridiculous, he felt a compelling desire for it to be so. He lay there, stunned beyond moving as she loaded the sponge with more tepid water, and he just about flipped out of his mind when she ran the sponge around his testicles.

Her humming morphed into singing. His breath shot in and out as he rode a wave of divine bliss. This was the most erotic, sensual, bizarre moment of his life. For the first time ever, he felt like a normal human being. His body, his hideous, diseased body, didn't repulse this woman.

He felt like he actually belonged in the human race.

He felt like he was someone who could be loved.

Calmness washed over him.

Nox wanted to stay in this moment forever.

Chapter Twenty-Eight

"Jesus babe, what are we going to do?" Rosalina couldn't believe what Archer was saying. She glanced at the sky, expecting to see the police helicopter in the distance, but it was long gone. Archer claimed nothing would be done about the attack from Iggy and even worse he didn't think the police were legitimate.

Both realities cast a chill up her spine. It meant Ignatius had a whole lot more power than she ever imagined. It also meant he wouldn't give up until he had what he wanted. And that put them in a very dangerous situation.

Archer cupped her chin, drawing her eyes to his. "We're getting out of here for starters."

Rosalina resisted the urge to jump for joy. She didn't want Archer to think she hated every moment aboard *Evangeline*. Although surely, he couldn't blame her. Between life-threatening situations and missing her family, it was a wonder she hadn't taken off weeks ago.

She looked up at him, and one glance into his dark brown eyes convinced her he was as nervous as she was. It was a look she hadn't seen on her fearless man too many times. He kissed her forehead and tugged her to his chest. "I'll instruct Jimmy to haul up anchor and cast off."

"Now?" A flutter skipped over her stomach at the thought of going home.

"No time like the present."

She squeezed her arms around him. "Where will we go?"

"It's time to get this treasure off *Evangeline*. . . so back to Italy. Besides, it's time I met your family.

She frowned up at him. "You've met my family."

"Not all of them. Not your father, or your younger brother."

Rosalina wasn't keen on seeing Filippo, not now that she had to confront him about all the hassles he'd been giving Nonna. And she hadn't seen her father in years. It wasn't that they'd had a fight, or anything that would make them estranged in any way. But when her mother died, he became increasingly distant. To the point where he rarely ventured into the main house. He spent his time in the winery and slept in one of the smaller cottages at the back of the property. Maybe the chance to meet her fiancé would entice him out of hibernation.

An idea formed in her mind. She pictured it as clearly as if it'd already happened. "We could have a huge luncheon in the vineyard. Jimmy and Ginger can meet my family too. Oh Archer, it'll be wonderful. I can't wait to tell Nonna, she'll love it. Thank you." She jumped up, wrapped her arms and legs around Archer and pulled him in for a kiss.

Then she wriggled out of his arms and climbed down. "I'm going to tell the others," she called over her shoulder as she dashed for the stairs.

As expected, she found Ginger and Alessandro in the saloon. They were sitting side by side at the table. Her hand was within his and they were both watching him trail his finger along Gingers palm as if he were reading her love lines. But their contentment evaporated when their eyes darted to Rosalina.

"What did the police say?" Alessandro's bushy eyebrows were a line of worry.

Rosalina slipped into a chair opposite them. "They kept asking questions about what we had on board that'd cause all these attacks."

Ginger's eyes bulged. "They didn't tell them, did they?"

Rosalina didn't justify Ginger with an answer. "They didn't seem to care about who attacked us."

"This's crazy." Ginger twirled one of her plaits around her palm.

"It certainly is. That's why Archer just told me we're heading home."

"Home?" Alessandro questioned.

"Yes. To Italy. To offload the treasure and see our families."

"*Fantastico.*" Alessandro turned to Ginger. "Would you like to meet my family too, *mia bella.*"

Alessandro's pleading look was one Rosalina had seen many times. She hoped Ginger wouldn't refuse him.

"I'd love to."

In a vivid fantasy, Rosalina imagined Alessandro and Ginger married and deliriously happy in love. The premonition tumbled from nowhere and she was delighted with the daydream.

Archer walked into the room, rubbing his hands together. "Okay, first stop Syracuse. Happy?"

"Very." Rosalina grinned up at him.

"*Sì, assolutamente.*" Alessandro curled a lock of Ginger's hair behind her ear and Rosalina could tell from the intense look on his face that he'd fallen hard. She hoped Ginger didn't break his heart like Rosalina unintentionally did.

"Good. Jimmy's setting the course. Alex, you and I need to get cracking on sorting out what to do with the treasure."

"Of course." Alessandro jumped up quickly, toppling his chair over. The noise was loud enough that Rosalina ducked for cover. When she realized it was his chair, she knew that heading home couldn't come quick enough. She tugged on her gold loop earring as a flush of embarrassment flooded her cheeks.

"And ladies, I'm starving, I don't suppose you could whip us up something to eat?" She was grateful Archer diverted the conversation to something that would distract her.

Rosalina contemplated what was in the pantry. "I think we can do better than that. This calls for a feast. Right, Ginger?"

"I reckon."

The men departed and Rosalina assumed they were heading to the office. As she walked toward the galley, she stepped around the monkey statue and realized no-one had asked Alessandro what he'd discovered about it. It was by far the most curious piece they'd found. Not only was it the biggest, except for the cannon, but as far as she was aware, it was the only one that displayed Egyptian hieroglyphics. She couldn't comprehend how something like that had become part of a vast missing treasure from Italy.

Archer won't be able to rest until that riddle is solved.

It was a bittersweet musing, because while she'd love to explore the origins of the monkey statue, she was also almost at the end of her treasure hunting endurance.

But for now, cooking was the ideal therapy.

As Rosalina tugged open the pantry and then the fridge, the concept of a table full of delicious tapas meals came to mind. She pictured grilled halloumi served with her homemade caramelized onion relish, glazed chorizo with fresh cherry tomatoes she'd purchased at the market stall yesterday, blue cheese and pistachio stuffed fresh figs wrapped in prosciutto and baked to perfection, chickpea and bacon balls with a mild chili sauce. The ideas burst from her mind as she tugged ingredients off their shelf and placed them onto the counter.

She set Ginger the task of making the chickpea and bacon balls while she assembled the other ingredients into order. Within an hour, the dining table would be presented with a feast to tempt anyone.

"Hey Rosa, what do you think will happen to the treasure?" Ginger didn't look up from the sizzling bacon as she spoke.

"I don't really know. I'm sure Alessandro will contact the museum in Florence first."

"It's going to a museum? Do we get to keep any?" Ginger's voice escalated.

Rosalina frowned. "No. How can we? These items are precious and deserve to be exhibited somewhere so everyone can enjoy them."

"Oh." Ginger placed handfuls of chickpeas into the blender. "Does the museum actually buy the treasure off us?"

"I don't think so." Rosalina ground a dash of salt and pepper onto the halloumi. She glanced down the hallway, watching out for the men. She was pleased they were all preoccupied, not only because it would take their minds off this morning's horror, but because it allowed her to surprise them with their feast.

"What, not even one piece?"

Rosalina laughed. "Ha, wouldn't that be nice. Which one would you keep?"

Ginger's face lit up. "Oh, it would have to be that bracelet with the large emeralds on it. It's beautiful." She turned back to the blender and the grinding noise filled the room with each press of the pulse button.

Rosalina contemplated what piece of treasure she would like to keep. But it was impossible to narrow it down. She'd want to give the pearls to Helen and the bracelet with the plaques to Nonna. Then again, she was pleased they would go to a museum, all the pieces deserved to be in a safe place where the whole world could appreciate them.

As Ginger set the table and placed each tapas dish upon it, Rosalina whipped up a fresh garlic aioli and pan fried lightly battered chili shrimps until they were crisp and golden. With the final dish nearly done, she sent Ginger off to find the men.

They must've been hungry, as no sooner had Ginger set off to get them when they all returned to the dining area.

"Oh, wow." Archer walked in with his arm around his mother's waist, guiding her to a chair. "Look at all this food."

Having lived at a nunnery for twenty years, Helen may not have seen a tapas feast like this in a very long time, if ever.

"Morning, Helen, did you sleep well?" Rosalina walked over and gave Helen a kiss on each cheek.

"Not too bad, thank you," she said.

Most of the time, when Rosalina had checked in on Helen, she was sleeping so soundly she looked like she was in a coma. Occasionally though, her face would be contorted in pain as she slept through one nightmare or another. Rosalina knew how disruptive they could be. She'd witnessed Archer's almost nightly horrors for years. Finding the Calimala treasure had been the key to unlocking and breaking him free from them. She wondered what Helen would need to stop hers.

"You ladies have been busy." Archer tugged a chair out from the table and sat beside his mother.

"Rosalina, as usual, this looks *magnifico.*" Alessandro's appreciation of her cooking was lovely, but she felt the suspicious glare from across the room.

"Ginger helped too."

Alessandro glided over to Ginger, reached for her fingers and kissed the back of her hand. "Wonderful. I can't wait to taste it all." He pulled out a chair for Ginger, helped her to sit, then sat beside her and whispered something in her ear that made Ginger's neck flush.

"Please. . . start eating before it gets cold." Rosalina nudged the shrimps to the center of the table and took her seat beside Archer.

"I know it's not even midday yet, but I'm gonna have a beer." Jimmy strode to the bar. "Anyone else joining me?"

"I believe you owe me a rum." Alessandro gleamed with the cheeky request.

"You want rum? Now!" Jimmy laughed. "You'll be off your rocker before we eat."

"I'll make it for you." Ginger jumped to Alessandro's rescue.

As Ginger passed the monkey statue, it jogged Rosalina's earlier unanswered question. "Hey Alessandro, I forgot to ask what you learned about the monkey statue."

"Si si, so much has happened since then." Alessandro steepled his fingers.

"Did you find out where it came from?" Archer reached for the plate of baked figs and handed it to Rosalina, knowing it would be one of her favorite dishes on the table.

"Not yet," Alessandro said. "But I do know where it didn't come from. It wasn't part of the Calimala treasure."

Jimmy sat opposite Rosalina and wriggled his eyebrows as he surveyed the abundant tapas selection. "So professor, how do you suppose it ended up on the *Flying Seahorse?*"

Rosalina would have bet her beloved coffee machine on Jimmy reaching for the chorizo sausages first. And she couldn't resist smiling when he did. She'd had him in mind when she made that dish. Jimmy was a man's man, and although she'd tried to tempt him on many occasions with all manner of other meals, his preference was always for the robust meat dishes.

Rosalina loaded her fork with a slice of fig, topped with the warm blue cheese and pistachios and a piece of crunchy prosciutto and popping it into her mouth. The delicious combination was summer and tropical sunsets all at once.

It took her back to a time when she'd made these for Archer while they cruised around the Whitsunday Islands. His reluctance to even taste them had been laughable. The way he'd carried on was as if he'd believed her possible of poisoning him. After the fuss, he eventually did try one and not only did he love it, he devoured several in a row. Now whenever she found fresh figs, she'd bake this dish. Unlike Jimmy, ever since that fig epiphany, Archer was ready and willing to sample all of her dishes. There weren't too many he didn't fancy.

Alessandro fastidiously topped his plate with a selection from each tapas plate, but he was yet to taste any of them. "First of all, it's obvious, just by looking at it that it's of Egyptian origin. Secondly, it's not a monkey, it's a baboon."

Jimmy huffed. "Monkey, baboon. Same thing."

Alessandro was gearing up for a technical response to Jimmy's remark but Archer jumped in with a question. "What's inside it?"

Alessandro paused with a chickpea and bacon ball on his fork. "I didn't open it. I think it would be wise to perform that in a controlled environment."

"Worried about booby traps?" Jimmy stabbed a slice of grilled halloumi, deliberately avoiding the roasted cherry tomatoes Rosalina had served with it.

Alessandro cocked his head at Jimmy. "Yes, as a matter of fact, that's part of the reason." He popped the nibble in his mouth and chewed only briefly before he swallowed.

"I was joking." Jimmy pushed the whole slice of halloumi into his mouth.

"I'm not. The Egyptians were known for their creativeness at keeping gravediggers from their valuables. I'm more concerned with damaging what may be inside."

"Oooh, like what?" Ginger grinned up at Alessandro like a lovestruck student.

Rosalina popped a shrimp into her mouth and bit off the tail. The tempura batter was crispy, the shrimp was full of flavor and the touch of chili in the aioli polished the delicacy to perfection.

"If there was a scroll inside, made of Egyptian papyrus for example, it is conceivable, because it's been sealed inside the statue, that it's retained a pristine condition." Alessandro ran his hand through his thick hair and it flopped back into place.

"Oh wow, imagine that." Ginger waved a slice of chorizo on the end of her fork. "Do you really think it would be okay?"

"I hope so. Because an artifact like that would be worth millions." Alessandro wiped his fingertips on his napkin.

"Millions." The word whispered off Ginger's lips.

"Not to mention what could be written upon it," Archer said.

"How could a bit of writing on a scroll be worth more than that?" Jimmy's eyebrows shot up.

The halo of gold flecks in Archer's dark eyes glimmered. "It could lead us to the rest of the Calimala treasure."

"Hell yeah. . . now you're talking." Jimmy raised his glass as a toast.

After the toast, they all fell silent but Rosalina was certain none of them were following the same train of thought she was on. They'd most likely be thinking about the treasure and the vast possibilities of what they may find, but she'd had enough of treasure for a while. All she wanted to do was go home and see Nonna, cook a grand feast for everyone and spend some time with her family.

"How long until we get there?" She had many dishes to plan before they arrived home.

Archer frowned. "Syracuse or Livorno?"

"Livorno." Livorno was the closest port to her home. From there it was just over an hour's drive to her hometown of Signa.

"We'll stop in Syracuse tonight and Positano tomorrow night, then we should be at Livorno before lunch on Sunday. How's that for a plan?" He grinned at her.

This fitted perfectly and it took all her effort to keep her excitement contained. "Fabulous. Thank you."

"You can thank me later." He tossed her one of his cheeky grins and she felt the heat rising up her cheeks as Helen, and indeed everyone else at the table, glanced in her direction.

She speared a slice of halloumi and a cherry tomato with her fork.

The afternoon rolled on with pleasant discussions centering around what to do with the treasure. Rosalina was amazed that Ginger could devour nearly as much food as Jimmy. Looking at her trim, petite figure, it was impossible to work out how she managed to fit it all in.

Helen, on the other hand, ate the smallest amount before she declared she was full. But at least she was reaching for the food on her own now. Rosalina had felt awkward at constantly having to prompt her to eat.

"Helen." Rosalina was always hesitant when it came to mentioning Archer's father, but she pushed on regardless. "Did Wade ever speak of the treasure being in Egypt?"

Grid lines formed on Helen's forehead and as she turned to face her, Rosalina could tell Helen was rolling the question around in her mind. Almost like a librarian, shuffling the volumes of index cards around until she found the right one.

Helen sighed. "Oh, there were so many. Half the time I wondered if he was talking in tongues because I couldn't follow what direction the conversation was taking." Her words were delivered with metered precision, as if she had to think about every single one of them.

Archer laughed. "I remember that too, Mom. He'd start talking about one treasure in say, South America, and before you knew it, he'd hop to China and detail a completely different, unrelated treasure."

Helen nodded. "He was as much a mystery as the treasures he chased." The smallest of smiles curled at her lips.

"On that note, we have much to do." Archer stood and rubbed his stomach. "Ladies, that meal was absolutely splendid. Alex, help me clean this up."

"Go, go. We'll clean up." Rosalina stood too and manhandled Archer and Alessandro away from the table. "You men have other important things to do."

"Yes, we do." By the look of Archer's smile, he was happy to avoid the cleaning up.

Jimmy stood up and belched. "Whoops, pardon me. I better start the engines and get us moving again." Jimmy shot out of there like a mouse avoiding a hungry cat.

That left the three women. Rosalina didn't expect Helen to help, but she started collecting the plates and transporting them to the kitchen's granite top. Rather than make a fuss over her, Rosalina let her continue. She wanted to ask Archer's mom a thousand questions. It would be great to know more about Archer's childhood. . . before the horrendous times that is. But Rosalina resisted. It was lovely having her around and she didn't want to scare her off too quickly.

"Have you been to Italy before, Ginger?" Rosalina pushed the food scraps into the bin.

The blonde shook her head. "Before I boarded *Evangeline*, I'd never been outside Australia. Actually, I hadn't even been outside of Victoria."

"Oh my goodness. Why did you apply for this job?"

"This," Ginger spread her arms wide, taking in the vast views of ocean outside the windows. "This's exactly why I wanted this job. To see the world. And to live on a magnificent yacht like *Evangeline* while I do it. I thought I was the luckiest girl in the world. Still do actually."

Rosalina wondered if Ginger had also hoped to find a rich boyfriend in the process. But she shoved the unfounded snipe aside when she reflected that Ginger's story wasn't dissimilar to her own. Before she went to Australia, Rosalina hadn't been outside of Italy. Despite their differences, every once in a while, she was reminded of how much alike her and Ginger were.

"Wade and I lived in Venice for nearly year."

Rosalina's heart nosedived at Helen's comment as she recalled a statement Archer once made that he'd never been to Italy. It had been the trigger to one of their biggest fights, because at that point she'd thought she had proof he was lying. In the end she'd believed him. But now, after Helen's declaration, she felt sick.

He had lied to her. She swallowed back the lump in her throat. "When did you go there, Helen?" Rosalina hoped the others missed the quiver in her voice.

"Oh, I don't know. It was well before Archer was born. . . "

Helen continued talking but her words faded into obscurity as Rosalina mentally punched herself for being so paranoid. It shocked her at how quickly she'd jumped to the conclusion that Archer lied. She was saddened by her reaction. *Was her trust in him ever going to be complete again?* She realized Helen had asked her a question. "Sorry Helen, I missed what you said."

"I asked if you'd ever been to Venice."

"Actually, I took my grandmother there for her sixtieth birthday. It was just the two of us. We had a fabulous time doing all the tourist things and eating in many wonderful restaurants."

"Mmm," Helen mumbled. "Wade and I ate at the same restaurant at least twice a week. It wasn't so much the food that we loved, though it was good, it was the ambiance. We sat at one of their little wrought-iron tables, barely big enough for our plates and a bottle of wine, and we watched the people go by." She laughed.

It was the first time Rosalina had heard Helen laugh and she was shocked at how similar it was to Archer's.

"Wade invented this game where he'd guess the occupation of the passing pedestrians. He was funny, because the more wine he sipped, the more his imagination would slip from occupations to their involve-ment in treasure somehow. From stealing it, to hoarding it, to selling it, to finding it. He was obsessed with treasure. I see so much of him in Archer." Helen looked at Rosalina.

All Rosalina wanted to do was wrap her arms around Archer's mom and give her a huge hug. It was like Helen had stepped back in time, a time before all the horrible things happened. Helen was talking about her life, like any mother would.

Rosalina sighed and wished Archer was hearing this. It was prob-ably a story he'd never heard before. "Hold that thought, Helen, I'm going to the loo. I'll be right back."

As Rosalina dashed out of the kitchen, she was grateful to hear Ginger continuing the conversation with Helen. She scurried along the hallway and burst into the office. Both Archer and Alessandro looked up at her in surprise. Archer slammed down the phone, obviously cutting off the person he was talking to, and Alessandro flipped over a notepad that was in front of him.

Rosalina's paranoia hit overdrive as her eyes darted from one gentleman to the other.

"What's wrong?" Archer jumped up and strode toward her.

It suddenly occurred to her that with everyone on edge at the moment, she may have driven their reactions by the way she pounced into the room. She really needed to drag her paranoia down a few notches.

"Nothing's wrong." She clasped her hands together. "In fact, it couldn't be better. Your mom's been telling us stories about restaurants she went to in Venice and games she played with your dad." She clutched his hand and led him out the door and in the direction of the galley. "You should hear her, Archer, it's like she's finally worked out how to talk."

"Hang on a minute, Rosa, I don't want to scare her by running into the room."

"Oh right." She stopped. "Okay, what should we do?"

He squeezed her hand and let go. "We're not going to do anything."

"What?" She gaped at him.

"Just hear me out. I think the best thing to do is to act normal around Mom. Making a fuss about her improvements might make her feel. . . I don't know, anxious. If each of her progressions, no matter how slow, are revealed without any fanfare, then maybe she'll keep improving."

He kissed her on the forehead, then turned her shoulders toward the galley and gave her a little smack on her bottom. "Now get back to the kitchen, you naughty girl."

Rosalina couldn't help but laugh. "Okay but come in soon. All right?"

"When we're done. Alex and I were in the middle of something when you came waltzing in and disrupted us."

"I noticed that," she paused, hoping he'd fill her in, but he didn't. She blew him a kiss and left him in the hallway.

She found Ginger and Helen still in the kitchen, still cleaning up, and both still having a conversation like everything was normal. It was like Helen had been released from a spell. Rosalina stepped up and began wiping down the counter.

After they'd finished, Rosalina went to the office with the intention of ringing Nonna with the details of coming home, but once again Archer and Alessandro nearly jumped out of their skin when she entered. This time she couldn't put it down to anything she did and her suspicion took flight.

"Are you guys okay?" She eyed each of them, searching for answers.

"Of course. What's up?" Archer put his elbow on the table and propped his chin onto his palm. She was certain he was trying a little too hard to look relaxed.

"Nothing is up, I'd just like to use the phone to call Nonna."

"Can you give me five minutes to finish up?"

"Okay." Rosalina shrugged, slipped into the chair opposite Archer's desk and turned to Alessandro. "So, how are the plans going?"

"The plans?" Alessandro actually looked frightful.

"Yes. The plans for the treasure once we get to Livorno. What's wrong with you guys? You seem on edge?"

Archer sighed. "Sorry, babe. I guess we're a little jumpy at the moment."

"Okaaaaay," she dragged out the word, openly showing her skepticism about Archer's reasoning.

"The plans are going well now that Alex has found the right people to talk to. We're making progress about where the treasure will be secured for cataloging and restoration."

"Great. That's a relief."

Archer stood. "Actually, I could do with some fresh air. I'll leave you to call Nonna." He kissed her before he left the room and Alessandro scooted after him.

Rosalina tried to calm her overactive mind by telling herself she was being ridiculous. She picked up the phone and dialed. Nonna was slow to answer and she sounded every bit her seventy-eight years of age. Her voice was as fragile as the bone china cups Nonna drank her tea from.

After a few pleasantries she asked the question she was dreading. "Has Filippo been behaving himself?"

Rosalina listed to Nonna's answer with building frustration and she was certain Nonna was still omitting some of the things her youngest brother was doing. Talking about Filippo's behavior was upsetting Nonna and Rosalina decided to change subjects.

"Don't worry about him, Nonna. I'll have a serious talk to him when I come home on Sunday." Rosalina waited for her grandmother's response to her news she was coming home. And it was wonderful. Nonna was so excited she spoke a thousand words a minute. And she grew even more excited as they discussed Rosalina's idea of a big luncheon with all their family and friends. An hour passed quickly and it was only when Archer popped his head into the room again that she wound up the call. She could talk to her grandmother for days.

"I love you too, Nonna. See you in two days."

The rest of the day drifted by as swiftly as the azure Ionian Sea they cruised across. As the sun was setting and the lights of Syracuse began to dot the port-side city, Jimmy guided *Evangeline* into a berth at Porto Di Siracusa.

Their night was uneventful and Rosalina was glad to see the town behind them as they set off early the next day, passing through the port entrance just as the sun kissed the horizon with its golden rays.

Archer maintained *Evangeline* at a constant distance from the ever-changing shoreline. After breakfast, she tried not to watch Archer and Alessandro with suspicion as they once again vanished into the office. She shrugged off the feeling as she sat at the dining table and began planning the menu for the family gathering.

It was mid-afternoon when Jimmy guided the yacht along the Amalfi coast and into Positano's sheltered harbor. Rosalina was enjoying the rugged coastline from her view on one of upper deck sun lounges when Archer sidled up beside her. His hand was warm on her knee. "You, my beautiful, need to pack a bag."

She sat up and shielded the sun from her eyes with her hat. "Why? Where are we going?"

"I thought you might like a night off *Evangeline*." His hand glided up from her knee and rested high on her inner thigh.

"Oh, I'd love to." She realized she sounded just a little too eager. "What I mean is, it would be lovely to have you all to myself for a night."

"My thoughts exactly. Come on then, get packing, we're here for less than twenty-four hours, so we need to make the most of it."

Rosalina rushed to pack and within minutes Jimmy had her and Archer in the tender, hanging onto their hats as they motored toward the Amalfi shoreline.

Chapter Twenty-Nine

Alessandro ran his thumb over the soft skin on the back of Ginger's hand as they stood at the railing of the lower deck. In the distance they watched Jimmy motor the small boat toward the sandy Positano beach to offload Rosalina and Archer. Positano was a pretty harbor-side town. It was a spectacular spot that hugged the steep cliff, allowing nearly every home a view overlooking the stunningly blue ocean. The colorful houses blended pinks, whites and terracotta like an artist's pallet. All the homes looked to be precariously stacked atop each other and appeared as if they were about to tumble into the sea at any moment.

He squeezed Ginger's hand. "I propose we grab a bottle of red chianti and cheese and crackers and watch the sun go down from the top deck."

"Yes please. Sounds lovely."

"It's a charming view already, but I bet it becomes even more beautiful as the sun sinks behind that cliff and the lights come on."

She glanced at the fireball in the sky. "We have a few hours until sunset then." Ginger turned to him. Her eyes were vibrant blue, as if they'd absorbed their color from the azure sea surrounding them. "Maybe you could show me the treasure. I'd love you to tell me the history behind each piece." She looked up at him, wide-eyed with interest.

Alessandro glowed on the inside. He placed his hands on her cheeks, leaned forward and lowered his lips to hers. It was a brief sensual kiss that conveyed volumes. For the first time in a decade or so, he felt free from Rosalina's clutches. When he pulled back, Ginger met his gaze. Her eyes softened and seemed to be absorbing his features. And her lips were slightly apart as if something important were about to whisper across them. In that instant Alessandro was eternally grateful to Rosalina for setting him free.

She beamed a wonderful smile. "Is that a yes?"

"Sounds like a marvelous plan." He reached for her hand and with their palms clasped together they walked inside. Alessandro did a mental check of all the amazing pieces of treasure that he'd saved from Iggy's clutches. There were still so many spectacular items to examine. "There is one piece I'd like to have another look at. It's the gold plate Rosalina discovered, the very first piece of the Calimala treasure we found."

"Oh yes, I remember it."

"I was wondering if the decorations around the rim of that plate match the small plaques on the gold bracelet you showed me."

"Oh." She reached for her long plait and flipped it around her hand. "What would it mean if they do?"

Alessandro shrugged. "It may mean both pieces were designed by the same artist. Or maybe for the same person." He opened the door to the office and directed Ginger toward the sofa. She sat and he strode to Archer's desk, took out the key and then opened the floor to ceiling doors at the back of the room.

He bent down and entered the combination to the safe. It buzzed and clicked open. Using the key, he opened the top compartment and reached in to remove the plate. Ideally, they'd have all the precious pieces secured like this, but the safe simply wasn't big enough.

He turned with the plate in his hands, and the smooth gold caught in the bright lights and reflected a flash of light down the wall. Ginger hopped up from the sofa and came to his side.

"Oh wow. I forgot how beautiful it is."

"I did too." He placed it on the leather trim of Archer's study desk.

"This is why I'm looking forward to seeing them on display in a museum."

A thoughtful moan tumbled from her throat. "So, I was wondering. When people find treasure, who gets the money?"

"It depends." He lifted the plate to look closer at the emblem embossed in the center. "Every country has a different law. For example, if you find rare gold coins in London, then they're returned to the royal family, though I'm sure the Queen would compensate you. In America if you find something in a public place, it really is finder's keeper's, but if you find it on someone else's property, then it would belong to the property owner." He ran his finger over the emblem embossed in the gold plate. It was three lily flowers, connected with a dotted line and the word 'Thopia' was engraved beneath the flowers. He never did get a chance to establish the significance of that name. But he relished the idea of tracing that bloodline sometime soon.

"What about sunken treasure? Who gets the money when that's found?"

"It can get really messy. If a diver finds a sunken ship with a treasure of galleons, that would likely end in a legal battle between the diver, the country, the ship's owners and the insurance company, *if* there was a claim when the ship sunk, that is. It could be tied up in the courts for years."

"But our treasure is so old, surely no-one can claim it but us?"

"Well, when treasure is verified as antiquated and has been lost for so long that the owners are dead or unknown, it's a different story again. The laws relating to this type of treasure differ from century to century, country to country."

"So, this is the category ours will fall into."

"Correct."

"Where will our treasure go when we get to Livorno?"

"I'm still working on that. These pieces are of historical importance, so we need to make sure they're secured in their rightful place. I have several museums already interested. But my preference is my museum the Accademia di Belle Arti. " He lowered the plate to the desk and sighed. "I still can't believe I'm here. Even though I've been surrounded by history my whole life, I've never really appreciated it until now."

She turned to him and placed her hand on his chest. "I'm glad you are." Her eyes seemed to be smiling and she tugged on her bottom lip.

"I'm glad I am too. Especially with you."

She moved her hands to his shoulders and in a flash, she jumped into his arms. As he clutched her bottom, her mouth planted on his. She parted her lips and he took the invitation to taste her. Their kiss was fierce, almost desperate and she grabbed his hair, pulling his mouth to hers. Tasting, savoring, exploring, and tantalizing his body inside and out. The kiss lingered, long, luscious and lovely.

Abruptly she pulled back, gasping and blinking at him. Her eyes were glazed.

Ginger was truly beautiful. Her skin was a milky shade of peach, unblemished by freckles or flaws, and her pale pink lips were perfectly formed. Not too full or too thin.

As if she could read his mind, she ran her tongue over her bottom lip. "You're a wonderful kisser."

Ginger said it like she was surprised and he couldn't resist the smile curling at his lips. "Thank you."

"No. I mean, really, really good kisser."

"Why does that surprise you?"

She hesitated with a shrug. "I. . . I don't know."

"I'm good at other things too." He wriggled his eyebrows.

Her eyes widened, then she latched her lips onto his again. She groaned and he groaned with her. He hitched her up and strode to the sofa. They were naked in a flash and he took a moment to enjoy the scene. Her body was breathtaking. He could almost feel the heat of her want radiating from her skin.

"I want to take my time with you, *la mia bella*."

"Okay, I'm ready."

He eased to his knees and slowly ran his finger from her thigh to her breast. Her milky skin prickled in his wake. "But we can't. Jimmy will be back soon. Too soon."

She pulled the cutest sad face. "Well, we could be really quick now and then. . . we can do it all again later."

He obeyed.

Never before had he had sex with such fierce intensity. She took him to staggering heights and joined him there. Her long neck was exposed to him, beckoning, and he spied the throb of her vein beneath her delicate skin. They climaxed together and his arms trembled as he held himself above her to watch her stunning performance. They both panted with the haunting satisfaction of impassioned sex once they finished.

She trailed her fingernails down his back. "Yep, you are good at other things."

"Thank you. As are you, *la mia bella*."

Chapter Thirty

Rosalina and Archer were met at the shoreline by a young buffed man in turned-up tan-colored pants and a white linen shirt, buttoned down to show off a gold cross nestled amongst a thick field of dark chest hairs. Rosalina liked him from the moment he held his hand forward to help her out of the boat.

"Good day to you. My name-a is Antonio and I be your guest for the week." His broken English was straight out of a B-Grade movie.

Rosalina stifled a laugh as she held out her hand. "Lovely to meet you, Antonio. My name is Rosalina and this is Archer." She spoke in English to avoid excluding Archer from the conversation. The men shook hands and Antonio guided her toward a waiting car.

As he whipped the car around the steep winding roads, Antonio gave them an accelerated guided tour. "You have chosen the most spectacular of all villa's in Positano. The Soprano Villas are build-a in the very historic watch tower of Positano. It dated back to thirteenth Century. You will experience momentous views that will take your breathing away." His eyes skipped from the cliff-defying road ahead to Rosalina and even though her heart was in her throat at every turn, the tour was as magnificent as it was exhilarating.

He stopped at a grand wrought-iron gate and honked the horn.

Seconds later the gates opened and they drove through them and down underneath the building.

He slammed to a stop and raced around to help Rosalina from the car. Archer grabbed their bags.

"You travel light to stay for week," Antonio said as he led the way.

"Oh no," she giggled. "We're only staying for one night."

He turned; a frown rippled across his features. "But you pay for week."

"That's correct, Antonio." Archer placed his hand on Antonio's shoulder. "But sadly, we can only stay tonight. Next time, we'll stay longer. This time, just one night."

Rosalina's mouth fell open.

Antonio plucked the bags from Archer's hands. "Very well, please follow me."

Archer reached for her hand and she squeezed it. "This must've cost a fortune."

"The website said it was Positano's most unique luxury apartment. The minimum stay was seven nights. But how could I resist?"

She loved that Archer appreciated the beautiful things in life.

"This gate leads you to your own private beach." Antonio poked the keyhole with his finger. "I will give you key soon."

Rosalina was mesmerized by the breathtaking views, revealed more with each step she climbed up the stone staircase. At the top, Antonio pushed an ancient looking skeleton key into the hole in the large wooden door. The door creaked open and she stepped into a stunning open-air room with an even more amazing view of the Amalfi shoreline.

"Welcome to your fairytale." Antonio grinned like an artist presenting his greatest masterpiece.

Rosalina was speechless. Antonio's well-rehearsed statement said it all, this really was a fairytale. While she vaguely heard Archer tip Antonio and say his goodbyes, Rosalina was drawn to the fabulous stone-lined private terrace. The outdoor setting, with sunflower-colored pillows and cobalt blue plates was a scene straight from an exotic travel magazine. Above the table setting was a thatched roof that was overrun with a bougainvillea, plush with vibrant magenta flowers in full bloom.

She stepped up to the railing and imagined she could see the other side of the world. Vast blue ocean stretched for miles and met with an equally intense blue sky. Not a single cloud blemished the scene. Far down to her right was the public beach set up with rows of neatly placed deck chairs. People dotted the beach and ocean like colorful confetti. Directly below her was their own secluded beach, ready with six sun lounges set up as pairs with individual white umbrellas. Their beach was deserted at the moment.

Archer came up behind her and wrapped his arms around her waist. "Happy?"

"Oh babe, this is magical."

"I agree."

Rosalina closed her eyes, breathed in the warm salty air and leaned back against him.

"You're a difficult woman to surprise."

She snapped her eyes open. "What? Why?"

"Because you kept walking into my office and disrupting me."

She bit her lip feeling terrible at her doubtful thoughts. "Oh. . . I'm so sorry."

"You're forgiven." He kissed her cheek and she rolled her head to the side and allowed him to thread kisses up her neck. His delightful tickle sprinkled shivers over her skin. He smelled so good, his favorite aftershave was all aromatic spices and candlelit dinners and always reminded her of their first date. It was some six years ago, and she'd known almost immediately that Archer was the man of her dreams.

"Should we eat, or make love first?" His hot breath was all throaty eagerness that had the hairs on her neck bristling with desire.

She swallowed back the yearning to tear his clothes off and turned toward the table. It was topped with a selection of food, along with a bottle of champagne and two crystal glasses. She draped her arms up over his shoulders and pulled him down toward her. "Both," she whispered.

He wriggled his eyebrows and when he smiled, small creases lined his eyes. "Sounds delicious."

Rosalina reached for his hand and molded her fingers into his. "Let's see what we have?"

She scanned the selection. Plump cherries. Strawberries served around a bowl of whipped cream. Fluffy golden pastries dusted with icing sugar. Delicate chocolate cups, no doubt filled with liqueur. Crusty bread with a selection of cheese, sliced meats, a variety of nuts, olives and bright orange caviar. Rosalina was salivating just looking at the decadent choices.

A loud pop drew her attention to Archer and the wave of bubbles that erupted from the champagne bottle he'd just opened. He'd removed his shirt and she ogled his muscular torso, thinking he too could've stepped from the pages of an exotic vacation magazine. She giggled as he tried to quickly pour the flowing bubbles while she selected a couple of bright red strawberries and plopped one into each glass.

He lifted his panama hat off, placed it on a chair and loosened his curls with his fingers. The sun threaded through the thatched roof in thin ribbons, offering just enough light to gild Archer's hair. It was much longer than he usually grew it and she liked it; it suited his carefree nature. She stepped up to him and with her hand on his bare chest, just below his gold pendant, she felt the warmth of his skin.

"A toast." He handed her a champagne glass.

"What shall we toast to?"

"Mmm, there are so many choices. Let's start with a toast to having you all to myself for a while."

She loved that idea. "Ahhh, a special toast indeed." They clinked glasses and Rosalina took a sip. The bubbles danced along her tongue, tickling her taste buds before she swallowed the delicious nectar.

Archer cupped his hand under her chin, drawing her eyes to his. "What yummy things are you planning?"

Her mind jumped to him naked, above her, his rippling muscles licked with a fine sheen of sweat. But she forced the lust down before she acted on it by refocusing on the food. "Mmm. There's quite a selection here. We could be here all day."

"Sounds like a grand plan to me."

She settled her champagne glass on the table. "In that case, I think we should start with savory and work our way through until we're exhausted." With both hands on Archer's magnificent pectoral muscles, she guided him to the oversized sun lounges.

"I'm at your mercy."

She smiled at that idea as she nudged him to lie down. He obliged, lying back with his free arm nestled in behind his neck. He looked relaxed, yet every defined muscle in his torso remained rock hard. His eyes sparkled with desire.

The urge to tear his pants from his body was so strong that she very nearly did it. She wanted to see him in all his glory, naked and exposed for the whole world to enjoy. But she dug her fingernails into her palms to resist the temptation, wanting instead to savor this precious time together. It'd been a long time since they were alone and she speculated that maybe it was why she was questioning her life with Archer. She loved him. He was her gravitational pull of love and lust and everything beautiful. He was the promise of an amazing future that she couldn't possibly have without him. Surely, once they get back home everything would be back to normal.

"You stay right there," she said.

He blinked slowly and when he inhaled his chest rose and fell. "Okey dokey."

Tearing her eyes away from him, she returned to the food. She swallowed a large sip of champagne as she surveyed the ample selection again.

She picked up a plate and chose some olives. The bowl contained three types, all marinated with a dash of chili. Perfect for getting the taste buds going. She smiled as she glanced at him. As he'd been told, Archer hadn't moved. In the midday sun, his small patch of chest hair glistened like it'd been dusted in gold flakes. His eyes followed her as she walked back to him, making her aware of her escalating arousal.

"We start with an aperitif of olives." Standing at his side, she plucked a Verdale olive from the bowl. The large green fruit briefly gleamed in the sun before she popped it into his mouth. He wrapped his lips around her finger as she slowly removed it from his mouth. Watching him chew, she chose one for herself and bit into it. The olive was meaty and sweet and showed no bitterness at all. "And?"

"It's nice."

She cocked her head. "Nice. Is that all you've got?"

He nodded and rolled his eyes as if unimpressed.

She spread his legs, stepped up to kneel between his knees, unbuttoned his pants and slowly rolled down the zipper to reveal the top elastic of his underpants. His breathing was deeper, slower, and his pendant, the solid finger of gold that he never removed from his neck, scintillated in the sunshine.

This time she chose the Kalamata olive and popped it into his perfectly formed belly button. The bulge in his pants grew before her eyes. She loved having this effect on him, but she wasn't ready to release him just yet. He'll have to play along with her little game first.

She leaned forward and started licking from the nest of curls at his pants line and followed the thread of hairs upwards. At his belly button, she circled her tongue around it a few times before she sucked the olive into her mouth with an audible pop. As she chewed on the Kalamata, savoring its robust salty flavor, he took a large swallow of his champagne.

"Did you enjoy that one?" The hard bulge, now threatening to burst from his pants, confirmed he did.

"It was. . . nicer."

She gasped. "Is that all? You're a hard man to please, Mr. Mahoney." As she climbed out from between his legs, she ran her hand over his groin. Just looking at his excitement, strained beneath the fabric, was enough to set her pulse racing. She reminded herself to take it easy, they had all afternoon to enjoy each other.

At the table again, Rosalina took another large sip of her champagne, allowing the delicious bubbles to tingle her throat as she selected her next temptation. She peeled off a slice of cured meat, took another drink of champagne and turned to Archer. "Let's see if this is better."

As she resumed her position between his legs, he gulped down the last of his drink and set his glass aside. Rosalina rolled up the finely sliced Culatello, put one end into her mouth and leaned forward so she was directly above him. As his hands cupped her breasts, he obliged by opening his mouth and allowing her to dip the end of the meat roll onto his tongue. He chewed. She chewed. They met in the middle. Rosalina pictured this ending with them delighting each other with a lovely sensual kiss but it wasn't possible without choking. She pulled back, laughing as she finished her half of the sliced meat. "That wasn't as sexy as I thought it would be."

He slid his warm hands up under the skirt of her dress and placed them on her hips. "Mmm."

The intensity in his eyes glowed. The golden flecks dazzled, both with the afternoon sun and burning desire. And his lips, sensual full lips that always fascinated her, were as plump as the cherries on the table.

With her hands on his chiseled chest she leaned forward and brushed her lips against his, closing her eyes to listen to his deep breathing and felt her own beating heart. When he opened his mouth, she ran her tongue over his lips, tasting the saltiness of the meat and the sweetness of the champagne. His hands glided up her stomach and she nipped at his lower lip when he caressed her breasts through her bra. She wanted to free herself from the lacy constraint and although she shuddered with anticipation, she mentally forced herself to slow down.

She slipped her tongue into his mouth to tango with his. A moan tumbled from the back of his throat, and with each flick of her tongue he matched it with his own delectable strokes. He tasted so good. He felt even better. She could spend the entire afternoon just kissing him. Archer managed to slip one of her breasts over the top of her bra and was teasing her nipple between his thumb and finger. She gasped as the sensation filled her with more want.

She sat up and playfully slapped his hand away. "What do you think you're doing?"

He grinned that sexy sassy smile of his, highlighting his dimples. "What?"

"I'm the one in charge here." She lifted her dress up over her head and in the brief second the fabric covered her eyes he grabbed her exposed nipple again and pinched it delicately between his fingers. Although his touch sent ripples through her body, and she wanted nothing more than to let him carry on, she flicked his hand away again.

"I said I'm in charge. You just have to lie there and take it. Like a man." She chewed on her bottom lip, trying not to laugh.

He swallowed. "Right. Sorry." His voice was a throaty whisper and his eyes; well, they were making love to her.

Rosalina slipped off the sun lounge again, and as she walked to the table, she lifted her other breast out so they both bulged over her lacy bra. It was slightly uncomfortable but at the same time, out on this terrace, and exposed, it was incredibly sexy. With her back to Archer, she cut a small slice of soft cheese and with no idea if this was a good plan or not, she stifled a giggle and wedged it between her breasts.

She topped up her glass, took a large sip and watched for the look in his eyes as she turned with the bottle in her hand. It was the reaction she wanted, his eyes snapped straight to her breasts and he pushed up on his seat, angling toward her.

"Oh baby, you're killing me here."

She strode toward him. "Mmm. Are you complaining?"

He held his glass forward, ready to top up. "I no complain."

She filled his glass until the bubbles threatened to overflow. He quickly captured them in his mouth avoiding a spill and this gave her another idea. But first the cheese.

She placed the bottle on the table beside the sun lounge. "Your next menu delight is hidden. You have to find it. With your tongue."

His tongue slipped over his luscious lips. She allowed him to gulp back half his drink before she straddled him, this time so her legs were either side of his hips.

His smile drilled the cutest dimples into each cheek and his eyes devoured her. "Let's see." He rested his hands on her hips. "There are so many places to hide things."

She placed her hands on his pecs, so his nipples poked through her fingers. "Don't get too excited." She could only imagine what the cheese would be doing squashed between them.

He cocked his head at her. "Honey, I think it's too late for that."

Rosalina giggled as Archer wrapped his lips around her hardened nipple. She gasped as the sensation sent her into overdrive. He sucked her nipple, flicked his tongue across the sensitive tip and then sucked some more. Then he showed her other breast the same faithful attention. She wanted to keep her eyes open to watch him savor her, but it was impossible. The muscles inside her tightened and tingled and the pulsing between her legs had her rocking back and forward, teasing him.

"You're not looking hard enough." Her voice was barely a whisper.

He fell back on the lounge. "Are you complaining?"

She opened her eyes with a laugh tumbling from her throat. "I no complain."

"I think you should come a little closer." He nudged her forward so her breasts dangled above his face. She closed her eyes and let him work his magic on her bosoms. He sucked, nibbled, caressed and then sucked some more. Finally, he licked his tongue up between her breasts.

"Mmm, I think I may have found what I was looking for."

She arched her breast towards his lips. "You need to dig a little further."

Archer obliged by caressing her breasts and running his tongue up and down between them.

"Tastes great." He licked his lips.

"Aha, so we've moved from nice to great. Now we're making progress." She sat back and resisted looking at her chest, certain the cheesy mess wouldn't look very appealing.

"I think you deserve a little reward." She wriggled back between his knees and climbed off the lounge again. She gripped onto the ankles of his pants and tugged until they came off. As she tossed them aside, she couldn't take her eyes off her man.

"I think someone is happy."

His eyes travelled down his body and back to her. "I think you're right."

Rosalina couldn't stand it anymore, she wanted to see all of him. The underpants were off in a flash and she wasn't disappointed. She slipped into voyeuristic heaven and it was her turn to make love to him with her eyes. He was more mouth-watering than any food could ever be.

"So, chef." Archer cleared his throat. "What's next on the menu?"

"Oh." She had planned on climbing on top and taking him right now. It was her turn to clear her throat. "I, um. . ." her voice was as shaky as her legs. "I think its dessert time."

She wasn't sure if her limbs could carry her. But she forged on, taking unsteady steps to the table. She gulped back her champagne and placed the glass on the table before reaching around to unclip her bra and toss it aside. Using a napkin, she cringed as she wiped the cheesy residue from between her breasts.

Scanning over food selection, the little chocolate cups caught her eye. For what she was planning, she hoped they were filled with liqueur.

She carried her glass back to the table and allowed Archer to fill it. After another quick sip, she resumed her position between his knees. She couldn't help but smile at the glorious view before her. Archer had an Adonis body, abs as solid as any fighter, sun-kissed skin and a tantalizing line of hair that said 'follow me' as it ran from his belly button to his dark nest of curls. He certainly had her attention.

With the chocolate cup between her fingers, she nibbled off a tiny corner, but instead of just dribbling out, the entire cup crumbled and the liquid and chocolate fell all over Archer's groin. "Whoops." She laughed and he laughed with her.

"I hope you're planning on cleaning that up." His eyes were full of suggestion.

"Of course." She leaned forward and licked every drop of that delicious, sweet liqueur from his body.

Archer ran his hands through her hair. "Oh Rosa."

The way he said her name was like a soft caress and the throb between her legs had her close to imploding. As she helped herself to dessert, his moans of pleasure sent the sweetest of sensations rippling through her body.

She wanted him. Now. She eased back, stepped off the sun lounge, slipped out of her lacy knickers and went to climb back on top.

"Hang on, baby." Archer pushed himself further up the chair. "It's my turn."

She stared, open-mouthed. He had to be joking. How could he wait? She was practically bursting at the seams. He must've seen her indecision, because he slipped off the lounge and with his hands on her waist, he guided her to lie down.

"You stay right there." As he walked to the table, she watched his perfectly round butt cheeks rise and fall as his muscles flexed.

The warmth of the sun on her skin was as heavenly as the champagne enchanting her insides. She reached for Archer's glass and drained the bubbles from it. Rosalina had never sunbaked naked before and she couldn't decide if it was the liquor, the golden sun or the anticipation of red-hot sex that was driving the tingles through her body, inside and out.

"As you didn't share the last one, I helped myself to a chocolate. Delicious."

She grinned. "So was mine."

The heat between her legs became a smoking hot furnace as he walked toward her stark naked with a handful of strawberries and the bowl of whipped cream. He knelt at her side, placed the strawberries on her stomach and when he ran his tongue over his lips, he stole the breath from her throat. She wanted him to stay right there, basking in all his sun-drenched nakedness for all eternity.

"So, my lovely, I'm going to show you how strawberries and cream should be done."

Rosalina had combined these two ingredients every which way possible and yet she was certain Archer was about to show her something new.

"Want to try one?" His voice was so husky she barely recognised it.

She swallowed. "Sure."

He selected one of the strawberries and held it towards her. She opened her mouth, and half expecting some kind of trick she sunk her teeth into the juicy fruit, biting it in half.

Archer laughed. "Hungry, are we?" The remaining half of the ripe red fruit he brought to her breast. He touched the cool strawberry from one nipple to the next, circling her now almost bursting buds and then dabbing the very tip. Despite his delicate touch, the sensation drove pulses that started at her nipples and ended with a delightful shiver between her legs.

Archer leaned forward and licked each breast clean. When he finished, he sat back. "And." His eyes shone.

She shrugged and it took all her might to keep a straight face. "That was nice."

Archer muffled a deep, throaty laugh. "Nice! Righty ho, then."

Rosalina chewed on her bottom lip as she watched Archer. She could almost see his mind working in overdrive. He grabbed another strawberry and this time he dipped it into the cream.

Using the strawberry as a brush and her body as the canvas, he spread the cream over her nipples, and when he was done, he cleaned up the artwork with his tongue.

Rosalina curled beneath him, sending the strawberries on her belly scattering as she reached a climax that'd been building within her for what seemed like a decade.

When she opened her eyes, Archer was smiling with eyes ablaze with satisfaction.

"That was much better," she said through gasping breath.

Archer stood and with purpose he moved to the end of the lounge. He stared at her naked body for a long delicious moment. She wanted him now and he could take every little piece of her; her mind, her body, her soul.

Archer climbed on top and kissed her like they'd never kissed before. Their tongues probed each other's mouth, tasting, licking, exploring. He pushed up on his hands so his chest hovered above her and his gold pendant toyed with her nipples. They finally made love, his eyes glazed, slipping into a world of bliss.

When he fell onto her chest, breathless and panting, they stayed as one for a very long time.

She ran her fingers through his unruly curls. "You know I'm never going to look at an antipasto platter the same again."

He chuckled. "Me neither."

Chapter Thirty-One

With each passing day Nox's wounds improved. As he surveyed his injuries, something he did every morning, the bruises that had dominated almost every part of his body when he'd drifted here gradually mellowed from as dark as a stormy sky, to light purple and yellow stains. He flexed the fingers of his pierced hand. It was wrapped in a clean bandage and still very sore, but it was a relief to have any movement at all. It looked like the wound would heal completely, hopefully without any lasting effects. He couldn't believe how lucky he was. He could've lost part of his hand in that fall. That time with the weird twins already seemed like a distant nightmare. He shuddered at the memory.

From his comfortable bed, Nox had a window view of a healthy garden in the foreground, a lush green paddock in the middle and the dark blue ocean in the very distance. Over the last couple of days, he'd been quite happy to just to lie there and watch the woman and the two kids through the glass pane. Every day the mother tended to her herbs and vegetables with as much care and attention as he'd witnessed first-hand on his body. While around her the boys played all sorts of games, from running, skipping and hiding, to little cars that they drove in and out of the garden until their mother shooed them off with a smile on her face.

It was a glimpse at family life that Nox had never seen before. Being abandoned at an orphanage and then transferred to the church to be in Father Benedici's care at twelve meant Nox had never witnessed, let alone experienced how a real family behaved. He was mesmerized. It was the calmness that he found fascinating. As if the world travelled in a slower gear here. Drifting along without stress or burden.

He wanted this. He wanted to know what it was like to wake up happy and content and go to bed feeling the same way. Darius, the dark-haired boy, was the older of the two. From what Nox could tell he was also the leader, constantly telling Arion how things were done.

Nox didn't know if he had siblings, although that memory, the one where he watched the woman spin around with the child in her arms, always made him wonder if that were his mother and brother. He would never know. Nox had no intention of ever tracking down his family. When he was rich and famous and dripping with the Calimala gold, if they ever came calling, he'd find a way to make them suffer for abandoning him. He'd make it a slow suffering too.

One of the red jewels in his ring glistened in the sun and he rolled the antique around so all three blood red jewels twinkled at him. Nox slipped the ring off his finger and rested it on the windowsill. Its glow was magical in this sunlight. The ring represented a turning point in his life. The point of no return. His thoughts drifted from his mushroom poison, to the first poison he'd ever used to kill Sofia, the stupid girl who had inflamed both unbridled arousal and burning hatred in him.

He had killed her slowly. Very slowly. And it'd been glorious to watch.

He'd found the perfect poison. Arsenic. Colorless, odorless and tasteless and readily available in an orphanage practically overrun with rats and mice. And perfect to sprinkle on Sofia's toothbrush in the most minute of doses. Having unlimited access to the church and the adjoining orphanage meant he could walk the halls unchecked whenever he wanted. And the secret passages and discrete spy holes ensured he could do it without fear of being discovered. Nox wanted Sofia to suffer. To watch her declining health was outstanding revenge. She gradually grew weak and pale. Her hair fell out in clumps and the beautiful Sofia was no longer pretty.

She was a fighter, though, and when she fell into a coma she stayed there for months. Nox even had the chance to visit her bedside. He held her hand and as he looked at the weird striations running across her fingernails, he told her everything. Although she didn't move, he was certain she'd heard every word he said, because she died the very next day. It took eight months from that first sprinkle to final gasp. Along the way Nox learned that he could be very patient. It was worth every ticking second.

The other spectacular spinoff was setting up one of Sofia's boyfriends, Raffaele, for her murder. Nox knew all along that eventually arsenic poisoning would be identified as the cause of death. His tapes with Raffaele and Sofia having sex, in addition to the box of rat poison they found hidden in his cupboard, were enough to ensure he was found guilty of murder. Nox had no idea if Raffaele even lasted the twelve years he was committed to. But he'd loved every minute of watching the trial and it was either by serendipity or a grand plan that Nox caught Raffaele's eye several times during his darkest hours. It was gratifying to know Raffaele suffered greatly.

The second boy who had belittled him had become one of Nox's trusted cohorts. Not by choice. Another tape showing Brother Bonito with Sofia in several disgusting sex acts was enough to ensure his silence for life. Nox wondered where the pathetic priest was now. The last time he'd seen him was when Nox had fired a couple of shots at the man. But Bonito had been in a boat speeding away from him at the time and Nox was quite certain he hadn't hit him.

Nox tried to picture what Bonito would have done when he returned to Italy. Would he go crawling to the *polizi* and tell them all about Nox? Or the treasure? Nox didn't think so. Bonito had done too many wayward things at Nox's bidding, several of them criminal.

A knock on the door dragged him from his mental drifting. It was the boys, both smiling and completely oblivious to the murderer they were looking at. Nox didn't smile back at them, he'd learned a long time ago that his yellowed teeth scared people off. "*Ciao.*"

The boys waved him forward with childish glee. He stood up and went to them. Each boy grabbed one of his hands and they dragged him outside, chatting excitedly in a language Nox couldn't comprehend.

He stepped into the sunlight and the three of them sidestepped along the gravel path that bordered the house. The boys led him through the garden Nox had been viewing from his window for days. He was deliriously happy just to be holding hands with these two innocent children. It wasn't until they arrived at the top of a hill that he saw their mother. She was seated on the grass beside what looked like an old wooden wheelbarrow. But it was tilted at a tragic angle, clearly broken.

The boys ran on ahead and Nox followed. When he arrived at her side, the mother raised her hand in a gesture that said 'help me up'. Nox did, and was actually eager to assist. With animated hand signals and with much undecipherable talking, she indicated that she would lift the fully loaded wheelbarrow, while Nox was to push the wheel back on. "Okay," she said. It was the only word he recognized.

"Okay." He nodded.

It was fascinating to watch her lift the barrow, she was all bosoms and brute strength as she simply bent her knees and lifted. Nox dashed in and wriggled the heavy wooden wheel into place. "Okay," he said. And the second he stepped back she lowered it with leisurely ease.

She smiled and patted his shoulder in appreciation. Without any fanfare, she gathered the handles, lifted the barrow and began pushing it up the hill. With each step she took, her enormous derriere shifted like two individual land masses and Nox, mesmerized by the glorious sight, couldn't shake his eyes from them.

The two boys giggled at him and embarrassed at being caught, Nox raced after her.

"Let me do that," Nox said as he reached her side.

She shook her head, as if understanding what he was saying. Nox moved to the front of the barrow halting her path. For the first time in his life he wanted to help someone and do manual labor. It was a miracle.

She stopped, put the barrow down and grinned so wide her eyes disappeared beneath her chubby cheeks. As she rubbed her left palm over her right, she shook her head with a worried frown. Nox's stomach fluttered when he realized she was concerned about his injured palm. He squeezed his fingers to make a fist, showing her he was fine. Then he sidled up beside her and gently nudged her aside. Using his bandaged hand, he gave her the okay signal, then he indicated for her to go on ahead. Because with her in front not only could he watch her bulging bottom, he could also avoid any humiliation if he started to struggle.

He lifted the handles and was horrified at how heavy it was. Regardless, he trudged forward. Within a very short amount of time he was puffing for breath and sweat tickled the hairs on his lower back. Occasionally, the woman would turn to him and he forced a nod and a grin and pushed on even harder. It took momentous effort to reach the top. But he couldn't stop there. After a brief rest he gathered the handles and began the trudge down the hill. The whole time he was pushing it, when he wasn't watching the woman and her two children, he was wondering where the man about the house was. Clearly there was a man, or at least there once had been, as Nox was now wearing his clothes. The woman had opened her closet to him and each day Nox helped himself to a clean set of garments that fitted him like they were his very own.

With relief he finally reached flat ground and he followed her to the edge of the garden where she indicated for him to tip the gravel at the end of the path. Sweat dribbled down his temples like a nervous confessor. Determined not to fail, Nox put everything he had into it. He bent his knees, put his hands on the underside of the barrow's handles and drove upwards. His heart pounded. He struggled for breath. But he did it. The grateful look on her face stirred little butter-flies in his stomach. Nox wished he could talk to her, but maybe it was better this way.

Nox patted his chest. "Nox," he said and opened his palm to her. "What is your name?"

She nodded. "Ophelia."

He patted his chest again as he caught his breath. "Nox," he said again then he pointed at the blond boy. "Arion." Then he indicated to the dark-haired child. "Darius." Then he met eyes with her. "Ophelia."

When she smiled at him her dark eyes again disappeared behind her chubby rose-colored cheeks and Nox felt like he could walk on water.

Chapter Thirty-Two

T he morning after their delicious Positano picnic whizzed by in a whirlwind and Rosalina was torn between exploring every market stall dotted along the beach and getting back on-board *Evangeline* so they could weigh anchor and head home. Although it was sad to leave Positano, she would forever have precious memories of the time they had together at the glorious seaside village. Jimmy pulled up anchor just after breakfast and Archer declared they should arrive in Livorno around midday. Rosalina quickly turned her attention to the meals she was planning for the family gathering.

Archer and Alessandro disappeared into the office again and Rosalina had no intention of interrupting them this time. She headed to the kitchen to begin cooking. Ginger offered to help, and to her delight, so did Helen. In no time she had several dishes on the go. The three of them worked together well and Rosalina slipped into her own blissful world of chopping, slicing, dicing, and sampling the food to create some of Nonna's favorite dishes from the recipes Rosalina knew by heart.

"Ginger, can I show you how to make the pumpkin and mozzarella arancini balls?" Rosalina tugged the large bowl of cooked Arborio rice forward that she'd already mixed with mashed pumpkin, onion and garlic.

"Sure." Ginger sidled up next to Rosalina.

"Okay, so wet your hands slightly and roll a heaped tablespoon of this mixture into a ball, like this." As Rosalina demonstrated, Ginger copied. "Now, press a cube of mozzarella cheese into the center of each ball and make sure it's completely concealed within the rice."

"Did you cook this for Alessandro?" Ginger asked as she copied Rosalina.

Dread inched across Rosalina's mind as she wondered where this question was leading. "I guess I probably did. It's a traditional Italian dish." She resisted the urge to look at Ginger.

"Cool. I'd love to learn how to make it for him."

Rosalina's relief was instant. The last thing she wanted to do was have a confrontation with Ginger. Especially not in front of Helen.

"Okay, what do I do now?" Ginger presented her arancini for inspection.

She'd done a great job. "Now we roll it in flour, then dip it in the egg and coat it in the breadcrumbs." She demonstrated with her own. "This way it will have a nice crunchy outside and yummy and moist on the inside. Okay?"

"Yep. Got it."

Rosalina left Ginger with the rolling and turned her attention back to the other meals and the table setting. She could picture the layout. . . crisp white tablecloths, the good gold trimmed crockery and the polished silverware. The good crockery only came out on special occasions, such as all her sibling's engagement and wedding announcements and Nonna's seventieth birthday. The last time was when Nonna prepared a mammoth feast to celebrate Rosalina's return from Australia after five years abroad.

Today she planned on setting the table up in the paddock nestled between the back of the villa and the bottom vineyard. It would be the perfect setting. She had invited all her family and although both her father and youngest brother, Filippo, were invited, it would be extraordinary if they both turned up. The animosity between them was as mature as her father's special blend of red wine he kept secured in the dark recesses of the wine cellar. Despite many attempts to find out what happened between them, Rosalina still had no idea of the reason behind their hatred for each other.

In fact, Filippo's friendliness towards her was very shallow too. Fortunately, being seven years her junior, she'd never really had much to do with him growing up. Then again, maybe that was the reason for their rift. Her oldest sister was seven years older than her, but there was one sister and three brothers between them and they were all very close. Rosalina often wondered if Filippo was an accidental pregnancy, but she'd never voice that aloud. As it was, the tragedy of his arrival was never spoken of.

Archer came into the kitchen just after ten o'clock; no doubt looking for coffee. Rosalina happily set about making it for him.

"I'll go see if Alex wants a coffee." Ginger skipped off down the hall.

"How are my two favorite women doing?"

Rosalina shared a smile with Helen, it was the first time they'd done that and it felt good. Archer sipped his coffee and when he put his mug down Rosalina noted the unusual look on his face; it was a curious mix of nervous anticipation and relief. "I'm glad I caught you two alone, I have something I wanted to show you." Rosalina's mind flashed to the pearl necklace. So much had happened she'd forgotten all about it.

"Here Mom, come and have a seat beside me." As Archer pulled back a bar stool for his mother, Rosalina grabbed her coffee and moved to stand at the counter opposite Archer and Helen.

"When we were going through the boxes the other day, Mom, we found something that I think you should have." He eased forward on his seat, slipped his hand into his pants pocket and removed the little present. "This is for you, Mom." Archer slid it toward her and his Adam's apple bob up and down.

A tapestry of wrinkles lined Helen's forehead. "What is it?"

"It's a gift Dad and I bought for you a very long time ago."

Helen blinked several times and confusion drilled onto her pale blue eyes. "Open it, Mom, so I can tell you." She threaded the white satin ribbon through her fingers.

"The man who wrapped it was so slow, like he had all the time in the world, and Dad was ridiculously patient."

Her eyes met his. "Really? That's not how I remember him. Nothing ever happened quickly enough for Wade."

Archer smiled. A genuine full smile. "Open it. You'll love it." Helen tugged on the ribbon and it gradually released.

"Dad and I rode a couple of donkeys along some cobblestone streets to get to the store. I think we were at Santorini, but I'm not sure. You should have seen his donkey, the poor thing looked like it was about to buckle under his weight." Archer spoke with boyish glee and Rosalina let her imagination drift to the boy he may have been, at least the boy he was before tragedy changed his life forever.

Archer explained the overcrowded alley where the jewelry store was and he went into great detail about the old man behind the counter. It was amazing what he remembered about that moment.

Helen had the box completely unwrapped now, but she paused with her fingers hovering over the lid of the box. "Wade was uncanny at finding things in the most unlikely places." She ran her tongue over her lips. Finally, she folded back the lid. Inside, curled around a nest of black satin lining was a simple yet elegant pearl necklace. The pearls were almost identical in size and color and the galley lights showed off their lovely luminous shine.

Helen cupped her mouth with trembling fingers and her eyes pooled. Archer lifted the pearls from the box. "I reckon Dad looked at every single pearl in that shop. I had no idea there could be so many different types. You wouldn't believe how long he took to choose these."

"Really?" Helen's eyes remained on the pearls as she reached out to touch the necklace. She smiled and for the first time ever, Rosalina noticed the dimples in her cheeks, just like Archer's.

"Oh yes. The shopkeeper had this enormous magnifying glass and Dad must've scrutinized everything in the store. He looked at rings, earrings, bracelets and necklaces. I thought he was never going to make up his mind."

Archer undid the clip. "Would you like me to put it on you?"

She nodded.

"As soon as Dad spied this necklace, he said this was it. I don't know what was different about this one, most of them looked the same to me, but there was something about this string of pearls that grabbed him."

Archer draped the necklace around her neck and she ran her trembling fingers over the strand as he did up the clasp.

"It's beautiful," Rosalina said.

"Yes, it is, isn't it?" The look on her face was one of complete reverence. "Thank you Wade, it's wonderful. I'm so glad you found it."

Archer tugged his mother to his chest with a huge sigh. "Me too, Mom. Me too."

~

As Archer had predicted, *Evangeline* cruised into Livorno's Marina Di San Vencenzo just before midday. Unlike most marinas they'd visited over the previous months, this marina not only supported Archer's super-yacht, it was capable of holding even larger ones. In fact, compared to some of the ones they passed on their way to their designated berth, *Evangeline* looked like a toy. This marina was relatively new, and as the treasure was set to remain on the yacht until tomorrow morning, the twenty-four-hour video surveillance and the secure controlled entrance was an appreciated bonus.

As soon as they were tied up and ready to disembark, Rosalina took charge of ferrying the food from the galley to the waiting cars Archer had pre-organized. Her stomach did delightful flips at the prospect of going home and, in particular, seeing Nonna.

The car couldn't get there quick enough, and the ninety-minute drive seemed much longer.

Nonna met her as the car pulled to a halt on the gravel driveway, and when Rosalina wrapped her arms around her, she noticed just how thin and frail her grandmother had become. Tears filled her eyes when Nonna placed her hands over Rosalina's ears and pulled her down to kiss her cheeks. It was the signature kiss Nonna had been doing since. . . since forever.

As each family member arrived and she showed off her engagement ring, they all embraced Archer with the traditional Italian welcoming. It was like he'd always been part of the family. That was how the Calucci family did it. The only awkward moment was Filippo's arrival. Filippo made a show of giving everyone a kiss on each cheek except Rosalina and Archer. She guessed it'd been at least six years since she'd seen her brother and his unfounded resentment toward her was a palpable as ever. Rosalina wondered what Nonna had said to get him there, because he made it obvious that he'd rather be anywhere else.

Filippo's appearance made one thing fairly predictable. Her father probably wouldn't be attending. It filled her heart with both sadness and anger. Her father was yet to meet Archer and she had hoped he would put whatever grievances he had with Filippo aside for her sake. Obviously, that wasn't to be.

Archer and Alessandro were constantly sneaking off, most likely to make plans for the treasure's transfer from *Evangeline* to the Accademia di Belle Arti museum tomorrow morning.

When everything was perfectly laid out on the table, Nonna rang the big cowbell that she'd been using to announce dinner for as long as Rosalina could remember. Within minutes, every person Rosalina loved was sitting at the long table that was just about overflowing with food.

Archer sat beside Rosalina, and from then on, the afternoon was a lovely patchwork of amazing traditional Italian meals, good old Calucci family humor and delicious Villa Pandolfini red chianti wine.

Archer reached for a bottle and she watched his gaze fall to the label. He turned to her. "You never did tell me about the black rooster." Archer was referring to a discussion they'd had in the cellar quite some time ago. They'd been fighting at the time and she didn't want to share her family history then. Now though. . .

Filippo huffed. "*Ignorante.*"

Rosalina snapped her eyes to her youngest brother and from the look on his face, he was shocked that everyone was looking at him. He must've thought he'd made his remark to himself.

"Did you want to say something, Filippo?" Rosalina wanted to include him in the conversation; so far, he'd remained decidedly quiet.

"*Si, certamente.*" Filippo eased back on his chair and when he jutted his chin out, worry bubbled in her stomach like a nasty chemical experiment and she grew nervous about what he was about to say. "I want to know how your treasure hunter boyfriend knows nothing of the emblem that's been around our family since medieval times. Does he even know you at all?"

"Filippo, there's no need--"

Archer squeezed Rosalina's leg to cut her off. "It's okay, babe. Let me answer this."

Archer rose to his feet. As he spoke, his eyes drifted to everyone seated around the table. "Thank you for your question, Filippo. Obviously, I don't know everything about your family's history. But here's what I do know. I know that you can be friends with someone for five years but barely know them at all. But you can be with someone for just five minutes and feel like you've known them forever. I feel like I've known Rosalina forever and I look forward to learning something new about my beautiful fiancée every single day."

"Hear, hear." Alessandro raised his glass.

Rosalina glanced at Nonna, who was clasping her hands at her chest and beaming up at Archer.

Archer held his palm forward and helped Rosalina to stand beside him. Archer handed her glass to her, then raised his glass to clink them together. "Here's to my beautiful Rosalina. Cheers."

"*Cin.*" The entire table cheered.

"*Cin.*" Archer repeated after them. "I like that. Now will someone please tell me what the rooster emblem is about, because every time I ask, we get sidetracked?"

Nonna's boney knuckles bulged white as she squeezed her hands together. "Did you know red wine has been produced in this area for over one thousand years?"

"No, I didn't. That's impressive."

"The Black Rooster emblem is as old as Villa Pandolfini." Nonna reached for her glass and swirled her wine around as she spoke. All those around her remained quiet. Despite her soft voice, when Nonna spoke everybody listened. She was loved and respected equally. Many had been deceived by her diminutive frame and learned the hard way that Nonna was a powerhouse when she needed to be.

Nonna held Archer captive with her dark eyes. "For seven hundred years this symbol has proudly represented wine grown from the Chianti *Classico* Zone."

Archer sipped the red wine, and as he made a show of appreciating its taste, Rosalina stifled a giggle. "But why did they choose a black rooster?" he asked.

"I am getting to that, Mr. Mahoney." Rosalina loved watching her grandmother in full form. Nonna was doing a marvelous job of suppressing her cheeky grin while she flaunted her authority on this deep-seated family tradition. Seeing her grandmother like this was wonderful. It was a relief to know she was in good health and still had her wits about her. Rosalina was certain Nonna had many more great years of living ahead of her.

"Sorry." Archer put his wine glass down and wrinkled his nose at Rosalina.

"The cities of Florence and Siena make feud over rights to farm this region for a thousand years. Finally, around the year 1200AD, they agree to competition. It was to put end to long running dispute. A challenge was put forward." She paused and looked at Archer, no doubt to ensure he was listening.

Archer inclined his head as if he knew the signal to get Nonna talking again.

"The idea was. . . at first morning crow of rooster, one horseman would depart from Florence and one horseman would depart from Siena. Wherever they met would. . . *determinare* the boundary lines." Nonna spoke as much with her hands as her voice. "The rooster was *necessario*, you see, because back then, how else could they communicate starting time. But!" She stabbed her finger in the air. "The Siena people were a little *stupido*, because they chose big fat rooster." She puffed her cheeks and pumped her arms out to the side like big chicken wings.

"However, we Florentines, we are wise. We chose starving black rooster. You see, Mr. Mahoney, starving rooster crow long before happy fat one. Our Florentine rider gallop off much earlier than his foolish rival."

Nonna clasped her hands together again. "The Siena horseman, much to his surprise, did not ride very far before two horsemen met. I give you comparison. Florence grabbed the barrel, while Siena folk barely filled a thimble." Nonna finished her fable with two fingers held an inch apart and a satisfied grin.

Archer laughed and clapped his hands. "That's fantastic. I love it."

"*Cin Cin.*" Nonna held her glass high.

"*Cin Cin.*" Everyone else at the table raised their glasses too.

The sun was hovering high off the horizon when the city clock tower chimed seven o'clock. Rosalina excused herself from the table to freshen up and Archer jumped up too. "I'll come with you."

They walked hand in hand back to the villa. "Your family are amazing, babe."

"Most of them." She shrugged her shoulders. "Filippo's behavior was appalling." When she had an opportunity to get him alone, she had every intention of telling him so.

"Yeah, he's not one of my greatest fans."

They passed through the kitchen doorway and Rosalina tried to ignore the mountain of dishes piled high in the sink. "It's not you Filippo resents, honey. It's me."

"You? What did you do?"

She sighed. "Come on up to my bedroom, there's something you should know."

He huffed. "Sounds a little daunting."

"Yeah. I guess it is." She didn't feel comfortable talking about her family's dark secret, although given his history of harboring life-shattering family secrets, Archer seemed like the perfect person to tell. It was a depressing quandary.

Rosalina led him to the bedroom that'd been hers since the day she was born, and as she'd predicted Nonna hadn't moved a single thing while she'd been away. No matter how far, or how long she was abroad, Villa Pandolfini would always be her home

"Have a seat, I'll be back in a minute." She ducked into the restroom. As she washed her hands, she glanced into the mirror and forced back the anxiety burning her chest. What she was about to tell Archer was something she'd lived with nearly her whole life, yet it still hurt like it'd happened yesterday.

She dabbed cold water on her eyes, inhaled a deep calming breath and returned to her bedroom. Archer was sitting on her bed and holding a picture frame that he'd lifted from her nightstand.

"Is this your father?"

She sat at his side and looked at the photo. Not that she needed to, Rosalina had long ago committed the picture to memory. "Yes, this was taken the day before Mom died. It was the last time I ever saw him smile." A tear trickled down her cheek.

"Oh Rosa, I'm so sorry." He captured the tear with his thumb and wiped it on his trouser leg.

"I've never told you how Mom died." To even say those words aloud after all these years still cut a slice from her heart.

Archer cocked his head and frowned. "No, I guess you haven't. You only ever speak of Nonna."

Rosalina swallowed the lump in her throat. "Mom died giving birth to Filippo."

"Oh no."

"She was thirty-eight and I can still picture her as my incredibly vibrant, loving mother. To look at her you'd never have guessed her age." Rosalina turned over the picture frame and slid aside the clips that held the picture in place. She felt Archer's gaze but he remained silent.

The back of the frame came away and as it did, a silver chain tumbled into her lap. She grabbed it before it slipped onto the floor. She realigned it so the tiny pendant on the chain was centered in her palm. The woman embossed into the front of the silver disk wasn't particularly beautiful, and Rosalina had always thought she appeared more ghostly than saintly. She didn't need to turn it over to know what was on the back. She'd long ago memorised the encryption: *Oh God, help me to see through the eyes of St. Rita. Help me to forgive my enemies. Give me the strength of faith, devotion and passion.* Rosalina had always questioned the strange choice of saints that her mom chose. She couldn't picture her mom ever having enemies. "Do you know what this is?"

Archer shook his head.

"This is Saint Rita, the Patron Saint of Forgiveness. I was terrified about Mom going to hospital to have the baby. I was young, just seven, and for some reason it scared me. Mom gave me this bracelet to hang onto until she returned with my new baby brother or sister." She released a long, heavy sigh. "She never returned."

Archer wrapped his arms around her and Rosalina felt the warmth of his body against hers. "My father was never the same after that. He blamed Filippo for her death and from that moment on, he treated me as his youngest child. I was terrible for allowing that to happen."

"You can't blame yourself for your father's behavior."

She sat back and rolled the silver chain around her palm with her finger. "Nobody knows I have this. My father looked for it for months after Mom passed away and I didn't want to give it to him. It's been hiding here, with the photo of my dad, ever since."

Archer reached for the bracelet. "Well, it's time it came out." He undid the clasp.

Horrified, she pushed backward on the bed. "No Archer, I can't."

"Honey." He cupped her chin and raised her head so she had no choice but to look into his eyes. Their usual smiling impression was gone, replaced instead with deep concern. "Your mother would've wanted you to wear it."

Rosalina rolled the statement around in her head as St Rita swung from side to side in his hands like a hypnotist's shiny device. Her mind slipped to that moment, in this very room, when her mother had removed the chain from her wrist and folded it in Rosalina's palm. She recalled her mother's words as if she'd spoken them this morning: "Don't worry about me, darling. Having a baby is the most natural, beautiful thing a woman can do." Rosalina had believed her at the time. But ever since she passed away, the idea of having a baby scared her beyond belief. Archer needed to know that.

"Rosa, we're putting this on. This is a special day for us and this is the best way to have your mother here too."

"But there's--"

"No. Stop. You're wearing this. Now, which wrist would you like it on?"

Knowing he wouldn't give up, she raised her left arm and while he did the clasp she glanced in the mirror behind her dresser. Her red-rimmed eyes looked hideous. "Oh God, I look terrible."

"You look wonderful." He leaned in to kiss her, just a brief touch of their lips. "Now, come on. Let's dance off some of that food before we're forced to eat any more."

"Now?"

"Yes now. It'll put you back in the right mood." He reached for her hand, tugged her to her feet, and by the determined look in his eyes she had no choice.

"Okay, but not too long. They're all waiting for us at the table."

Archer led her up the stairs to the third floor. Nine months ago, when she'd first taken Archer to the ballroom, she'd been embarrassed by the neglected area. For nearly a decade the grand room, once the picture of elegance and celebration, had been used as nothing but storage space. The dust that covered the beautifully polished floorboards had been heartbreaking enough, let alone the collection of cloth-covered furniture abandoned in the corner.

Archer pushed through the double doors and the refreshing smell of pine is what caught her attention first. Someone had cleaned the floors. Archer flicked on the lights and her eyes widened in bewilderment as hundreds of fairy lights lit up the room. The furniture was gone and the fireplace at the far end, that hadn't been lit in years, was dancing with flames.

Rosalina covered her gaping mouth as she slowly scanned the room. "Oh Archer, did you do this?"

With one foot forward, he held his hand towards her. "May I have this dance?"

She swallowed back overwhelming tears of happiness and could barely breathe as she stepped towards Archer and accepted his request. As he cupped her hand, she fitted into the warmth of his other hand as he placed it on the small of her back. With a twinkle in his eye he led her onto the dance floor and twirled her around the freshly polished floorboards with an elegance that belied his rugged appearance. After a few dips and twirls that had her head spinning, he pulled her close so their bodies molded together. "I love you, babe."

"I love you too." She reached up on her tippy toes to kiss him.

"All right you two." Rosa turned to see her oldest sister and husband step into the room. "Stop hogging the dance floor." Her brother-in-law took Francesca in his arms and dashed her across the dance floor towards Rosalina and Archer.

As they arrived at their side, Archer leaned over to kiss Francesca on the cheek. "Thank you for all your help, Francesca. I couldn't have done this without you."

Rosalina gasped at her sister. "You sneaky little thing." She playfully slapped Archer's chest. "You two are in so much trouble for keeping this from me."

"Can't believe we did it so quickly, but *complimenti* to you, little sis," Francesca said. "We're so happy for you two. I hope you enjoy your little engagement party *il mio dolce*." Francesca turned to her husband.

"Quickly darling, take me away before that ring on Rosalina's finger blinds me forever."

"Thank you, Fran, you're the best." As her sister was whisked away, Rosalina twisted her diamond around her finger and was captured by its beauty in the twinkling fairy lights.

"My turn to dance with the lady," Jimmy demanded as he strode through the doors. Rosalina recognized his voice, but that was about all. Her mouth fell open. Jimmy, dressed in a tuxedo, looked truly debonair. He'd even slicked back his hair.

"Jimmy?" She uttered his name as he walked across the floor towards her.

He assumed his position as her dance partner. "I scrub up pretty good, don't I?" He spun her around with a few clunky moves that had her laughing.

"Oh Jimmy, you have to stop, I'm getting dizzy."

He clutched her to his chest. "Shall we tango?"

"I'm not sure--"

She hadn't finished her sentence before he forced her to move with him. They strode toward the fireplace at such a pace she wondered if he'd stop. He did, and when he spun her around, she couldn't believe what she was seeing. As a four-piece band started setting up in the corner, her family trickled in through the doorway and began dancing in pairs around the room.

"Aha, my date has arrived," Jimmy said as he dipped her backwards and then just as quickly yanked her upright again.

Confused, she glanced at Jimmy hoping he would finish his statement. Instead he gripped her again and strode with her across the dance floor to meet Archer on the other side. Jimmy cast her off into Archer's waiting arms and strode off in the opposite direction. "This is the most amazing thing that you've ever done for me, Arch. Thank you."

"You're the one who's amazing." He kissed her and resumed his dance hold. "Shall we?"

She laughed. "Yes please."

Archer glided her over the dance floor as if they floated on air. At every possibility he stopped to make sure she said hello to everyone in the room.

Out the corner of her eye, she saw Jimmy take Nonna into his arms. Rosalina said a silent prayer, hoping he'd treat her gently. Nonna would likely snap in half with Jimmy's spinning moves.

A woman walked into the room who made Rosalina gasp. "Tracy? Oh my God, it is you." Tracy squealed and bounded across the room to her.

"How did you get here? When did--"

"It was all Archer's doing." Tracy wrapped her arms around Rosalina and she squeezed her best friend that she'd left behind in Australia. Leaving her nearly a year ago had been one of the hardest things.

"Show me. Show me." Tracy reached for Rosalina's hand and turned it over to reveal her engagement ring. "Oh, my Godddd. That diamond is positively enormous."

"I know, can you believe we're engaged." The last time she'd seen Tracy was to tell her she'd broken up with Archer. Her mind boggled at how much had happened since she left Australia. They had so much to talk about.

"I always knew you two would hook up again." Tracy jiggled on her feet.

Rosalina clutched her friend's hands in hers. "When did you arrive?"

"An hour or so ago."

"How long are you staying?" So many questions pummeled through her mind and she wasn't quite sure where to start with all the excitement buzzing around the room.

"Just a week, but Archer has arranged for a place to stay in Positano. I can't wait. But we'll have all day tomorrow to catch up." Tracy squealed and bounced on her toes. "I can't believe I'm here."

"Me neither." She turned to Archer. "You're incredible. Thank you."

"He's a keeper, honey." Tracy kissed Archer on the cheek again. "Thank you. Now if you'll excuse me, my dance partner is waiting."

Rosalina looked ahead of where Tracy was walking and saw her boyfriend Peter, waiting patiently. She waved to him, blew him a kiss and he blew a kiss in return.

The music beat picked up and Archer glided her around the dance floor with ease. After countless spins and twirls, they cruised up beside Nonna and Jimmy. "How are you going, Nonna?" Rosalina appreciated the moment to catch her breath, she didn't know how Nonna would be keeping up.

"Nonna?" Jimmy gushed. "What about me? This woman's a wildcat."

Nonna laughed and the sparkle in her eyes made Rosalina laugh too.

A loud thundering crash startled her. She turned toward the noise to see Filippo on the floor next to the band, tangled up in amongst the noisy cymbals. Archer and her older brother dashed to his aid, but Filippo brushed aside their help. He stumbled and swore as he tried to get up.

"Oh dear." Nonna had her hand over her mouth and the look of concern in her eyes was heartbreaking.

"It's okay, Nonna. He's just had a bit too much to drink. Archer will look after him." Rosalina put her arm around Nonna for reassurance.

Filippo was on his feet and the two men were guiding him out of the room.

"It's all good folks, just a little slip," Archer said as Filippo shoved Archer's hand away. "How about another song, Luigi?" Archer called to the band before he stepped through the doors.

The guitarist strummed a few notes and the rest of the band joined in. Gradually all the guests resumed dancing again.

Rosalina turned back to Nonna and her grandmother's eyes fell to Rosalina's wrist. The look in her pale blue eyes shifted from the concern over Filippo that they'd portrayed moments ago to a darker cloud of distress.

"What is it, Nonna?"

"*Mi scusi.*" Nonna walk away and Rosalina started after but stopped with a jolt when she remembered the bracelet hanging loosely around her wrist. As she rubbed St Rita between her fingers, Archer re-entered the room with a woman on his arm who she didn't recognize. He nodded in her direction before he guided the woman toward Jimmy.

"Hey Dad." The young lady said in a prominent Australian accent.

Jimmy stared open-mouthed at the woman for the briefest of moments. "Pauline?"

"Look at you. You look fantastic." Pauline wrapped her arms around Jimmy and he nearly squeezed her to death in his muscular arms. Rosalina was fairly certain she saw tears in his eyes. Jimmy held his hand forward to shake with Archer. Rosalina had never met Pauline before but she knew Jimmy had been trying to see his daughter for years. It looks like the offer of an Italian vacation was all that was needed. Archer's generosity knew no bounds. Her heart filled with love and awe for the man she cherished.

For the rest of the evening, Rosalina drifted along like she was in a fairytale. Archer had thought of everything and everyone. When Archer and his mother took to the dance floor, the crowd eased back to give them space. Their dance was fluid, elegant, almost poetic as they glided across the dance floor. Rosalina's already bursting heart swelled even more as she watched Helen move with grace and poise while Archer led her graciously over the dance floor. To see Helen so happy, and Archer for that matter, was the highlight of the evening. Their dance ended with a twirl and a dip. As the crowd began to clap, Helen laughed and Archer pulled her in for a hug. He looked over his mother's head in her direction and was beaming with happiness. Rosalina's chin quivered as she grinned back at him. Archer guided his mother back to her chair, sought her out from amongst the crowd and set off around the dance floor with her once again.

When the distant town clock chimed midnight, Archer let go of her hand and strode toward the band. She assumed it was to ask for a song. But he grabbed the microphone instead.

"*Ciao posso avere la vostra attenzione.*" Rosalina cupped her mouth in surprise as Archer asked for everyone's attention in Italian. He really had been busy.

"*Spero che hai avuto una grande notte.*" The crowd cheered and clapped and she couldn't agree more. But it wasn't just a great night, it was more spectacular than any engagement party she could have ever dreamed of.

"Sorry, that's all I can say in Italian. Where's my wingman? Come on, Alex, help me out here with the translation." Alessandro nodded and stepped to Archer's side.

"On behalf of Rosalina and I, we would like to thank you all very much for coming tonight, especially those who travelled all the way from Australia at very short notice. Pauline, Tracy and Peter, thank you."

"Our pleasure." Tracy clapped her hands.

"I especially want to thank you all for keeping this a secret. Rosalina is a hard woman to surprise."

Rosalina palmed her chest and then blew her husband-to-be a kiss. "I'm sorry, baby."

"You can apologize to me later." He winked at her and a flood of embarrassment heated her neck. "So. My lovely fiancée and I are heading off now. I have a hot date planned on *Evangeline*." The crowd cheered and whistled. Rosalina's hot flush shot up to her cheeks.

"Rosalina, would you like to say anything?"

"Yes please."

"Of course she does, Rosalina always has something to say." He rolled his eyes yet his grin lit up his face.

She kissed Archer on the lips as she reached for the microphone. "I can't believe you all kept this from me." She pretended to be mad but giggled too.

The crowd cheered again.

"Archer baby, thank you. You never cease to amaze me. To manage something like this must have taken an incredible amount of planning."

"If you weren't constantly spying on me it would've been easier."

She poked her tongue at him.

"Thank you everyone for making this an incredible night. I love you all."

She handed the microphone back to Archer.

Archer held it up to his mouth. "You have the band for another couple of hours so please enjoy." He handed the microphone back to the band member, then wrapped his arm around her to bring her close. "You have ten minutes for goodbyes before the car arrives. Okay?"

"Thank you." Rosalina spotted Tracy and Peter in the crowd. She could hardly miss her; Tracy's fiery red curls were as rich as candied strawberries. "Hey, Tracy."

"Hey. Tell me, is this your home? My God, woman, you never told us you had a grand ballroom."

"I guess, because I grew up here, it's just normal to me. Say, what are your plans for tomorrow? Shall I take you to lunch in Florence?"

"Yes please. Sounds perfect. It's been crazy mad since Archer called us three days ago."

Rosalina's mind raced. Three days ago, was when they left the Greek Islands. She couldn't believe Archer had organized all this in such a short amount of time.

"He's so generous paying for our flights and accommodation."

"Oh yes, you'll adore Positano. And the food is fantastic." She smiled as she recalled the wonderful time they'd had there. "I assume you're staying here tonight."

"Yes, Archer has arranged a room for us."

"Great. Okay, I've got to go, but I'll pick you up tomorrow before lunch." She wrapped her arms around both Tracy and Peter and squeezed them together.

Rosalina was overwhelmed as she did a quick dash around the room, trying to personally thank everyone before Archer came and grabbed her. Her head was spinning as he led her from the room.

"I can't believe you did all that for me. Thank you again."

"I can't believe I got away with it."

As Archer had said, a car was waiting for them in the driveway. But it wasn't just any car, it was a very long white stretch limousine. The driver opened the door for her and helped her inside. She fell into the soft leather of the back seat and felt completely exhausted. Archer slipped in beside her, draped his arm across her shoulders and pulled her to rest against his shoulder as the limousine pulled away.

"I love you, baby."

"I love you too, sweetheart." He tugged her closer, kissed her forehead and she settled in for the long drive back to *Evangeline*.

Chapter Thirty-Three

Archer was dismayed at the amount of traffic still on the road at this time of night. Despite that, the driver was able to maintain maximum speed most of the way. They cruised into the marina parking lot and as the driver pulled to a stop Archer gently shook Rosalina's shoulder and kissed her forehead. "Hey baby, we're here."

She groaned. "Oh, did I fall asleep?"

"Yep, almost the instant we left the villa."

She blinked her eyes open. "Sorry."

"It's fine. We've had a huge day."

The driver jumped out to open the door.

"Thank you, Giovanni."

"*Grazie*, Mr. Mahoney. Call me anytime you need."

"I will." Archer slipped a five hundred Euro note into the driver's hand and Giovanni's eyes threatened to pop out of his head.

The moon was a misty light, filtering down through low-lying clouds as an eerie ivory haze. It was more spooky than romantic. Archer wrapped his arm around Rosalina and as he led her toward the main gate, he fished his security card from his pocket.

"I hope you're not too tired." Before they'd left earlier today Archer had slipped a bottle of Bailey's Irish Cream and a box of chocolates into the fridge and he'd hoped to replicate a little Positano action with Rosalina before the night came to an end.

"Of course not. I'm all yours, baby."

"I hoped you'd say that." Although he had counted on the full moon being more prominent. He still had every intention of enjoying Rosalina within full view of the night sky. He wasn't worried though, no matter where they went, it'd be the perfect end to a perfect night.

He removed his arm from her shoulder to swipe the card. But it didn't work. He flipped it over to try again. Still nothing. There was minimal light and he could barely see what he was doing. He glanced around looking for a light switch. But couldn't find anything. He looked up at the light and frowned at the jagged teeth of broken glass that glimmered with a blue tinge. Archer stepped back and something crunched beneath his feet.

Glass!

A streak of dread curled up from the base of his spine. With a blaze of urgency, he stepped up to the gate and swiped the card for the third time. The gate popped with a sharp click and he shoved it open.

He turned to Rosalina and cupped her face. "Stay here."

"What? Why?"

"Just stay here until I come and get you."

She clutched his arm, her nails digging in. "No, Archer. I'm not going to just sit here. Tell me what's wrong."

"I don't know. Please Rosa, stay here. I'll be back for you in a minute."

Archer turned and sprinted along the main pontoon, guided only by the subtle blue lights illuminating the way. He was nearly halfway along when he saw something that shot dread from the base of his spine right up his backbone. A helicopter. On top of *Evangeline*.

"Fucking bastard," Archer screamed as he fist-punched the air. "Call the police."

His heart was set to explode as he sprinted with the determination of a panther chasing prey. For the first time ever, he hated how his beautiful yacht was always relegated to mooring at the outer pontoons. Twenty-one pontoons. That's how far he had to run to get to her.

Eight. Nine. Ten.

"Call the *polizi*." He screamed as he ran, hoping Rosalina, or anyone heard him.

His left knee throbbed with his unrelenting pace, but he didn't stop.

Thirteen. Fourteen.

The throbbing beat of a motor cut through the silence and he looked up to the chopper. But its rotors remained still. Thank Christ. Ignatius would be the pilot. He was certain of that. Archer planned to strangle that bastard with his bare hands. A light in the distance caught his eye. It was beyond the last line of boats. A powerful spotlight skimmed across the black water as the boat carrying it sped away from the marina.

Away from *Evangeline*.

"NO!" Archer screamed, clenched his fists and pumped his arms back and forth in an attempt to go faster.

Seventeen. Eighteen.

Then he heard the noise he'd been dreading. Whomp. . . Whomp.

"Son of a bitch."

Nineteen. Twenty.

The sound of the helicopter's blades spinning was unmistakable. Archer had no idea how long the startup would take. One minute? Two? Five? He hoped like all hell it was five.

Whomp. . . whomp. . . whomp.

He hit pontoon twenty-one at full speed. His feet pounded on the wooden slats. His heart pounded like a galloping horse in his chest. And his brain pounded through his limited options trying to formulate a plan.

Archer reached *Evangeline* and, not bothering with the gate, he jumped over the railing, crossed the lower deck and raced up the back stairs. He stopped at the keypad and tried to ignore his trembling fingers as he punched in his access code. But the alarm wasn't set. He had double-checked it was set before they left.

That meant one thing. Iggy had deactivated it.

Whomp. Whomp. Whomp.

He yanked the sliding glass door open, sprinted past the lower bedrooms to the internal staircase. There was no point checking the downstairs hold.

The Calimala treasure would be gone.

His clenched teeth hurt as he allowed that despicable reality to drive his anger.

His knee screamed in pain. But he didn't stop. He climbed the spiral stairs to the main deck two at a time, gripping the railing to increase momentum. At the top he dashed through the saloon, dining room, galley and up the stairs to the upper deck. Another fleeting thought bolted across his brain. *How the hell did Iggy know where they were and that the yacht would be unoccupied for so long?*

Could it be Ginger? They barely knew her.

No! He refused to believe it.

The answer hit him like a wrecking ball. Iggy knew their moves. That's what the thugs had done. Jimmy was right that the attack didn't make any sense.

It made perfect sense now. They'd planted a bug.

WHOMP WHOMP WHOMP.

The chopper was jet-propeller loud and Archer hoped he had more than thirty seconds before it took off. Because if he didn't, he was set to miss it. A sudden brainwave had him dashing to the padded leather cushions. He snatched the cushion off, tossed it aside, reached in and blindly fumbled around until his fingers found what he was looking for. The gun.

He'd never fired a gun before but the thought of using it on Ignatius Montpellier felt so fucking good.

WHOMP WHOMP WHOMP WHOMP.

The blade's tempo increased and Archer's heart was a thundering mess as he pictured the chopper taking off. He dashed to the last set of stairs and as he looked up at the spinning rotors his fear was realized. The blades were at full speed, spinning so fast he couldn't even see them.

He scaled the stairs two at a time. The wind, the sound, the crazy situation, it all hit him like a chemical explosion. He aimed the gun at the cockpit and pulled the trigger. Click. Nothing happened.

He searched the gun, desperate to find the safety clip he figured must be on. To his horror, the helicopter skids lifted ever so slightly. But just as quickly they dropped back down.

"No!" Archer cursed.

He found the safety. Clicked it off, aimed at the glass dome and fired.

A bright spark burst from the glass as the bullet ricocheted off.

The darkened cockpit lit up, and Archer saw his nemesis. Ignatius Montpellier.

The bastard stared at him, then an evil grin split his lips. The cocky bastard started laughing.

Archer heart lurched. The damn glass must be bulletproof. Acid churned in his stomach. The gun was useless.

Ignatius waved at him and then pushed the gear stick forward.

The skids lifted and the speed with which they did confirmed there was no stopping it now. He clamped his jaw until it hurt and watched on helpless as the helicopter gained airspace.

"No!" Archer screamed, then before he knew what he was doing, he put the gun between his teeth, ran at the chopper and dived.

Archer caught the landing skid and the chopper dipped with his weight. He wrapped his elbow around the rail and desperate to hang on, he swung his legs in a frenzied attempt to hook one of them over.

Yes! His left leg hooked over.

Gasping for breath, he looked downward.

What he saw terrified him.

It wasn't that he was about six feet in the air. It was Rosalina, on her knees, looking up at him with wide fearful eyes.

But damned if he was about to let Ignatius get away with his treasure. He was going to hang like this until Iggy touched down again.

The chopper rose higher.

His heart beat faster.

And he had no fucking idea what he was doing.

His tongue tasted the metal of the gun and he reached for it with his free hand. An idea catapulted his head. It wasn't great. It was far from great. But it was worth a shot. . . or two.

With his gut twisting into knots, he aimed the gun at the spinning rotors, intensified his grip on the skids, closed his eyes and pulled the trigger. The gun kicked in his hand and he heard the thunder of release, but nothing happened.

He'd missed.

"Shit!"

Determined to keep his eyes open, he aimed and fired again. Nothing. He knew his direction was right but couldn't believe the bullet had gone right through the blades. Archer had no idea how many bullets were in the gun. *One. Two. None!*

Oh God, please don't let it be empty.

He aimed again but then he remembered the tail rotor and in a snap decision changed his aim to it instead. He squeezed the trigger.

The chopper bucked. And everything went to hell.

His world spun as he fell from the sky. Fast.

Archer gripped for his life. His world whizzed by past at frightening speed. The gun flung from his hand and he reached for the rail as the drag threatened to pull him off.

He saw the ocean, *Evangeline*, the ocean.

They were going to crash. He was going to die.

It spun so fast he was in a vortex. His body was being sucked off the skids. His brain hurt.

He was slipping. He clawed at the skids, scraping his fingernails over the metal. He squeezed his leg muscles, desperate to stay in place.

A cry burst from his throat as he flung free. He flew through the air like rubbish in a tornado. Before he had any chance of regaining his bearings, his back hit the water.

His breath slammed out of him and as he drifted below the surface he watched in horror as the helicopter crashed into *Evangeline* and exploded into a huge fireball.

His chest squeezed with the agony of broken bones, and as he gulped huge mouthfuls of bitter water, he cried out for Rosalina.

Chapter Thirty-Four

Nox didn't miss the irony in Ophelia asking him to make rice for dinner. His specialty back in Italy, in the kitchen deep in the bowels of the church, was mushroom risotto. The last time he'd cooked it was special. His perfectly cooked rice, laced with poisonous mushrooms and lashings of his special mushroom powder, had ensured a quick end to Father Benedici's life.

As Nox stirred the big pot of rice with a wooden spoon he watched the boys set the table. They had obviously done this many times over and knew exactly where everything went. Dinnertime in this house was a family affair with lots of food and conversation, most of which he had no comprehension of at all. It was his favorite time of the day. But it made him realize he'd missed a significant part of normal human behavior growing up, and it only made him hate Father Benedici even more.

Ophelia chopped the chicken and vegetables with a heavy knife then she tossed them into a saucepan equally as large as Nox's pot. She grabbed his hand and her touch alone sent sparks through his body. Still holding the wooden spoon, she moved his hand to her pot and motioned for him to stir it too. He did as he was told, alternating his stirring from one pot to the next, but with every opportunity he watched her. The woman was a colossal bundle of homely bliss, and it wasn't just her size that made him think about her that way. She fussed about the food and the kitchen, cleaning with equal measure, and at every available moment she'd wrap her arms around both boys, hugging them to her ample bosom and kissing the tops of their heads before she let them go.

With each ingredient she tossed into the chicken pot she grabbed his hand and stirred. It became a little game in which he deliberately went too slow so she would grab his hand and guide it around the pot with vigorous stirring. The aromas that quickly emanated from the cooking were as delicious as her frequent touches, and once again Nox reflected on his good fortune. He couldn't remember a time when he'd ever been so. . . happy.

There had been glimpses of happiness, like eating a stolen chocolate, or smoothing down the fur of his beloved cat Shadow or seeing his plans for revenge come to fruition. But never had his happiness transcended over days, let alone weeks. He considered fate had dealt him yet another hand and he'd always been destined to meet Ophelia and her two rambunctious boys. This scenario, with a family that loved and cared for each other, was new to him. But he already knew it was something he wanted in his life permanently.

Ophelia placed four plates before him and with her usual flamboyant hand movements she indicated that he spoon on rice and then top that with the chicken dish. He did as he was told and as each plate was filled, the boys took turns ferrying the plates from him to the table.

Once all the plates were placed, they each took their designated seats at the table and put their hands together for grace. It was Arion's turn and as the little boy spoke in Greek, Nox said grace in Italian. He couldn't remember the last time he'd said grace, but, for probably the first time in his life, he really was grateful for something.

As it promised to be, dinner was delicious and Nox cleaned his plate with a slice of Ophelia's homemade cornbread slathered in butter. Together they placed all the dishes into the sink and he knew that once the boys had gone to bed, Ophelia would clean them.

They moved to the lounge room and Ophelia switched on the television and assumed her position in her favorite chair. Nox took his place in a chair to her side, that way he could balance his gaze between her and the television. The two boys played with little cars on a rug at their feet decorated with roads and houses.

Ophelia pressed the buttons on the remote until she found the news channel she watched every night. The screen flashed to a fiery explosion and Nox's heart jumped to his throat as he did a double take at the television. The enormous yacht in the foreground was *Evangeline*, he had no doubt about it. He'd followed that boat around the Greek Islands long enough to have memorized every aspect of its sleek lines. A reporter came on and her lip movements didn't match what she was saying. Whatever language she was speaking had been dubbed over in Greek. That meant the report wasn't coming from the Greek Islands.

The screen skipped back to grainy footage, like it had been taken on a mobile phone or similar device. It gradually cleared as the picture zoomed in. A helicopter hovered several feet above *Evangeline*. He launched forward on his chair as the footage focused on a person dangling beneath the helicopter's landing gear.

"Is that Archer?" He stared open-mouthed at the screen.

The helicopter suddenly spun out of control. Flicking around like a popped balloon. The man beneath it dangled by just an arm and one leg and he gasped when the body flung off. Barely a second later, the chopper crashed into the yacht in an enormous explosion. The fireball engulfed the back of the yacht as the helicopter broke up on impact. The tail sheared off and fell onto the lower level of the yacht. Through the smoke and flames he saw the blades spinning, until they both snapped off and flung in different directions, hitting the water with sizable splashes. Flaming helicopter pieces rained down into the black marina water.

"Holy hell." Nox leaned further forward on his chair.

The dark-haired reporter was back on the screen. She was talking into a microphone and in the background was *Evangeline*. Black smoke billowed from the top and firefighters poured a stream of water from their small boats at the side of the yacht up onto the top of the helicopter remains. The camera panned around the marina and Nox read several signs, convincing him the yacht was in Italy.

Did they leave Greece because they'd found all the treasure?

He bet they had. Archer wouldn't leave the dive site until all the pieces were recovered.

A photograph of Archer's smiling face flashed onto screen. It was exactly as Nox remembered him. Wavy hair, dark eyes, olive skin and an air of cockiness about him that said 'I am invincible'. The photo couldn't be any older than a year or so. *Was he dead?* Nox's weighed up the positives and the negatives of that being the case. Dead was what he wanted. But not yet. He still needed to use Archer to help him find the rest of the Calimala treasure.

Nox had learned from the scroll that the treasure had been divided into thirds many centuries ago. He thought he was the only person in the world who could possibly know that. But Archer and his crew may have worked it out somehow. It already surprised him how much they'd accomplished. Obviously, they knew what they were doing. Which is exactly why Nox needed Archer alive. For now.

He'd been dreaming of the Calimala treasure for decades. Its vastness, as described in the scroll in his bedroom wall, was enough to fill three ships. That being the case, it was impossible Archer had found it all in such a short amount of time. The question was whether or not the treasure was still onboard *Evangeline?* Nox scanned the background, looking for any sign displaying the name of the marina. And there it was, a big blue sign with Marina Di San Vencenzo Livorno. He was right. They were back in Italy. It occurred to him that this accident could have something to do with the valuables. He balled his fists at the thought of someone trying to steal it.

The reporter was back on the screen, her excitement showing in her rapid words and hand movements. Nox groaned when the screen flashed to a picture of himself. A bald, pudgy picture of him, but by the gasp from Ophelia, a still very recognizable picture. In the photo he wasn't looking at the camera and with his clenched jaw and wide eyes, even he had to admit he looked evil.

He couldn't figure out where the photo had been taken. There weren't too many happy moments in his life that involved capturing the occasion. The camera gradually panned back from the photo and when Nox saw the plaid shirt he was wearing he figured it out. It was taken in the office where he hired the boat in Athens to chase Archer around the Greek Islands. They must have had security cameras in that office.

Mental juggling slotted the puzzle pieces into place. The hired boat was never returned. The boat hire place reported it stolen. And his name would have thrown up a red flag after Archer and Rosalina reported what happened at Anafi Island. He remembered all the forms he'd filled out at that boat hire place and he punched his fist into his own palm at his foolishness. The authorities would now have his full name and address.

He stood up and rubbed his beard stubble as he paced. If they knew where he lived, it's possible they would've searched his bedroom in the church. He'd left so quickly that he didn't have time to hide anything. Not that he would have anyway, because at that point in time, he'd had every intention of returning. He drove his fingers through his hair as he thought over what was in his bedroom. His tapes. His scroll. His supply of poisonous mushroom powder. They were the three things that meant everything to him. He was certain the scroll was safe. The brick in the wall it was hidden behind was identical to every other. So, unless someone knew of the secret compartment hidden behind the bricks, they'd have no reason to start searching. The other two items though would provide more than enough evidence to convict him of murdering at least a dozen or so people.

It was inconsequential though, because as far as Archer, Rosalina and the police were concerned, he'd drowned in the ocean with a spear in his belly.

Nox was a dead man walking.

His eyes drifted to Ophelia. She was staring up at him, her lips slightly ajar as if poised to say something but couldn't get the words out.

Her small almond shaped eyes that usually disappeared behind her chubby cheeks with a smile, bulged with mortal fear.

Chapter Thirty-Five

Rosalina gasped for air; every breath scorched her throat. Black smoke stung her eyes and a loud buzz tortured her ears. The blistering heat was terrifying. She tried to back away but couldn't.

"Archer!" She cried out for him. Her despair was a living, breathing thing, engulfing her with uselessness. He'd been up so high when he fell. Hitting the water would have hurt him, or injured him, or worse. She shuddered. Bracing against the pain in her legs she pushed to sit up. But couldn't. She wiped her eyes, trying to clear the grit.

"Help." Her throat hurt. She swallowed, tasting ash and fumes. "Help."

When the helicopter had spun out of control she'd stared in horror as Archer was flung around. She'd watched his plummet. She heard him scream.

That was the last she saw of him.

Through smoke and stinging eyes, she saw flames, high above her on the helipad where she had been. Now she was on the dive platform two story's below. No wonder her hip was agony. When she'd hurled herself off of the top deck, she'd planned to hit the water. But she'd hit the deck instead and landed on her hipbone.

"Help!" Through her blurry vision she saw why she couldn't move; the tail end of the helicopter was across her legs.

She could wriggle beneath the twisted metal, but not enough to pull her legs out. She was trapped.

Turning her head, she searched the black water less than three feet from her head.

"Archer!" With fiery agony she pushed at the metal pinning her legs. But the twisted contraption refused to move. Pain radiating from her shins was as excruciating as the pain in her hip.

"Help!" Tears streamed down her cheeks, as much from her stinging eyes as for Archer. He's a good swimmer. He would be okay. She repeated the mantra over and over as she wriggled beneath the metal.

She heard voices. "Help." Relief flooded her veins.

People were shouting and lights were illuminating surrounding yachts.

"I'm here. Help me." She beat her fists on the metal as she scoured the black water searching for the man she loved. "Archer!" Her throat was a burning inferno. "HELP."

"Oh my God, are you okay?" It was an elderly man, in blue polka dotted pajamas. He climbed down the steps and knelt at her side and she smelled talcum powder and mothballs.

"My fiancé. He fell into the water. Find him, please."

"But what about you, you're--"

"I'm okay. Please, he fell from the helicopter. Go. Go get help. Now. Please." She begged over her frantic tears.

"Okay. Okay. I'll get help." With agonizing slowness, he pushed up off his knees, and she alternated her gaze from watching his crawl up the stairs to the still, black water beyond her.

Several people she didn't recognize came running down the stairs. "Did you find Archer?"

"Who?" said a man with a thick head of silver hair and a matching mustache.

Rosalina slammed her fist onto the wooden decking. "My fiancé. He fell from the helicopter. He landed in the water. Please find him. Before he drowns."

The man with the mustache jumped up and ran back up the stairs.

Deep wracking sobs cut through her body and rivers of tears trickled down her cheeks as her heart shredded into hundreds of little pieces. She fell back, gasping for breath. She had no comprehension of what was going on.

People around her were talking to her but she was in a cloud.

They were touching her arms and legs, but her body was anesthetized.

Everything was numb. Her mind, her body, her heart.

An engine noise cut through her distress. She looked over her shoulder. It was a small rubber boat cruising across the water. The people in the boat were searching the blackness with a powerful light. Rosalina didn't take her eyes off that circle of light, desperate to see Archer and yet at the same time fearful of what she might find. She had no comprehension of time and no idea how long ago he'd hit the water. Was it seconds? Minutes? Hours?

Her world faded into blurry misery as she sobbed until she struggled to breathe.

Suddenly Jimmy was there, and Alessandro. "Rosa. Rosa. My God, are you okay?"

"Jesus. Jimmy, I can't find Archer. He fell from the helicopter and into the water." A thought of horrific proportions hit her. If Jimmy was here, then at least an hour had passed since the helicopter crashed.

A cry burst from her throat.

As she wept in Jimmy's arms, her heart crumbled to dust and drifted away with the mild ocean breeze.

Chapter Thirty-Six

Ophelia's gaze at Nox changed from pleasant indifference to fear and loathing in the space of seconds. It was not pretty to watch. His beautiful, cherubic, welcoming Ophelia became wide darting-eyed, and she gripped the chair as if fearful he was about to attack her.

He held his palms up in a calming gesture and wished he could tell her he would never hurt her. But, how could he? He took a step toward her and in a move that completely stunned him she leapt out of her chair and smashed the remote control over his head.

Nox stepped back, blinded and disorientated. He blinked the fuzziness from his brain and shook his head. When he reached up to feel where she had clobbered him, he couldn't believe he was bleeding.

He turned to her, but she was gone. As were the children. But the wooden floorboards in the kitchen revealed their escape route. Nox strode to the kitchen and was greeted with a red-faced Ophelia. The boys were gone, no doubt they'd shot out the open door to her right. Ophelia was holding the knife she'd used only an hour earlier to cut the chicken and vegetables. A slice of carrot was still clinging to the blade.

Her lips trembled as much as the fingers she had wrapped around the handle.

Nox again tried to calm her by offering his open hands. She spoke to him and her usual singsong voice was now a feverish, high-pitched

244

hiss. He stepped toward her and she swung the knife, slicing the air before his chest with a quick slash. He was certain she had no intention of actually using it, but the speed with which she swung it sent the carrot slice scuttling across the room.

Ophelia's eyes locked on his and blazed with fear.

A trickle of sweat dribbled down her left temple and over her rosy red cheek. Nox noticed his own body odor oozing from his skin. It was back, the pungent stench that had ruined his life had returned with every drop of its vile fury.

A growl erupted from Ophelia's throat and she lunged at him. Nox was stunned and thrown off guard. He dived for cover behind the table and avoided being stabbed in the heart by barely an inch. But Ophelia didn't stop there. She lunged at him again and this time the knife sliced through his shirtsleeve. He stared in bewilderment at his arm as blood seeped out over the shredded cotton.

Nox gaped at her. He didn't recognize who he was looking at. She'd transformed completely. She'd become a wild animal.

Ophelia dived at him again, he twisted aside at the last minute and grabbed her knife-wielding arm. With brute force he smashed her hand on the table, scuttling the knife to the ground.

Twisting her arm behind her back, he used it as the driver to slam her face first into the wall. Ophelia screamed when she hit and several wall mounted photos tumbled to the ground with her. She scrambled over onto her back to face him.

Nox ignored the blood splattered across her face as he pounced onto her, straddling his legs either side of her immense hips. He wrapped his fingers around her throat and centering his attention on her esophagus he squeezed. She fought back, punching, scratching, kicking her legs. He stared into her eyes, clenched his jaw and squeezed harder.

She looked right back at him and the happy peacefulness that he'd fallen in love with was gone.

Her eyes began to bulge. She gasped. Her tongue poked out. He dragged his eyes away.

Nox spied the dislodged photo to her side. Through the shattered glass he gazed upon a picture of Ophelia sitting in a bright red lounge chair. On her lap were her boys, sitting either side of her bountiful bosom. They were all smiling. Happy. Peaceful. In love.

Nox stopped squeezing, and as if struck by lightning he jumped back. Ophelia gasped for breath, clawing at her throat. His heartbeat pounded like a freight train as he climbed off her.

It was as much a surprise to him as it probably was to Ophelia that he was going to let her live. He knelt at her side, placed his hand on her arm and watched as the color flushed her cheeks pink and her breathing returned to normal.

It occurred to him that he must truly love this woman to allow her to live. *But how could he kill her?* She had shown him love. She deserved to see that he was capable of it too. When he stood, a set of car keys hanging on the side of the fridge caught his eye.

He snatched them off the hook and without even a final glance in her direction he strode out the door.

From now on, Nox wasn't just a dead man walking.

He was marching.

And he knew exactly where he was heading. Livorno.

Chapter Thirty-Seven

The men made the twisted tail end of the helicopter look like a featherweight as they lifted it off Rosalina and moved it aside. Despite protests from everyone else, she begged Jimmy to carry her up the stairs and into the saloon.

"*Per favore* Rosa, we need to take you to a hospital." Alessandro's shaky voice was emotion-choked as he followed behind them.

"Absolutely not. I'm not going anywhere until I know where Archer is."

Jimmy was puffing by the time he lowered her onto the leather lounge. She reached for his hand. "Is. . . he. . . ?" She couldn't even say it. It wasn't possible that Archer was gone. Not possible.

"We don't know, Rosa. He hasn't been found yet."

"He'll be okay, I'm certain." But even as Alessandro said it, his eyes darkened with fear and he turned his back and walked away.

"Are you hurt?" Jimmy touched her shoulder but his eyes travelled to her legs.

She flicked her skirt down to cover her legs, ignoring the bruises she knew would be there. "I'm good. Archer's a good swimmer, Jimmy. He made it to safety. I know it." She reassured herself by forcing conviction into her words.

He squeezed her hand. "I know." Jimmy clenched his jaw, squaring out his chin. He'd removed his black jacket but his bow tie hung loosely around his neck. Her fabulous engagement party now seemed like a lifetime ago.

"What happened, Rosa?"

She relayed the details to Jimmy, but the whole time she was talking, she was listening to what was going on upstairs. Black water streamed down the outside of the yacht as firemen continued to pour water over the smoldering helicopter. There was a sudden commotion and the water stopped. A grinding noise erupted from above and sparks rained down the outside.

"They're cutting him out," Jimmy said with a sneer on his lips.

"Who?" She frowned.

"Ignatius."

"Oh." Archer had dominated her thoughts so much she hadn't wasted even one moment on Iggy. Of course, no-one could survive an explosion like that. If by some miracle Iggy did, she'd strangle him with her bare hands and she wouldn't care who watched her do it.

The noise stopped and the men above spoke in muffled tones. It was a full ten minutes before a stretcher was wheeled through the saloon. Thankfully a white sheet covered the body but the stench of burned flesh made her gag. Rosalina glanced at the cloth-covered body briefly before she turned away. She felt no remorse for the man.

The putrid smell lingered for a long time after they were gone and she tried to block it away by turning her attention back to Jimmy. "You know he took the treasure, don't you?"

"I figured as much." Jimmy hissed the words out of his thinned lips.

"It's probably gone forever. All that hard work for nothing." She shook her head and winced at a stabbing pain behind her eyes. Ignatius had a way of making treasures vanish. Archer had once told her that he was hoarding it all, and one day, when Iggy was captured, all those stolen treasures would be his demise. Then, finally Ignatius Montpellier would be revealed as the thief he really was.

Jimmy rolled his clenched fist in his other palm. "Lucky he's dead. Or I'd kill the bastard myself."

Alessandro walked into the room and the solemn look on his face turned her heart to ice. "What is it? Did they find Archer?"

Alessandro's eyes bulged. "Sorry Rosa. No. I still haven't heard anything. I umm, just checked downstairs." He clutched his temples. "Ignatius took everything. The whole lot."

"Not everything."

Rosa's eyes shot in the direction of the all too familiar voice. "Archer!"

Archer stepped from the hallway and an avalanche of emotions bombarded her. Shock and disbelief were at the top. Fire and ice flooded her veins. She wanted to run to him, to wrap her arms around and crush him with her embrace. But her body was jelly.

He looked ashen, ghostly even. Dried blood smeared his chin. Dark smudges lined his eyes. As Archer hobbled toward her, tears spilled down his cheeks. Every step he made looked crippled with pain.

He fell to his knees at her side and they clutched at each other. She couldn't breathe and the lump in her throat was impossible to swallow.

"I love you so much, babe. When that helicopter crashed, I. . ." He let the sentence hang.

"I thought I'd lost you too. You didn't resurface. . . and I thought. . . I thought you'd drowned." She sat back and slapped him on his shoulder. "Where the hell have you been?"

"I'm sorry, baby. I don't know what happened. I woke up in an ambulance." He cupped his hand behind her neck. "They were dragging me off to hospital and I couldn't make them stop. The first chance I could, I snuck out and grabbed a taxi back here. I couldn't even get a message to you, my phone's dead."

Jimmy placed his oversized paw on his buddy's shoulder. "Jesus, mate, you trying to give me a fucking heart attack." Archer stood and winced when Jimmy tugged him into a firm bear hug and slapped him on the back.

"Just keeping you on your toes, buddy," Archer said.

Alessandro took his turn hugging Archer and welcoming him back from the dead.

"How did you guys find out what happened?"

"Rosalina rang us and said you'd gone off screaming toward *Evangeline* like a crazy man."

Rosalina only vaguely remembered that call, she must've sounded hysterical. And that was before she'd even seen the helicopter.

A wave of exhaustion brought heat and burden to her body. She'd been awake for nearly twenty-four hours. And it'd been a crazy twenty-four hours too. Her legs felt alien. Foreign in every sense of the word. They throbbed but were numb. They were stiff yet felt strangely loose. She resisted the urge to draw back her skirt and witness the trauma she knew would be there. Archer was the one who needed help, before he passed out in front of them all.

Alessandro cleared his throat. "Excuse me, Archer. What did you mean Iggy didn't take everything? There's nothing downstairs."

Archer pointed to the end of the bar. There, glistening in the bright galley lights with its big swollen belly and cheeky facial features, was the monkey statue.

"Yes." Jimmy punched the air. "They missed the one thing that wasn't hidden."

"Oh, and we still have your father's notebooks and the diary," Alessandro said with a renewed glint in his eye.

It suddenly occurred to her that Ginger wasn't here. "Where's Ginger?"

"She'd already gone to sleep when you called, so I left her," said Alessandro. "She doesn't even know about all of this."

A line of suspicion cut through Rosalina's thoughts. "She must've fallen asleep quickly, weren't you with her?"

"Not when you rang." Alessandro shook his head. "I was helping Nonna with the dishes. You know what she's like, I couldn't convince Nonna to leave it to the morning."

Rosalina wanted to punch herself for thinking such horrible thoughts. Ginger was a sweet girl and her mistrust toward her was unfounded and appalling. Rosalina's head was a painful staccato. She needed caffeine. And a strong coffee at that.

"Alessandro, could you make me coffee please? Make it a double shot please."

"Oh sure." He scooted off.

Archer drew up alongside Rosalina and it took all her might to curl her legs aside so he could sit on the lounge. "So," Archer said, "Iggy may've taken this lot. But there's still two thirds of that treasure just begging to be found. Now that both the crazy priest and Iggy are gone, we're in no danger to search for it now."

"I don't know, Arch," she said.

Archer turned to face her. His hooded eyes pleading.

She shook her head. "I'm beginning to wonder if the Calimala treasure is cursed."

"Cursed. No way." Jimmy waved away her comment.

"Jimmy!" Rosalina drilled her eyes into him. "Before you dismiss it so quickly, let me summarize. First, way back in 1348 when the treasure was stolen, there were plagues and earthquakes. Then the *Flying Seahorse* sank, probably killing everyone on board and now, in the short amount of time we've been chasing it, four people have died."

"Four?" Alessandro ferried a coffee from the galley toward her.

"Yes. Four. Nox. Brother Bonito, the man who helped Nox. That thug who drowned. And now Ignatius. Four." She held up four splayed fingers for emphasis.

"But they were all bad." Jimmy's mischievous grin lit up his face.

They all fell into silent contemplation as she reached up for the coffee Alessandro handed down to her. As she clasped the steaming mug between her hands the anticipation of what she was about to say drove adrenalin through her weary body. "I have a suggestion." She blew on the black brew and took a sip. "How about we forget about the Calimala treasure for a while--"

"Hang on a min--"

"Jimmy! Wait till I'm done." She glared at him and he huffed. Rosalina waited until his clenched jaw relaxed before she continued. "It will take some time to get *Evangeline* repaired and shining again. But after that, I think we should forget the Calimala treasure for a while and follow the *Awa Maru* trail instead."

Archer squeezed his hand on her thigh.

"Hell yes." Jimmy slapped his palm on the dining table.

Archer turned to her, drawing his beautiful gold-bedazzled eyes to her. "Are you sure, babe?"

She nodded and ran her hand up his arm. His skin was on fire, but it was the fire in his eyes that convinced her she was doing the right thing. As much as she needed a very long rest, and as much as she would have preferred to keep her feet on solid ground for a while, she couldn't leave it like this. The three men before her, Alessandro, Jimmy and especially Archer, looked like their hearts had been torn out by what Iggy had done. If they left it the way it was now, the bad guys won. "We can't end it like this, with nothing to show after months of hard work. And now like you said, with Nox and Ignatius gone, it's safe."

Alessandro cleared his throat. "Well, on that note, I think we need to get the both of you to hospital and healed quickly, because. . . I didn't want to mention it before but. . . after chatting with one of the modern history professors at the Accademia yesterday, I think I may know where the *Awa Maru* treasure is."

Archers palm was a furnace that he placed against her cheek. His gaze flicked from one eye to the next, searching her for the truth. She nodded, smiled and her shoulder was pure agony as she raised her coffee mug. "To treasure hunting."

"Okay then." Wincing, Archer raised his mug. "To treasure hunting."

DEAR READER, THANK YOU FOR CONTINUING WITH ARCHER AND Rosalina on their crazy treasure hunt.

. . . but now the enemy is closer than they think. When Archer finds a clue to a vast missing treasure, stolen during World War II, they're plagued with bizarre clues, endless dead-ends and deadly traps as they cross the globe hunting for it.

When Rosalina is kidnapped by a madman hell bent on getting his hands on those riches, it all becomes very, very personal.

If you've followed Archer and Rosalina this far, you won't want to miss the final explosive episode in the Treasure Hunter Series – Treasured Dreams.

OR KEEP TURNING THE PAGES FOR DETAILS OF MORE ACTION-PACKED **books by Kendall Talbot.**

P.S. Reviews are like finding gold after a long hard treasure hunt. . . they're priceless. It would be wonderful if you could do a review of this book for me.

Lost In Kakadu

Together, they survived the plane crash. Now the real danger begins.

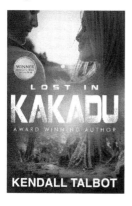

Socialite, Abigail Mulholland, has spent a lifetime surrounded in luxury… until her scenic flight plummets into the remote Australian wilderness. When rescue doesn't come, she finds herself thrust into a world of deadly snakes and primitive conditions in a landscape that is both brutal and beautiful. But trekking the wilds of Kakadu means fighting two wars—one against the elements, and the other against the magnetic pull she feels toward fellow survivor Mackenzie, a much younger man.

Mackenzie Steel had finally achieved his dreams of becoming a five-star chef when his much-anticipated joy flight turned each day into a waking nightmare. But years of pain and grief have left Mackenzie no stranger to a harsh life. As he battles his demons in the wild, he finds he has a new struggle on his hands: his growing feelings for Abigail, a woman who is as frustratingly naïve as she is funny.

Fate brought them together. Nature may tear them apart. But one thing is certain—love is as unpredictable as Kakadu, and survival is just the beginning…

Lost in Kakadu is a gripping action-adventure novel set deep in Australia's rugged Kakadu National Park. Winner of the Romantic Book of the Year in 2014, this full-length, stand-alone novel is an extraordinary story of endurance, grief, survival and undying love.

Two lovers frozen in ice. One dangerous expedition.

Holly Parmenter doesn't remember the helicopter crash that claimed the life of her fiancé and left her in a coma. The only details she does remember from that fateful day haunt her—two mysterious bodies sealed within the ice, dressed for dinner rather than a dangerous hike up the Canadian Rockies.

No one believes Holly's story about the couple encased deep in the icy crevasse. Instead, she's wrongly accused of murdering her fiancé for his million-dollar estate. Desperate to uncover the truth about the bodies and to prove her innocence, Holly resolves to climb the treacherous mountain and return to the crash site. But to do that she'll need the help of Oliver, a handsome rock-climbing specialist who has his own questions about Holly's motives.

When a documentary about an unsolved kidnapping offers clues as to the identity of the frozen bodies, it's no longer just Oliver and Holly heading to the dangerous mountaintop . . . there's also a killer, who'll stop at nothing to keep the case cold.

Will a harrowing trip to the icy crevasse bring Holly and Oliver the answers they seek? Or will disaster strike twice, claiming all Holly has left?

Extreme Limit is a thrilling, stand-alone, action-adventure novel with a dash of romance set high in the Canadian Rockies.

Jagged Edge

A grieving detective with nothing to lose.
A dying town with everything to hide.

After the shocking death of his daughter, suspended detective Edge Malone who seeks oblivion in a bottle and plans to photograph a rare blood moon in isolated Whispering Hills, California. But his night takes a deadly turn when a high-tech drone is shot from the sky—and a ruthless gunman murders an innocent bystander who dares to visit the crash site. Driven by instinct, Edge seizes the drone and escapes into the woods.

Now being hunted, Edge unwittingly thrusts Nina Hamilton into the chase—a street-smart beauty who is no stranger to men with dangerous motives. But when the drone data leads them to a shocking discovery, they quickly learn that no one in Whispering Hills can be trusted. The truth of the small town is anything but quiet, and the price of secrets runs six-feet deep…

Jagged Edge is a full-length, stand-alone thriller that will have you turning the pages all night long.

Fans of Robert Ludlum's Jason Bourne, Tim Tigner's Kyle Achilles, L.T. Ryan's Jack Noble, Jeff Carson's David Wolf, Lee Child's Jack Reacher, and Steven Konkoly's Ryan Decker will enjoy this pulse-pounding thriller.

Deadly Twist

An ancient Mayan Temple. A dark family secret. A desperate fight for survival.

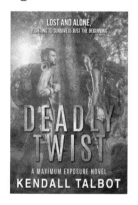

When a mysterious ancient Mayan temple is discovered by a team of explorers deep in the Yucatan jungle, the world is entranced. But Liliana Bennett is shocked by the images sweeping the headlines. She's seen the temple before, drawn in detail, in her late father's secret journal.

Now, the explorers at Agulinta aren't the only ones digging up secrets. Liliana is consumed by the mysteries surrounding her father's sketches and, refusing to believe she's out of her depth, she heads to Mexico, determined to see the temple for herself.

To reach the heart of the jungle, she'll have to join forces with Carter Logan, a nature photographer with a restless heart and secrets of his own. But a journey to Agulinta means battling crocodiles, lethal drug runners, and an unforgiving Mother Nature.

Lost and alone, they stumble upon something they should never have seen. Liliana's quest for answers becomes a desperate race to stay alive. Will Agulinta be the key to their survival? Or will Carter and Liliana become victims to the cruel relentless jungle and the evil men lurking within?

Deadly Twist is a gripping, stand-alone, action-adventure novel with a dash of romance, set deep in Mexico's Yucatan Jungle.

Download Today at Amazon: Deadly Twist

Zero Escape

To survive, Charlene must accept that her whole life was a lie.

For twenty years, Charlene Bailey has been living by the same mantra: pay in cash, keep only what you can carry, trust no one and always be ready to run. That is until her father is brutally murdered in New Orleans by a woman screaming a language Charlene doesn't understand. When police reveal the man she'd known all her life was not her biological father, Charlene is swept up in a riptide of dark secrets and deadly crimes.

The key to her true identity lies in a dangerous Cuban compound run by a lethal kingpin, but Charlene can't reach it alone. After a life of relying on herself, she'll have to trust Marshall Crow, a tough-as-nails ex-Navy man, to smuggle her into Havana.

The answers to Charlene's past are as dark as the waters she and Marshall must navigate, but a killer in the shadows will stop at nothing to drown the truth.

Zero Escape is a heart-pounding, stand-alone, action-adventure novel with a dash of romance that crosses from New Orleans to the back streets of Havana, Cuba.

Download Today at Amazon: Zero Escape

Double Take

A crime of love. The chance of a lifetime.

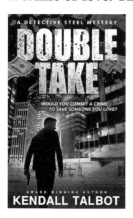

Jackson Rich is at risk of losing the love of his life, and he'll do anything to save her. Even if it means robbing a bank. So it's time to call in a few favors from his old gang because they owe him. Big time.

Gemma's spent her entire life doing the right thing. Now doing the wrong thing could be the best decision she's ever made, if she's brave enough.

When Detective Steel gets a tip-off of a planned heist, he doesn't know where the robbery will be. Only that it's going to take place during the famous horse race that stops a nation—the Melbourne Cup. And when it goes down, he'll be ready.

Except what happens next, only one of them sees coming. And for the others, it's suddenly no longer about the money. It's about retribution.

A fast-paced, stand-alone crime thriller that will keep you guessing until the final page, from award-winning, best-selling author of thrill-seeking fiction, Kendall Talbot.

Download on Amazon today: Double Take

What readers are saying about DOUBLE TAKE:

"This story is so well planned and well written, it was as if it had actually happened! I was riveted to my chair while reading the twists and turns. If I could give it 6 stars, I would." ★ ★ ★ ★ ★ Multi-Mystery fan.

Made in the USA
Middletown, DE
22 June 2021